PENGU

SACHIKO

Clive Collins was born and brought up in Leicester. He has worked as a teacher in West Africa, Northern Ireland and Japan. His praised first novel, *The Foreign Husband*, was published in 1989.

CLIVE COLLINS

SACHIKO'S WEDDING

PENGUIN BOOKS

PENGUIN BOOKS

Published by the Penguin Group
Penguin Books Ltd, 27 Wrights Lane, London W8 5TZ, England
Penguin Books USA Inc., 375 Hudson Street, New York, New York 10014, USA
Penguin Books Australia Ltd, Ringwood, Victoria, Australia
Penguin Books Canada Ltd, 10 Alcorn Avenue, Toronto, Ontario, Canada M4V 3B2
Penguin Books (NZ) Ltd, 182–190 Wairau Road, Auckland 10, New Zealand

Penguin Books Ltd, Registered Offices: Harmondsworth, Middlesex, England

First published by Marion Boyars Publishers 1990
Published in Penguin Books 1991
1 3 5 7 9 10 8 6 4 2

Printed in England by Clays Ltd, St Ives plc

for Cheryl Alexander Malcolm

'There are no women in this country.
There are only daughters and wives.'
Takeshi Ebisaka

ONE

My father tells me this is the happiest day of my life, as if he could order that as he has ordered everything else today. But what would he know of my happiness, or anyone else's for that matter? He has not thought of a single other person's feelings since the day he was born.

And yet perhaps I should be happy. It is my wedding day. I am dressed as the advertisements in the subway say a bride should be dressed. The train of my dress is made of lace from Belgium, and it is two metres longer than the English princess's was. All I lack is a prince, the one thing my father could not buy. I am seated next to Mr Ueno, the man I am in the process of marrying. He is most decidedly not a prince. We are at a table lavishly bedecked with flowers — these flowers alone have cost my father 400,000 yen — in the Heian Room of the Hotel Okura. As my father kept telling me all this morning, it is the largest, most expensive room in the most expensive hotel in Tokyo. For most girls all this would be a dream come true. For most girls, but for me it is a nightmare.

I exaggerate. It is not a nightmare. It is not anything. I almost feel as if this marriage is happening to someone else, another Sachiko Miura. Once I read about a man who had decided he had no reason left to live and so he swam out to sea. Not caring for his life anymore he had no fear of the ocean and let it take him where it would. His spirit became detached from his body, he said, and looked down upon it from the air, like a seagull. It was just one more piece of flotsam. That is the way I feel.

Of course the man was found by a fishing boat and taken from the sea. He survived his disappointment and wrote of the experience; then, when his book was published, he became a celebrity. His photograph was in the most fashionable magazines, and he appeared on all the late-night television shows with the porno-actresses and foreign personalities who amaze us because they can speak our language which, as anyone with any sense knows, is impossible for a foreigner to speak. My father does not usually watch these shows because he is a successful man and so is seldom home by eleven o'clock, but when he is he refuses to believe what he sees and shouts at the screen. Because the images continue undisturbed by his threats and questions he turns to my mother and tells her that speaking to the television is much like speaking to his family. My mother usually ignores him.

My mother at least does not think this is the happiest day of my life. This morning, before we left for the hotel, she came into my room and gave me a piece of paper. My name was written on it — *kofuku-no-sachi*, 'happiness'. She said it was all the happiness I had the right to expect in this life. She said she was speaking from experience. Of course, she has been married to my father for forty-three years.

The first time I met Mr Ueno he told me he would take an apartment for us in one of the new mansion blocks that are being built in Shibaura, close to the water. If it seems a little forward of Mr Ueno to have spoken in such terms at our first meeting, it must be understood he already knew he was going to marry me. My father had assured him of that. I think I almost believed Mr Ueno when he spoke of the home we would have, although, as I look at him now, uncomfortable in his wing-collared shirt and tail-coat, with his greased hair that obstinately keeps its distance from his skull, and his face red because of the scrubbing he gave it this morning, well, he would look rather out of place in such surroundings. Perhaps all he was doing when he spoke thus was sharing a dream with me, a dream of cleanliness and space, white-walled, sparsely-furnished rooms with wooden floors. The sort of rooms where lithe girls sit in their underwear in the morning sunlight, drinking coffee while they talk on the telephone, or incredibly handsome boys with perfect hair come in from the rain to open refrigerators filled with American beer. I know that Mr Ueno watches television a lot. The advertisements have furnished him with a fantasy life.

The white gloves he held during the wedding ceremony are by his plate. They are stained with the sweat of his hands. Poor Mr Ueno, he is not enjoying this very much either.

Well, we are not going to live in a dream home by the bay. We are to spend our wedding night here, in a suite my father assures me is the most expensive the hotel can furnish, then we go to Europe for five days, which is all the time Mr Ueno can take off from his job at the Ministry of Finance. When we return to Tokyo we shall go straight to Mr Ueno's parents' house in Azabu. His mother is so looking forward to our arrival, for she hates me and anticipates the pleasure of making my life miserable. The opportunity to tyrannize a daughter-in-law is something she has waited for all her life.

When I wept as I told my mother I was to go to Mr Ueno's house, she said that she had suffered for most of her married life at the hands of my father's relations, and now it was my turn. It seemed as if her hardship was an heirloom it was time for her to pass on to me.

Five days in Europe, two in London and three in Paris. In London we are to stay at the Savoy, in Paris it will be the Georges V. Again, the choice was made for Mr Ueno by my father. My father's money gives him great power over Mr Ueno and his family. I give them great power over my father. London-Paris, as we say, Lon-Paree, cross-eyed. Mr Ueno has cross-eyes that even his strong glasses cannot either correct or disguise. Perhaps our honeymoon destinations are appropriate then. I remember when he proposed to me in that also entirely appropriate restaurant, I was unsure whether it was really me he was asking, or the young woman at the next table.

Look at my parents, seated right at the back of the room. I must squint to see their faces, my mother's expressionless, like one of the masks that hang in the tourist shops. It is the face she has always worn, never betraying herself to joy or anger or sadness. It is how she has coped with her life. It is, I suppose, how she has survived. My father does not have her self-control. He is trying hard to look as vapid as the others, but underneath the set of his mouth a grin of self-satisfaction is evident. It is the day of his triumph. Finally, he has managed to marry me off.

Mr Ueno's head of department is beginning his speech. He is an Assistant Deputy Director at the Ministry and an important man. I think it was the fact Mr Ueno said this man would agree to act as our go-between that convinced my father to seal the marriage with him. Of course, the Director himself, or the Deputy Director, would have been better, but even someone with as insatiable an appetite for the best as my father cannot have it all the time.

Mr Ueno's head of department does not know me or, for that matter, Mr Ueno. It is a very large department. When Mr Ueno was promoted in the spring, he was moved to a desk a little closer to the window. It was, he assured me on one of the occasions when I was made to meet him before today, a significant step up. I asked him whether he meant a step across as he was actually moved sideways, but he did not appear to understand what I was saying.

The Assistant Deputy Director will do no more than read the short life histories with which Mr Ueno and I provided him when we went to his house last month. I have not seen Mr Ueno's life history. If it is as short as mine then this speech at least will be over quickly. I doubt it will be, however, he probably does not have as much to hide as I do.

It is only three-thirty, and we have the room until seven. I keep looking around at the faces turned senselessly towards us as if expecting a saviour to rise up from amongst them, a knight in shining armour, a prince who will cut through the forest of thorns and waken me from this dreadful sleep,

which is not sleep, with a kiss. When my father asked me
what music I wanted at the wedding — he has hired the
string section of the Tokyo Philharmonic to play during the
interval which will occur when I go off to change my costume
— I told him the only song I would like to hear would be
'Some Day My Prince Will Come' by the Dave Brubeck
Quartet. For a moment I actually thought he would strike
me across the face, as he had once before. He did not, but
there will be no princes here today. Oh Michael, you were
my prince, my Irish prince. You said that once your family
had been princes among your people. Why do you not come
for me?

Last night, as I tried so hard to find escape in sleep, I
remembered a film we watched together, you and I. The
hero took his love from the altar, and locked the groom and
all the wedding guests inside the church with a huge cross
jammed against the door. How my heart beat as I imagined
you and me, I in my bridal gown with the train which is two
metres longer than Diana's, running out into the streets of
this city. But it was only a dream. Such things do not
happen, except in dreams, except in films.

I wonder where he is now, my Michael. The man who
loved me, who would do everything and anything for me
except the one thing he could not do, marry me. In Sligo,
with his wife and children perhaps. He used to tell me he
would take me there and we would watch the wild western
sea beat upon the shoreline beneath a slate-grey sky. Well, I
did go to Sligo, and I did watch the sea beat upon the
shoreline, and, yes, the sky was the deepest, bluest grey I
have ever seen. But I was not with you, my love, I was with
my mother. We went to Sligo to see the grave of William
Butler Yeats, whose poetry I read at my university, and the
island of Innisfree and the mountain of Ben Bulben. We were
supposed to leave England for France, our trip to Europe
having served the two purposes of making me an even more
attractive proposition for Mr Ueno, and getting me out of the
way so that the scandal of Michael's desertion could die
down completely.

I told my mother that Ireland was more fashionable than

Paris, that it was becoming more culturally acceptable and she, who knows little of such things, agreed to the change in our itinerary. But I did not come to see some dead poet's grave, I came to look for my love, my lover, believing that if I could only see him once more his eyes would meet mine as they do in the books and all our troubles would melt away.

I did not see him, of course. We were alone by the sea, my mother and I; the only proof that any other living beings had ever been where we stood was a used syringe, discarded upon the strand.

This marriage is a farce, a piece of theatre. We are all pretending to be something we are not, actors, uncertain of our lines, and paying to watch our own performance. Nothing is real. When I came here with my parents to arrange the order of events I wanted to scream with laughter at the seriousness with which each idiocy was presented to us. The cake cutting, the candle service, the giving of bouquets to our families. Everything with its appointed time, and everything with its appointed price. Everything with its appointed price, like me.

So, soon I shall take Mr Ueno's hand in its sweat-marked glove and stand behind a plastic wedding cake that soars up towards the ceiling like an architect's model of a skyscraper in west Shinjuku, and then I shall take Mr Ueno's hand in its sweat-marked glove and walk around this room gripping a candle skewered on the end of a short sabre. Of course, the cake was the most expensive on offer, the cheapest being manufactured of slightly faded cardboard. We shall pose for the photographers, then plunge the silver dagger into the real cake hidden from the eyes of the spectators at the back of the plastic cake, and smile at each other. I find it hard to believe though that Mr Ueno will be smiling at quite the same thing as I. Finally, we shall take the prescribed flowers to our parents at the prescribed time, and our parents shall shed the prescribed tears, as if we had paid for those as well as the candles and the cakes and the flowers.

We went through a marriage ceremony in the hotel's chapel, although neither I nor Mr Ueno, or for that matter anyone in our families, is Christian. Anyway, it would not have mattered what kind of ceremony we had as the only legal way of marriage is to register with the local ward office. Once, when I had some business at the office in Nakano ward, I saw a marriage registered, among the cigarette smoke, and the clerks in their tracksuits and slippers, the grimy drinking fountains, the seats with their cheap plastic covers. Perhaps that is why so many of us are willing to ransom our lives for the romance the hotels and wedding centres offer.

I am only surprised that my father does not want us to register this marriage at once. My father who was so jealous of my virtue, he reserved two seats on the train each time I travelled home to Kyushu so that no man might sit next to me. My father who drove me to and from school each day for three years in order that he might forestall my meeting boys on the street. Is this the same man who tonight will happily leave me alone with a stranger to whom I have no legal or emotional connection? A man who will steal the virtue my father imagines he has been guarding all these years?

My father still thinks I am a virgin, in spite of everything. When we entered the chapel together after the priest had rehearsed the favoured congregation in the appropriate responses to his words, we were obliged to pause in order for my father to break a garland of white flowers strung across our path. The significance of this was not lost even upon him, and he turned to me with an almost tender look upon his face, gripping my arm more tightly for a moment. It was the first time I remember him ever showing a feeling other than displeasure to me in the whole of my life. In fact, those moments when we walked together towards Mr Ueno were the first time I remember my father touching me.

It was difficult to keep from laughing during the service. I had heard the minister rehearse the congregation as I waited outside in the corridor with my father. Mr Ueno was there as well. It was the first time I had seen him for almost a month, and what immediately struck me about him was how uncomfortable he seemed in his tailcoat and starched collar. Well, he wanted a June bride, and so he was having to pay the price, for the hotel was hot in spite of the air-conditioning. He got hotter and hotter all the time we were in the chapel, and with his face red from the scrubbing he had given it he soon came to look like a lobster boiling in a pan of hot water. When he took the ring from the Bible where it had rested while the minister blessed it, quite a large amount of sweat ran down his wrist and onto the open pages. The minister seemed most displeased, which upset Mr Ueno even more, and he dropped the ring. There was quite a search for it then, of course, until it was found to have lodged itself in the cuff of Mr Ueno's dress trousers.

No one could quite manage to time their responses correctly, in spite of the minister's sturdy coaching, and I was glad the service was quickly over with, even allowing for Mr Ueno's losing the ring. We might have had something rather grander, but this was one item in the progress of my wedding day my father was unwilling to spend money on. Perhaps it was because only the families were to attend, and so he did not have any of his business contacts to impress. I remember so little of it really, the lack of assurance in the congregation's amens, Mr Ueno's little mishap, and then the damp feeling of his touch as he put the ring on my finger, the first time his flesh had touched mine. Oh yes, and at the beginning, someone broke wind noisily.

The talk the priest gave was entirely inappropriate, so concentrated was it upon the word love. What do we Japanese know of love in marriage? For that matter, what do we Japanese know of love? Oh, we talk of love, we sing of love, but always in a tortured way. We only believe we love if we can feel pain. It is the pain we are really interested in. We are a passionate people, yet our passion has nothing to do with love, we revel in the passion of the senses, and this frightens us. So, we guard against it with social rituals and formulae, and arrange certain spaces, little holes in the organized fabric of our days, where we can abandon restraint entirely. We have our pleasure quarters, we have our love hotels. There we conduct our adulteries and our cruelties, there we inhabit our own private fictions without the caution that is necessary in our public lives.

I remember once Michael shouting at me about how a

people could change so much, and when I told him I did not understand, he said he was talking about the war. We were so cruel an enemy, he said, and yet now he could not believe that the salarymen he sat by in the trains, men reaching the end of their working lives, the men in blue suits, carrying their briefcases, reading their newspapers and comic books, that these men, these grey-haired executives, in other times, in other clothes, had marched European women and children to death through the jungles of Malaya, had cut open the bellies of pregnant Chinese, and buried their prisoners alive for the crime of being prisoners, had raped and looted and tortured an entire continent under the flag of a blood-red sunrise.

For the first time, I answered him back. I looked at him, and said nothing had changed, it was simply that one area of indulgence had been closed down to us temporarily. Michael went out that night and did not return for a long, long time.

No, the Christian service with all that talk of love was not appropriate. It would have been better to have had a Shinto ceremony, in spite of the clothes and heavy wig I would have to wear at such a ritual. I suppose my father declined it because he is, these days, something of an internationalist. Although he detests foreigners, he is sometimes forced into their company because of his business.

He always likes to remind us that he was a naval officer during the war and, as he says, he may have surrendered his sword, but he did not surrender his spirit. To hear my father talk you would think he had been a great hero, a kamikaze pilot perhaps, denied the final dignity of a death in blood and fire by a perfidious enemy whose atomic bombs confused the God-Emperor for a moment and brought about an unnecessary, unlooked-for capitulation. In fact, like our recent prime minister, my father was a member of the naval pay corps and never set eyes on the enemy throughout the length of his service.

It is because of this unsurrendered spirit, he tells us, that he can deal with the foreigners on equal terms, and not as a member of a defeated race. He is even a leading member of the International Friendship Circle of Japan and has twice been president of the local chapter. Personally I think his interest is less in the furthering of international understanding than the business he does through the other members. The only time he was ever called upon to tie the knot of brotherhood, as the Circle's charter puts it, he refused. Some exchange students were in Japan on IFC scholarships and were visiting Kyushu. My father was asked to entertain them, but when he discovered that two of the students were Korean he declared he would not have any of the group in his house.

For all that, he has done well from his foreign connections. Who would have thought, twenty years ago, when he purchased his first fried chicken franchise in Miyazaki, that today my father would be rich enough, important enough, for the American head of the company's Japanese office to feel his presence necessary at my wedding?

Indeed, the American attends the opening of each new franchise now, for my father is indisputedly the king of the fast food business in Kyushu, and consequently an important personage. I also must attend these things, for one day, my father supposes, his kingdom will come to me, or, from today, to me and to Mr Ueno. Inside the new store, its doors closed still to the common herd, the priest begins the ritual: he shakes his bough of sakaki and begins to intone the ancient words, but then the ancient words evaporate and we come to the real reason for his presence. For this priest is here not to appease the spirits of the place to ensure good fortune for the building, he is here to ensure good fortune for my father, good fortune being money, the prize and passion of his life.

I always have to cup my laughter in my hand as the priest, already incongruous in his heavy silken robes among the red and white tiles, the plastic tables and seats, the gleaming stainless steel fryers, begins to chant, 'May the profit of this American Fried Chicken franchise increase for the president and workers of the company.'

That question Michael asked me, perhaps now I could answer it more precisely, if a little less succinctly. We have replaced war with the pursuit of money. We will do anything for money, we will lie and cheat, we will consort with foreigners even. Money is power; with money we will accomplish what we could not accomplish with bullets and tanks and airplanes. With money we will conquer the world. Before, in the old days, the Americans had more bullets, more tanks, more airplanes than we ever dreamed possible. Today we have more money than the Americans. It is as simple as that, and with this money Japan will conquer the world.

Before, in the old days, we thought of the Emperor as a god, today we know that money is the god, and we carry its images about with us. It is at the centre of all our rituals. It is at the centre of my marriage.

Mr Ueno is marrying me for my money, well, not my money, but my father's money, and for all that it represents, the power, the prestige. It matters to Mr Ueno that I am considered beautiful, that I am well but not overly educated, that I have travelled abroad and speak English and French; it matters that my father is an important man, that he is courted by gangsters and members of the ruling party; it matters that a distant cousin of my father's was a class three war criminal, that my uncles are doctors and important lawyers. Yet none of this matters as much to Mr Ueno and his family as the fact that my father is rich.

It is my father's money that has erased my past for them. My father may actually believe that I am a virgin, but the Ueno family know I am not. They have had detectives checking up on me, it is of course a part of the marriage ritual. They will have discovered some of my secrets, some of the men I have slept with, if not all of them. They will know about Michael. They will have seen my medical records. It is my father's money that makes all of this count for nothing in their eyes. If this information was used at all it was only to ensure that I should take Mr Ueno's family name rather than he take mine, which my father may have wished for. After that, my father's money wiped my past from their minds.

So perhaps it is significant that when Mr Ueno came to my parents' house to seal the marriage agreement, he came bearing a large sum of money, which was ceremoniously placed in the alcove of our best room, in front of our oldest, most special scroll. It was to my father a trifling sum compared to the amount he was to spend upon the wedding, compared to the amount Mr Ueno might expect to inherit, but the amount was unimportant. It was a token, an item of truly religious significance. Later, Mr Ueno gave me a ring, a diamond so vulgar my father actually admired its grotesque presence upon my finger, but it was the money that really announced our betrothal and it is money that has constantly attended me ever since.

Of course, we know all of this, what Mr Ueno did was not unusual, it is a tradition with us now, as this garish procedure that I am presently engaged upon is a tradition with us now. It is surprising, is it not, how swiftly traditions are established with us Japanese these days? It is like the clothes designers who proudly emblazon their goods with 'founded in 1982'.

But, there again, perhaps this tradition does have rather more ancient precedents. Was it not common in the past for Japanese fathers to sell their unwanted daughters to brothels, and what am I if not an unwanted daughter? I have read of these girls. No princes came to rescue them either.

TWO

Mr Ueno's head of department has finished reading the outline of my life that I gave him, all the details of my school career have now been made public, my studies at university, my degrees, my recent travel abroad, interests and accomplishments. Listening to him, I was almost impressed myself, almost. What a well-rounded young woman this Sachiko Miura is with her English and French, her work as a translator — but no mention of what I translate, my mother felt a little discretion was called for — and yet still so unspoiled by it all, still so — still so Japanese. And yet this woman does not exist. So much is left out she is a fiction, for we create untruth as much by omission as by invention. Could I have said more? Could I have told everything? I would have liked to. It really would have been the perfect revenge; the first, the last, the only and ultimate revenge upon my mother and father. To have sat here in this ridiculous room, in these ridiculous clothes, with these ridiculous people, and watched their faces as my life, my real life, unrolled before them from the mouth of this almost important man, yes, it would have been wonderful.

I'm dreaming again. As Miss Sekiya used to say, I have a lavish imagination. She would almost thrash me with the word. 'Over-imaginative', she would write on my essays, as if it were the most terrible fault in a student. Perhaps she worried my imagination would bring me to a bad end.

Perhaps she was correct. Perhaps it has. It has brought me to Mr Ueno.

I can see Miss Sekiya now with the others. She looks satisfied, like a cat. The cat that drank the cream, the English say. Why she looks so smug, that I cannot tell. Does she think I have been saved from the fate she saw for me, or finally succumbed to it? I do not know. I do not care.

I do have a strong imagination, even Miss Sekiya was perceptive enough to notice that. It fed upon the books I read, surviving everything, even the indescribable dullness of my teachers, the indescribable dullness of their classes. I forgot my boredom by actually reading the books they made us translate line by line, hour after hour. I read Jane Austen and George Eliot and Thackeray, and I read Maupassant and Flaubert. *Madame Bovary* became my constant companion. Not even my teachers could kill the excitement of those books, although, believe me, they tried. I did not read correctly, they said. I allowed too much of myself to enter the characters, they said. I was too imaginative, they said. I was always too imaginative. Of course I was. Of course I am. I do not need Miss Sekiya or any of the others to tell me my fate, I know it, I knew it, I read it in those books. The fate of women is to die or else be married off to some fool. It comes to the same thing in the end. I wrote this in the thesis Miss Sekiya despised so. 'The product of a lavish imagination,' she put in that exquisite hand of hers, so exquisite, so dismissive. If she had had her way I would not have been given my MA, but in the end the university had no choice. The trustees wanted money from my father, an endowment to help pay for a new extension to the library. He would hardly have given it to them had his daughter failed her postgraduate degree.

Death or marriage. Death and marriage. I have often imagined my own death, and the events after it. Particularly the events after it. My parents are distraught because I have thrown myself beneath a train. My mother's sorrow is due to the too-public nature of my death; my father's because he must pay for the mess to be cleaned up and he begrudges spending money when there is nothing to be gained from it.

Then, they discover my diary. No, that is not right. Then, they discover my *journal*, to the pages of which I have committed every detail of every day since I was a child. This is a mess no amount of money can clean up, and although it is not public it will always be there with them for as long as they live. Nothing can erase the knowledge gathered by the human heart. The mind perhaps, but not the heart. Nothing. Never.

It is a pity then that I have never kept a journal. I have not even kept a diary. I have meant to. Each and every new year for as long as I can remember I have bought a new book filled with dates and blank spaces, my head filled with good intentions. Each November I come across it in some drawer, the pocket of some unused handbag, the spaces blank still, the good intentions vanished. For a long time now I have taken to supplementing the ritual through buying a Letts' diary. So English. But the empty days remain empty for all that Englishness.

Perhaps I have not kept a diary because I have never known where to begin. It isn't enough to start at that first empty space. There must be a beginning for the beginning, and I remember so little of my childhood I sometimes feel that I have no beginning. When I think of my childhood — when I think of my childhood, what do I remember? I remember that house, my father's house, and its shadows and dark places. I remember my terror each night as I lay in the room next to where my grandfather's shrine was, his little dark house of death. I remember the coldness of my mother and father. I remember my grandmother. When I think of my childhood I do not remember love, I remember darkness, and coldness, and fear. I remember my grandmother.

I have always been frightened of darkness and dreaded the coming of the night. When I was a child my grandmother would take me down the long dark corridor with its black wooden floorboards the maids laboured over for so many hours each afternoon. She would take me to the room where my bedding had been laid out. I know my fear grew with each step, for in my eyes the black, polished floor was the oleaginous surface of a river, its slow current sweeping me relentlessly towards that kingdom of shadows where my grandfather and all the other demons waited for me. When we passed the room where the little house of death was I closed my eyes. When I slipped beneath my bed quilts I closed my eyes. It was my belief that if I did not, a demon would come from out of the walls and bite my head off. There were so many demons in that house, and I was intimately acquainted with all of them, I knew their habits and I knew their habitations. My lavish imagination again, I suppose, but it was well-furnished. At Obon all of the temples in the town were decorated with pictures of hell. They haunted me, those pictures, the agony of the tormented, the pleasure of the tormentors.

I look about me now and it seems the pictures have come to life. Mr Ueno's one accomplishment, as far as I am aware, is that he can transform his face into a very passable imitation of a demon by ruffling his hair so that it stands up completely straight, and grimacing. So, at last, the demons have got me, just as my grandmother said they would.

When I was a child our house did not have a flush toilet. My grandmother told me that if I was a wicked girl, and to hear my grandmother talk I was always a wicked girl, a demon would reach up through the lavatory trough and pull me into the murk. There I would endure unmentionable horrors until the men came to empty the cistern. So terrified was I of this particular demon I used to wait and wait to go to the lavatory until I could wait no longer. Then, adrift in pain and fear, and my own stench, I would beg my grandmother to go with me, to wait for me as I exuded my wastes, all the while sobbing out my pleas for her to stay by the door in case those black, demonic hands should reach up to lay hold on my ankles. When I was finished, and had somehow scrambled my clothing about me again, I would emerge to find that spiteful old woman was no longer there.

She hated my mother. My grandmother hated my mother. Hated her. No, hatred is not quite enough. My grandmother hated and despised my mother. My mother, my grandmother would tell me with delight, was a peasant, and I, in my childish innocence, would repeat this to my mother in the form of a question. I would ask her, was it true, as my grandmother said, that she was a peasant. I would ask her if it was true, as my grandmother said, that my father had married beneath himself. Of course, I was too young to know what I was saying, too young to know the pain I caused my mother, and I could not see it because somehow, at some point in the years of torment she suffered in my grandmother's house, she had turned her face into a wooden mask.

My grandmother knew so much about pain. My mother does not come from peasant stock, but Grandmother Miura treated her as if she did. My mother's father was a civil servant, a man greatly respected in our prefecture. In fact, I now know that the marriage was distinctly advantageous for my father because Grandfather Miura died in disgrace, and by his own hand. He was a doctor by profession, but he improperly treated the wife of another of the town's physicians, and she died. Nothing was done to reprimand my grandfather officially for his incompetence and so he took his punishment upon himself. He closed his office to the public one spring morning. A week later he hanged himself in a wood near a pretty river, the ground beneath his feet bright with fallen blossom. Of course, officially it was said that he had died of a heart attack, but that is not the story I heard later, when I was a schoolgirl.

That was a very trying time for the Miura family. A few months after my grandfather's death my father's younger brother was involved in some sort of sexual scandal which, had the Miuras not been such an important family, would undoubtedly have resulted in his arrest and imprisonment. As it happened, my grandmother sent him to live with a distant relative in Tohoku, and he was never spoken of openly again. These events made it very difficult for my father to find a wife, and when my mother said she would marry him it was, I have heard, generally agreed that my father had been extraordinarily fortunate.

Perhaps it was for this reason that my grandmother behaved as she did towards my mother, in order to salve her own hurt pride. She called my mother a peasant, and she treated her as a servant. I do not exaggerate, she treated her as she did the serving women who worked in our house. When my mother's mother, my grandmother Fujishira, came to the house, she was required to use the kitchen door, just as if she were some sort of trades person, or perhaps the mother of a servant. And she was never invited beyond the confines of the kitchen, never entertained by Grandmother Miura who, as far as I am aware, did not see or speak to Grandmother Fujishira again after the day on which my mother and father were married.

As for me, I never saw my maternal grandmother, and I do not believe that she ever saw me. Grandmother Miura took me from my mother's arms when I was only a few days old and carried me off to her private rooms. There a wet-nurse waited for me, a woman who stayed with me until I was weaned. After she was sent from the house I was left alone with my grandmother, who took it upon herself to instruct me in what knowledge she thought necessary for my future development. Principally this consisted of my ingesting to the core of my being the fact that I had disappointed the two people who mattered most in the world, my grandmother and my father, by having conspired with my mother to be born a girl. The virulence with which this was driven into me increased as I grew older and no further children of either sex appeared. I remember that once, when I was six or seven perhaps, I was sent to tell my mother that she had a womb like a dried apricot. My grandmother made me rehearse this phrase again and again before she entrusted me, dumb parrot that I was, to deliver it to my mother in the kitchen.

When I think of my father — when I think of my father — nothing. He was a blank space in my life. I saw less of him than I did of my mother, who was at least permitted the same access to me as the serving women. She would bring food for me to my grandmother's rooms, and she attended to my bathing. I assume that my father spent much of his day out at business. I know, for some of my school friends delighted in telling me, that he spent many of his nights in the company of a certain geisha who bore him a child, a child he could not acknowledge as his own. So, somewhere, I have a half-brother or sister. I think of that ghostly sibling from time to time, and wonder if it is happier than I am. I expect it is.

The only real memory I retain of my father from my early childhood is also the first memory I have of him. It is not a distinctive memory, except for the central facts which are very strong. I believe the events that happened must have taken place in the autumn. It was an autumn evening, a late autumn evening I suppose, for even in Kyushu the hours after darkness fell were becoming cold. I had been taken to bed by my grandmother but, because my sleep in recent nights had been disturbed by dreams more horrific than was usual even with me, I was allowed to have a flashlight with me in my bed, and the doors of my room were left open so that the light from the electric lamps in the kitchen and sitting-room might drive away the darkest of the shadows in the corridor.

I could not sleep that night, perhaps because I had experienced a particularly terrifying dream the night before. I do not know, I remember only that I could not sleep. I know this because I recall my father's voice coming from the other part of the house. Then I heard the unmistakable sounds of him beginning a meal, the mashing and slurping noises that nauseated me then and nauseate me still whenever I am in the company of Japanese men and they are eating. The noise made it certain that I should not sleep and so I began to play a game I had discovered on the first night when I had been entrusted with the flashlight. I began to explore the deeper reaches of my bed.

How swiftly the demons of darkness are banished by light. With the electric torch my room was transformed from a domain of fear to one rich in enticing mysteries. I was Aladdin, and at the touch of a button I could summon from my magic lamp the amicable and trustworthy genie of light, a kindly familiar whose presence made me immune to the terrors of the night. My genie could cut through the body of darkness and send the shadows scuttling into the corners like so many black spiders.

Especially I loved to delve with this light beneath the covers of my bed. Where once I had found fear lurking as I lay down each night, keeping my knees pulled tightly against my chest in case a foul hand might catch hold of my legs, now I was a dauntless diver in some cottony sea. I went gladly, gleefully, deep beneath the heavy waves. It was this stranger happiness that brought about my downfall, but then I should have expected that in such a house of dislike.

I had just surfaced and was laughing for joy, an element as precious to me as air to a real diver, when I heard my father curse the noise I was making from the kitchen. The noise? I was a child, I was laughing and this to my father was a noise? A few moments later my grandmother appeared and a light far harsher than the gentle beam of my wonderful lamp took the darkness away completely.

Grandmother snatched the flashlight from me, and then took hold of my empty hand, pulling me from my ocean of quilts, the sea of my happiness. She stripped my sleeping garments from my body and then roughly told me to dress. It was quickly done, and I stood, afraid beneath the hard, bright light in my school uniform, but Grandmother continued to pull clothing from the tall dresser where my things were kept. Then, when what seemed to me to be every garment I possessed had been dumped on the floor next to the pile of my deserted bed, she began to stuff the clothing into the old canvas satchel my father had brought back with him from the war. Slowly it came to me that what I had done was something so monstrous, so beyond the bounds of acceptable human behaviour, I was being sent away. And I was.

My arms were forced into the coat I wore whenever I was taken out into the streets in winter, and then my grandmother seized me by the arm and lugged me from the house into the dark garden. In her free hand she carried the canvas satchel, and I remember that even then, in the very moment of the nightmare, I could not help remarking the size of her hands, the strength of her hands. Perhaps, if I could see those hands today they would not be as huge as they appeared then, but at that moment, that moment of night-mare, they seemed possessed of such power.

And it was truly a moment of nightmare. No matter how awful the world within my grandmother's house might be, it was Paradise, a safe and sacred haven, when set against the world outside. I learned an English expression once, 'Better the devil you know'. I knew and feared the devils inside my grandmother's house. I was as yet unacquainted with the ones outside, but I understood that they were there, and what I did not know of them made them a hundred, a thousand times more terrible than the spirits who already haunted my days and nights.

My grandmother put me into the corner where the brooms the gardeners used were kept. She said I was to stand there all night and that, in the morning, when the men came with their cart to empty the cistern, they would be given money to take me away with them because I was an ungrateful and unruly child, because I was the child of a peasant woman.

She left me then to go back inside the house, but she paused in the slice of yellow light that broke in upon the night's darkness from the kitchen to add to my torment. She said, of course, I might not still be in the garden when the morning came, for there was a great and terrible demon who circled the house at night, sitting astride the wind as if it were his horse. She told me to listen to the trees, they would tell me of his coming. She said she hoped he would come that night, she hoped he would gather me in his arms and carry me off with him to a place beyond the stars so that I might never be seen again. She said she did not love me. She said my father did not love me. She asked me if I understood that.

She asked me again if I understood that she did not love me, that my father did not love me, and it was only when I said yes, yes, I did understand, that she went inside, leaving me in the darkness among the trees and the stirring wind to wait for the demon's embrace. I heard her turn the key in the lock.

Afterwards, years afterwards, when I was older and I began to look at paintings, I saw those European depictions of princesses chained to rocks, live bait for dragons and sea monsters. I was able, when I saw the paintings, to understand exactly how the princesses felt, and I was able to envy them, for at least their stories had an ending, a prince who would come riding up on a white horse, with steady lance and shining sword, to rescue them, to slaughter the monster and break through the chains that held them to the cruel rock. Even then, as I waited in the dark garden and watched the movement of the trees, even then I knew no valiant warrior would arrive to succour me. I could expect only the demon.

It was a pile of leaves swept into the corner, where I was standing, with the brooms, that announced the demon's presence. Lifted suddenly by the wind they struck the bamboo broom-poles with a dry, almost metallic sound, and then swirled about me like a magician's enchanted doves. And I too began to turn, caught up in the maelstrom, flailing with my useless fists against the great and sudden presence that had come upon me. I began to scream, to scream, to scream.

For what seemed like a long time there was nothing but the sound of my screams and the leaves flying about me in the darkness. Then I found myself in a place so strange that I truly thought I had been carried beyond the stars. My mother was there, and I remember I asked her if she too had been taken by the demon. For the first time in my life that I was aware of she smiled upon me. I loved her for that, and I loved her for the gentle way she spoke to me, telling me that I had become ill and was in a hospital where I must stay until I was better.

I was ill, and I was ill for a long time. I had developed rheumatic fever. I stayed in the hospital for several months and I believe that, despite my illness, the white room in which I lay framed the happiest period I had known in all my life.

I am quite sure that my illness had nothing at all to do with the hysteria my grandmother's cruelty induced. The fact that the fever had begun by the time a doctor was summoned to deal with my fit was mere coincidence. However, my illness, following as it did immediately upon the heels of my being sent into the night, gave my mother a key with which she was able to unlock some of the fetters in which my grandmother had kept her for so long. And it was another illness that allowed her to break the old woman's power for ever.

In my last year at junior high school Grandmother Miura began to exhibit the first symptoms of senility. Within a few months it was she who had been whisked away to a place beyond the stars, or at least, that is how I thought of it, for the person who was fed by my mother, was bathed by my mother, who had her urine-soaked diapers changed by my mother, who lay for hours at a time in an upper room, her limbs restrained with cords which had been tied by my mother, this person was not Grandmother Miura. She was someone else entirely.

In fact, it was because of me that my mother's attention was drawn to the beginning of Grandmother's sudden and rapid decline. Each memorial day for my grandfather it was my task to take the food he had loved in life and place it on the altar before his photograph. I disliked doing this because I disliked the dark little altar itself, a house of the dead within a house of the dead it seemed to me then, a perfect image of our situation. I also disliked it because in the evening I would have to remove the bowls of food from the altar and take them to the kitchen where the contents would be mixed with our own meal because, of course, on that day we ate the food my grandfather had enjoyed eating, and my grandmother would not tolerate any sort of waste in her household.

She had, she would say, lived through too many days of hunger to stand and watch as food was thrown away. It was probably one of the few things in life upon which she and my mother agreed. They were people who had come through the war and the years of deprivation that followed. How that time of austerity marked those who survived it, and how it shaped what they built up afterwards. Michael once said he knew of no other country where people exchanged with delight and gratitude gift boxes of cooking oil, and soap, and cartons of beefsteak. Well, no food, not even food for the dead, was to be discarded in Grandmother Miura's kitchen, but I always felt sure that I could taste the food from the altar mixed in with the rice, a bitterness that came upon the tongue beneath the flavourings of miso and tamari, and black sesame seeds, themselves the colour of death. I would not eat, and my sudden fasting, for normally I had a more than healthy appetite, always drew some sharp phrase from the old woman's tongue.

On one of the memorial days Grandmother watched as I carried the food into the room where the altar was kept and put it in its place, but then, when we walked back to the kitchen and I said I must hurry or else be late for school, she turned from me and went back along the corridor muttering something about my disobedience and that she would place the food upon the altar herself. I thought that this was strange, but I had not lied when I said that I was late for school and so I picked up my satchel and ran out of the house. It was when I returned home in the late afternoon and found my grandmother kneeling before the altar repeating to herself over and over again that she could not find Grandfather's rice when it was in the place we had put it in the morning, I knew something was very wrong, and I went to find my mother.

In fact, my mother had been away visiting an aunt for much of the day. When she returned and I told her of Grandmother Miura's behaviour she said nothing, but she must have understood then that the old woman was having life prised from her iron fingers, must have known that, at last, time had given her the victory for which she had waited. Before the year was out Grandmother Miura had passed into another state of being; her strength flowed from her and she became that tearful, babbling baby which could not feed or dress itself, or attend to even the most elementary tasks essential to maintaining the façade of human dignity. And her every movement seemed to me haunted by demons more real and more truly terrible than any that had haunted me.

It seemed to me, even then, that we would have done better to send her away, but, of course, a family like ours could not possibly behave in such a way. So it was left to my mother to care for the wreck of this woman who had made each day she lived in her husband's house a misery. I do not know how my mother coped in the years before my grandmother died. When I think of it I can still hear the screaming, and I can still smell the odour of decay that hung about every room. I do not know how my mother coped? I do. I can remember the way she would look at my father after she came down from tending to the old woman. She had in her eyes the look of someone who has won a long war. Each tray of food she carried up to my grandmother's room, each fouled diaper she brought down from it, was a battle won, a battle she had won.

I am swimming again. Everything is distant from me, the lights, the smells of food and clothes kept in cupboards, all these faces, the mouths opening and closing like machines. Sometimes my senses seem to alternate between the chatter of the crowd and the surge of the water, the world of air and noise and the strange green place beneath the surface, so silent, so utterly other, it might be the land of the demon my grandmother terrified me with, away beyond the stars. When I am there, in this other place momentarily, then I observe my wedding guests, the shining suits and shining faces, and I see each one as if for the first time, with the clarity born of distortion. Oh dear, Miss Sekiya would never approve. My imagination again. In a way I suppose it is my imagination that has condemned me to this wedding, and yet, I know as well it is my imagination that has let me survive the years of my life. I have, for example, imagined the things that were not mine. I have imagined love.

I have wanted love so much. I was perhaps sixteen when I understood, finally, that even my mother did not love me. Grandmother Miura had been dead for a little more than a year. In that period I had spent more time with my mother than ever before. She had become someone utterly wonderful to me. She was so beautiful, I woke each day just to see her. I worshipped her. I rejoiced in her presence, the texture of her hair, the paleness of her skin, the colours of her clothes. The faint sensation of her cologne upon the air after her passing could make my heart race. If I returned to the house and she was not at home, I would run to her room to throw open her dresser and closets and satiate myself with her, the touch of her silks and stuff upon my skin, the smell of her in my nostrils, the sense of her all about me. Once, once I shed my clothes and rolled upon the wooden boards of her room just because her own naked feet had been upon them. My love burned me, it was so intense, but I was utterly faithful to my passion. If ever I looked at the mothers of other girls it was only to find fault with them in comparison to mine, my mother, my love. Perhaps it burned too brightly, that flame I held for her in my heart, which is why it was so quickly extinguished.

I was returning home from school one evening in early winter, alone for once, my father being away on a business trip. I remember we had been surprised that weekend by an unexpected fall of snow and there were still banks of the tired, besmirched scrapings on each side of the street while the cars went carefully over the ridged and treacherous surface beneath their tires. I was late for I had stayed behind with the other members of my volley-ball circle for practice. I was hurrying along in the cold; a miser with time, I wanted only to be with my mother. I hoarded the moments I could be with her, cursed those when I could not.

I know that I looked before I began to cross the narrow road in front of our house, but suddenly the cars were upon me and I had the taste, the quite specific taste of death in my mouth, that sudden rush of bile beneath the tongue which is almost pleasant, like a seducer's knowing kiss. I was caught in the glare of headlights on my right and my left and, understanding that nothing I could do would save me, I stood still, frozen in terror, frozen like the frozen filth under the soles of my shoes. Life and death were mine to choose between no longer, now one of them would choose me. I could only wait and, as I did, I remember feeling the sensation of a great coldness entering my legs, as if death had already placed a hand upon my body.

Of course, it was done in a moment, but for me the moment went on forever, the sound of engines, the lights, the roaring noise as the rubber slid across the rutted snow. I saw the reflection of my face in the window screen of one of the cars. I saw my pale skin, and the glaze of terror in my eyes. I did not then, and do not now, know how the drivers managed to stop their cars, but their curses freed me, broke the spell of the enchanter and released, I ran away from the lights and the shouting, through the gate and into the for once welcome darkness of our garden.

I shouted for her, I screamed, Mamma! Mamma! The house was empty, the only sign of a human presence the smell of cooking, but the maids were gone from the kitchen and I could not find my mother. I ran upstairs, defying the steepness and the uncarpeted, polished wood, more treacherous to my feet in their white socks than the frozen snow outside. My mother was in the new lavatory. I knocked on the door, fell in front of it, calling to her again and again like a pilgrim prostrate at last before the holiest shrine of some great and holy place. I begged her to come out to me. At last she answered me, but coldly, telling me to wait. When she did come to me she asked what was so important that she must be disturbed in such a place. Suddenly it came to me that I could not tell her what had just happened and so, simply, I said that I loved her.

She looked at me with the same contempt in her eyes I had grown used to seeing in the eyes of Grandmother Miura when she looked at my mother in the days when my grandmother had the power in our household. She did not speak, and after a moment she walked away, leaving me where I had fallen. At the foot of the stairs she turned out the light, and the darkness I had thought was gone away came again.

THREE

This morning, when I had finished dressing and my hair and make-up were complete, my parents came to see me, as is the custom. As is expected I bowed and thanked them for everything they had done for me. It was difficult for me to get to my knees, and I think the women who had attended to my toilette were rather shocked at what they perhaps imagined was the unaccustomed extravagance of the gesture. For my father it was neither extravagant nor unaccustomed, it was what he is used to. Each time I return home I go to my father's room and prostrate myself before him, telling him my name and the fact that I am home. It is not that the ritual is required as an act of courtesy, even my friends find it excessive, nor does his memory fail him so that I must remind him of who I am. It is much more to remind myself of who I am. It is, like so much else in my life, like so much else in the life of my nation, a repeated lesson in submission. When I look back, it seems to me that I have spent much of my life bowing, to my father and to other men. It is as if submission is the only form of communication they can understand.

That moment, when my parents came to me this morning was one I had anticipated for a very long time. I might almost say I had dreamed about it. In my dream, instead of mouthing the expected, meaningless formula, I would look from my mother to my father and say, well, now are you satisfied? Then, while my father was still too shocked to react, I would tell him that I was about to marry a man I considered to be as far beneath me as my grandmother had considered her daughter-in-law to be beneath my father, and that I was doing so because it was the only way I could break free of someone I hated with great passion, the single great passion of my life. I would say that he ought to understand how great my hatred of him was by the fact that I was willing to give the rest of my life to bringing forth and caring for the children of a cretin in order to spite him. In my dream I said this, just as, in my dream, I ran from the altar with Michael, dress and veil singing in the speeding wind. Of course, the truth was, I said nothing, I simply put my face to the carpet and held it there until, at last, my mother touched my arm, bidding me to rise.

My father seemed satisfied. Perhaps he imagined that I had spoken, but the white veil and the flowers in my hair stopped my words from reaching him, or perhaps, as I have said, with my father bowing is the one form of communication he is capable of understanding. Certainly, whenever I have tried to talk to him I might have been talking to myself. When I think of it though, I have never, truly, spoken to anyone, not even to Michael. I have spent my entire life bowing and talking to myself. I do actually talk to myself. It is a habit those who are alone for much of the time adopt, and I have always been alone in the truest sense, I see that now.

I keep looking at the idiots seated before me. The men are all wearing their heavy black suits, the married women are all wearing their black kimonos, the unmarried girls, my cousins, my fortunate friends, in unlikely party dresses. They look like giant children who got lost on their way to some birthday party and came in here instead. I can see my cousin Sayuri. She looks pretty in her bright clothing, even if it is as much a uniform as any of the others, a young girl's uniform, at least it speaks of life. Next to her is the man she will marry in the autumn — I do not recall his name. Like mine, this husband was found for her. She too has accepted her fate and will live with a man who is a stranger to her. He looks like one of the caricatures of a Japanese that still appear in the foreign children's comics with his teeth and heavy spectacles. Poor Sayuri. So for her this will probably be the last occasion when she can dress in her pretty clothing, soon she will fold the clothes of her girlhood and take up the sombre veils of a wife and mother. I'm sure she will conceive on her honeymoon. For all their ineptness in bed, the fumbling uncertainties and sudden outraged displays of masculinity, these men still succeed in pushing their seed into us, where our idiot bodies embrace it, making out a child in due course.

The room is growing hot with all the lights, and the waves of naptha rising from people's clothing are choking me. When the waiter pushed that plate of vichyssoise soup in front of me just now, I thought I would vomit. I turned my head towards Mr Ueno, but he was looking at his professor who had just begun his speech and all I could see of him was his back, the thin blades of his shoulders pushing against his coat. In the books the bridegroom's shoulders are broad, and his bride, as she settles back in the rich leather seat of his touring car on the sweeping road that will lead them to the sea, removes the confetti that has lodged there with her gloved hand, feeling the heavy muscles tense as she does so, and as she does so anticipates, with an electricity that shakes her whole body, the pleasure she will share with him so soon. I, however, know that all I shall shake from Mr Ueno's shoulder will be the scurf that has fallen from his drying scalp, and when I touch him I shall feel nothing.

I look at the plate of soup again and for some reason I am reminded of semen. I want to rinse my mouth with the champagne that was served a few minutes ago when the toast was offered to the bride and groom, but there is another wedding due to take place in here at seven-thirty, and the waiters, for all their smiling manners, are quite relentless: my glass is gone. Well, in moments, the plate of soup will be gone as well, I can at least look forward to that. Yes, it really is only a matter of moments. It is all only a matter of moments.

I am thinking of my childhood again. It is these lights and this food. I was eleven. I remember leaving the house early in the morning for school, and my grandmother calling after me that I had forgotten my umbrella. It was June, perhaps that is why that day came so suddenly into my thoughts, that and other things, our thoughts weave such a tangled thread to link them one to another. Well, it was June, I remember it quite distinctly now. I remember the clear drops of rainwater that lay upon the leaves of the hydrangea bushes, I remember the tight heads of the flowers, how the blue of the petals had not yet quite shaken free from the stemmy greenness that once enclosed it. I have always loved the hydrangea. This morning, before I left my apartment to come here, I put my face into the wet leaves of the bushes by the gate, but the flowers had been broken by last night's downpour, and the pale blue, veiny blossoms were wiped across the stony path, their delicacy broken by the weather, and the heavy tread of a man, perhaps the paper-boy or my landlady's son. Today also I left home without an umbrella, the difference is that I shall never return home again. That day, the day I am thinking of, I did.

I remember it did not seem as if it would be different, that day. It is true we had visitors at the house, my aunt Mie, my father's sister of course, was staying with her son, Kenji. He was a little older than me, perhaps a year, and I detested him. Why he was not at school I do not know, I simply recall his presence in the house. Perhaps he was ill. His mother always treated him as if he were a little prince, pampering him, acceding to his slightest whim. Sometimes I hate Japanese women as much as I do Japanese men. We are slaves who breed our own masters.

We were to have a physical education class at school that day. Gym was something I enjoyed. It was the only time in my life I have been physically strong, and I exulted in my strength, the pliability of my body, and my mastery of the tasks the teacher would give us. Then I could climb higher, run faster, swim further than any of the boys in the class. At play, if one of them came to torment my friends, I would wrestle him to the ground in moments. Once, I remember, I gave a boy a bloody nose. He complained to his teacher, and when I was disciplined I was told that my crime was not so much that I had struck the boy, but that I had behaved in a way that was forbidden to my sex. I was a girl, and I must learn to behave like one.

We did not go to our gym class that day, at least the girls did not. Instead the class was segregated and the boys went off into the puddled schoolyard and I followed the others of my sex, one more starched sailor's blouse, another billowing blue skirt, towards the science room. We were told we would watch a film instead of playing games. The film, we were told, was more important, so important that we must say nothing of what we would see to the boys when we met them at lunchtime. I remember that, afterwards, after the film and the silence which followed it, I envied the boys so careless at their play. Perhaps I have never stopped envying them.

The film began with a girl bleeding from her nose and then, pursuing a logic still mysterious to me even now, explained that girls could also bleed from other parts of their bodies. I watched breathless in the general air of stupefied silence that had fallen upon my class as cartoon figures of girls, dressed as I was dressed, suddenly transmuted into sections of human beings, their sex organs exposed so that the process of menstruation and the means necessary to contain it might be demonstrated.

I think the film was meant to be reassuring, for I remember pretty pastel colours and sweet music, and words like beautiful, pure, delightful, brightness being repeated again and again. At the end of the film two of the cartoon girls called at a pharmacy on their way from school where a reassuring older woman in a bright pharmacist's smock sold them packs of sanitary supplies and wrapped them up in candy-striped bags. Then the girls went home, I thought at the time they must be twin sisters so alike were they, where they shared their new secret with their mother who smiled knowingly and then served them tea.

There was no tea for us, but an embarrassed teacher asked us if we had all understood what we had seen. When no one spoke we were told to return to our own classroom. On the way there I kept my eyes straight before me. What I had seen might be waiting in the future for the other girls in my class, might already have to some of them for I had seen those candy-striped pharmacy bags in one or two of my classmates' lockers, but I was determined it would never happen to me.

My resolve did not last very long. I wanted to talk to someone about the things I had seen, but who could I talk to? My grandmother? My mother? After lunch I stood for a while with a group of girls as they shared their pretended knowledge and more honest ignorance and said nothing, but the fears of that conversation found a fertile soil in my heart. So I became haunted by another demon, one that waited for me not in any room, not in any corner, but in my own body where the shadows were thicker than anywhere else. That night, instead of thoughtlessly tossing my undergarment into the bag for dirty washing I examined it, furtively, desperately, for signs of blood. It became my new ritual, and blood, my blood, became my new obsession.

I had been aware of the small receptacles that stood in the corners of the public lavatories for a long time. Even before I could read the character upon them I knew that they contained something that was filthy and disgusting — I suppose I was told not to touch and asking why received that as an answer. If it was my grandmother that I asked, and I assume it was, then I would have known even at an age too young for me to remember now not to enquire further. My new knowledge aroused my curiosity again, however, and one day, a month perhaps after I had been taken with the others to see that film, I squatted in a lavatory at the main station, my eyes fixed upon the grimy yellow bin. I knew what I was going to do as soon as I entered the cubicle and everything else was preliminary. I think, as well, I knew what I would find inside, but it did not lessen the surge of revulsion that came upon me as I lifted the lid and put my face over the revealed horror. I fled from that place and at home that night, before I took my bath, I scrubbed and scrubbed myself, raising welts upon my body that took days to subside.

It came to me, of course, in the end. I waited for almost a year, my belief growing that I had escaped. I knew that most of the girls in my class had equipped themselves as the film had quietly urged them to do; it was after all the product of a feminine hygiene company, but how many had begun to use the supplies they had acquired was a secret. I was in my grandmother's house.

It was late afternoon and a dark, heavy rain fell upon the garden, striking against the broad leaves of early summer, spattering the windows of the house. I was sitting on the floor of the room where I slept, looking out across the corridor towards the wet garden. It seemed unreal in the half-light the rain had brought with it. I had homework to do — I always had homework to do — when I had finished I went to the lavatory to wash my hands. It would have been so much easier to wash them at the sink in the kitchen, but my grandmother would not tolerate the washing and drying of hands in the kitchen by anyone except servants. I washed my hands, shook them dry and then went to squat over the trough. I saw at once that my undergarment was stained, but it was dark and I could not make out what the stain might be. I took my panties off and went with them to the window, not daring to touch the light switch for my grandmother was at home and she had long forbidden me to turn on lights before six o'clock in the summer time.

Still, I could not make out what it was upon the cloth, only now I could see that it was not one mark but several, and of what seemed to be a dull, brownish colour. I began to worry. Certainly it was not what I had feared and expected, it was not that.

I heard my grandmother come out of the kitchen and I went to her. She crumpled the garment in one of her big hands so that it might not be seen and took hold of my wrist with the other, pulling me back towards the lavatory. I was terrified, it was, to me, like the night she had taken me into the dark to wait for the demon who rode upon the wind. She said nothing, only gestured me to stand by the sink as she began to wash the stain away, rubbing at it with a huge piece of white soap as if all her strength was needed to drive away such a disfiguration. When it was done, and my panties were rinsed, she turned again to me, lifting my skirt. I trembled before her gaze on my nakedness.

She said I was to go at once to the bathroom and wash myself. I had expected some emotion in her voice, anguish perhaps at my condition, or anger that I should have brought such an infection into her house, for I was now quite certain that I had a disease, some awful, unnameable disease. There was nothing there, her words came to me flat and toneless. Obediently, I turned from her and went to clean myself again.

When I was done and made to leave the bathroom I found a small package on the floor of the passageway just beyond the door. I unwrapped the cloth, inside was a clean pair of panties and two of the things the cartoon girls had bought from the friendly pharmacist in the starched white smock.

I could not eat my evening meal and for once my grandmother did not comment upon my loss of appetite. Perhaps it was because the food did not go to waste, my cousin Kenji ate the portion that should have been mine as well as his own. I asked to be allowed to leave the table and went straight to my room where I began to cry, bitter, bitter tears for the terrible thing that had come to me, for my lost childhood, for the years that awaited me now as a woman. For once, I was glad of that house with its darkness and shadows. In the darkness I could hide my shame. The next day my grandmother gave me money and, as I came back from school, I went into a pharmacy and bought all that I would need to see me through my courses.

I was sullen as I set about my homework in the afternoon, and when I saw my mother passing along the corridor I called out that I was not hungry again and asked if she would intercede for me with my grandmother to be excused from dinner. My mother said only that the meal was to be served late that night, we were to wait for my father and, for once, eat as a family, and perhaps by that time I would feel like eating. I made no reply and went back to my homework.

My father came home early that night, and brought a box of cakes with him, although it was not a Friday. I heard the word 'cakes' pronounced with a greedy glee from the front part of the house by Kenji, which nauseated me. Kenji adored my father and always waited for him by the door when he visited our house. It was an affection I think my father returned, and he would give the boy money and occasional pats upon the head, gestures of a feeling he never showed towards me. Or perhaps the bastard he had sired with the geisha, my ghostly sibling of indeterminate sex, was, after all, male, and my revolting cousin reminded him of this other child, the son he had made but could never, publicly, acknowledge.

I came to the table on unwilling feet, indeed it was only my mother coming to my room to say that the food was ready and my father wanted to begin that got me moving at all. I knew that if I displeased my father I would have to answer for it the next day to my grandmother. As I entered the room I was at first shocked by the terrible brightness of the lights and then, taking my place beside Kenji, horrified to see the bowls of beans and rice that had been prepared, the colour of the beans almost identical to that of the marks I had caused the day before upon my undergarment.

Kenji was loudly demanding to know why we were to eat red beans and rice, what had happened, was it someone's birthday? His wild speculation drew neither confirmation nor denial. Nothing was said. Nothing was said, but my grandmother's eyes took in my aunt and then my mother, yes, even my mother, and in her look I could see a sudden web of feeling being spun between her and the two other women. I knew then that my grandmother had not kept the silence with which she had greeted my unbidden guest's arrival. Only Kenji, still bawling his demands to know in whose honour this festive meal had been prepared, and perhaps my father, remained in ignorance. As for me, I sat, my face flushed with blood and beginning to burn, burn bright as the lights in the room. The lights and the blood and the red rice, the red rice, my blood- red badge, burning clear for all the world to see.

Of all the cruelties my grandmother inflicted upon me that was the one I thought of most often as I grew into adolescence. I thought of it that night as I lay ashamed in my quilts. I thought of it the next day and the next night, and the next day and the next night again. And I thought of it on all the days when the demon had taken my grandmother away to that place beyond the stars. I would look at her face then, that old woman's face with the expression of an imbecile child grinning through it.

Those were the days when I thought it was my turn to share a secret about her with my mother. I was wrong. I had no secret to share, no conspiracy to enter, or if I had it was something soon betrayed. When I looked into my mother's face this morning I could not find even an imbecile child there. Only the silence that answered my cry of love all those years ago.

I nursed my returning wound alone, not knowing then what I was to slowly learn, what I know now, that I would always, must always, nurse my wound alone.

FOUR

I am tired and want to sleep. A moment ago my thoughts became dreams, drifting into a new dimension as I followed them away from here, lulled by the sound of Mr Ueno's professor tenaciously making his way *ad libitum* through his speech; but then, as if I was riding a train, my head slowly coming to rest on the pillow of my neighbour's shoulder, my body snapped forward and I awoke. If only I was on a train, then I could simply murmur a meaningless apology and get off at the next station. Here there is no apology to be made, and nowhere that I can get off. Well, not today.

Of course I am tired, I did not sleep last night. My mother was with me until late, cleaning my apartment. She said the migrating bird does not leave a soiled nest behind it. Somehow this piece of folkloric whimsey sounded foreign in my mother's mouth. Perhaps she was indulging herself, acting out a fantasy of being the mother she has never actually been. She was almost fussing last night. Not over me, over the filth, as she called it, in my rooms, a store of rubbish accumulated over the years, like my past. Tomorrow she will begin to throw it all out, and when the bags and boxes are piled up by the landlady's front gate, my mother will telephone the refuse department for the men to come and cart it away. Perhaps that is how she thinks of my wedding, a carting away of the rubbish. Why not?

Once, when I was teaching English, I used a textbook called *Japan — The Uncommon Place*. It was the usual thing, written by some foreigner to tell us how unique we Japanese are, and the culture shock this causes the poor intruder; the same facile insights, the half-legible print on cheap paper, illustrations so smudged and murky they illustrate nothing. I used it for the same reason all the other teachers use such things, to fill in the dreadful minutes of the classes, forcing the half-truths and errors down the students' throats line by tedious line until they are accepted as fact and we come to believe them ourselves. It occurs to me that perhaps this wedding also is a lesson, with its ranks of teachers and would-be teachers, each stating the obvious one after the other. And there is nothing to be learnt here, as there was nothing to be learnt in the classroom even when it was my classroom.

What am I thinking of, oh, the book, yes, in this book there was a section on marriage, and how middle-aged women talking among themselves would refer to their husbands as the big piece of rubbish. Yet my mother, in spite of everything, no, because of everything, if she ever used this term I am sure she would have used it about me.

I never once remember my mother saying a bad thing about my father. Whenever she spoke of him to me it was always with the greatest respect. Your father is a busy man, she would tell me if I asked why he could not come to see me play volley-ball on a Sunday, but he works so hard to provide a future for you. Your father is greatly respected, she would say, if I asked what he did, for I never clearly understood how he spent his days until the time when the chicken restaurants began to open and it was pointed out to me that they belonged to him.

What she really thought of her husband I do not know, if she spoke of it at all it was not to me. Of her marriage she had kept her own counsel until that moment when I wept before her because I had learnt I was to go to Mr Ueno's parents' house. I told her then, for the first and only time, that the marriage with Mr Ueno was not the marriage I wanted. She said that very few could have the marriage they wanted, and that I, especially I, must make do with the marriage I could have. Then she told me I was not even to think that I could escape from this marriage either before or after it took place. My father was, she said, a respectable man who had worked hard for me all his life and she would not allow him to be disgraced.

My parents provided me with the traditional gifts of marriage, as I expected they would, the bedding and the dagger. When I saw the knife I understood its true significance for the first time: I was not meant ever to return to their home. I had, as they say, been disposed of — like a big piece of rubbish.

No, I did not sleep last night. I felt as I felt when I was a child and sleep would not come because school was to begin again the next day after a long holiday, or worse, when the sunrise would usher in a morning on which I must visit the dentist. I lay throughout the hours of darkness, turning and turning in my bed, wanting so much to sleep because with sleep would come a momentary forgetting, but knowing I would not. I watched the light gradually whiten my curtains, and then the sun began to feed upon them and it was my wedding day. I went from the bed to the lavatory thinking to relieve myself, but when I got there I lowered my head like a condemned queen before her executioner and vomited.

I have so often escaped the world and its necessities in sleep that it is like a drug for me. Last night I was an addict denied my supply. In sleep there are so many possibilities and there is so much to hope for: the blows will not fall, the man will be gone, the prince will come. When I was a little girl and I saw the film of Sleeping Beauty I remember that I could not understand what all the fuss was about. By falling into her sleep for such a long time the princess went through her life without enduring the sorrows of those who must stay awake, for even a princess must acquaint herself with sorrow at some point, and then, as if this was not enough, when she did awaken it was in the arms of a prince, strong and handsome and courageous. I thought she was the luckiest girl in all the world. When I got home and went off to bed I remember I lost my fear of the darkness for just long enough to hope that I too might dream through life until, at last, at the right moment, my eyes would be opened by the kiss of a handsome prince.

Michael used to wake me with a kiss. He even called me princess much of the time. Good morning princess, he would say. I never slept so well as the time I was with Michael. He seemed to drive all the demons away. And I never knew such delicious wakenings, slow and loving and filled with so many happinesses. He would bring me cups of herb tea, sweetened with honey, and prepare a breakfast for me as I lay in bed reading the newspaper and drinking the infusion he had made.

I close my eyes and I see his face, his blue eyes and blond hair, the pale skin and lips, his eyelashes longer than a girl's. I open my eyes and I see Mr Ueno's shoulders with a shower of the dry skin from his head on them. I turn from him and see strangers, friends, relatives. My cousin Kenji is here with his sad-faced, bashful wife. They have been married for several years now and his wife grows sadder each time I see her, which is usually at a wedding like this. Perhaps she is sad because such events remind her of her own wedding day, or perhaps she is sad simply because she is Kenji's wife. Perhaps it all comes to the same thing in the end.

My cousin is a salaryman somewhere in Tokyo, I have no idea what he does. I have no idea what any of those salarymen do. I have often thought that if it is men like Cousin Kenji who make the economic miracle all the foreigners talk about, then it is a miracle indeed. Kenji has grown fat in the way Japanese men grow fat, from the chest to the knees. His tie is badly knotted and he needs a haircut. He drinks heavily. Kenji has got drunk at every wedding I have attended in our family. My father no longer favours him, if he ever did. For his part Kenji no longer fawns upon my father. Once I was afraid of him, now I simply despise him, and after today, there will not even be that for I shall be swallowed up into the Ueno family and probably never see Kenji again unless he attends the funerals of my parents.

Once upon a time Kenji was driven by a great and impure passion for me or, at least, for my body. It was August and he had been sent to us for the duration of the school holidays. I was, I think, fourteen. One night I woke to find him in my room, standing by my bedding in the darkness looking at me. I stared back angrily and he went away, fading noiselessly into the shadows like one of the ghosts that, even then, I remained convinced haunted the house.

The next night he came again, and the next. That third time he touched me, or rather, he touched my clothing. I was awake when he came, having half-expected him. With his foot he took the sheet from me. Then he began poking at me with his big toe until he had pushed my pajama jacket up around my neck. Quite why he did this I could not understand, for my breasts were still quite undeveloped and he would have seen more cleavage ogling himself in a mirror. He stayed looking at me for ten minutes before he used his feet to restore my clothes and bedding to more or less the same state they had been in when he entered my room.

His mother arrived the following day to stay for the weekend, which restricted Kenji's nocturnal wanderings as they slept in the same room, but when she left to return to my uncle in Tokyo, Kenji came again. This time, perhaps because he had peeked at his mother at some point and found out what I, and he, was missing, he removed my pajama bottoms. After this and because, I suppose, I made no move to restrict or protest his actions, his boldness grew with every visit and he would pull and push me about as if I was some large doll, poking his fingers into me. One night he sat crouched above me, dribbling spit between my legs from his mouth. I said nothing. I did nothing. I did not understand why then and I do not understand why now. Perhaps I had expected to be taken by a demon for so long that when one finally appeared in the guise of my cousin, I was almost grateful that it should at least be dressed in a familiar form.

Again my aunt came to stay for the weekend, again I was left to sleep in peace. The day she was to leave we all went shopping together, my aunt, my cousin and me. Aunty told my father she wanted to buy some small thing for us, to amuse us through the long, hot August days. All I wanted from her was that she take her son back to Tokyo when she left, but what I actually got was a box of coloured pencils and a charm to hang upon my schoolbag. Kenji asked for, and received, a flashlight. My aunt could not understand why he should want such a thing in the summer. I could, but dared not tell her.

In fact, the flashlight was what saved me from Kenji's attentions. He came the next night and found more obstructions to his lust, or curiosity, or whatever it was that drove him to my room, than he normally did. During the afternoon I had begun to feel unwell, my head hurt and my body temperature seemed to race between extremes of heat and cold. I thought perhaps I had a fever or, the fear suddenly gripped me, had taken some terrible infection from the spittle my cousin had drooled upon me, but then the pain trickled from my head like sand falling through my fingers and settled down, like an unwelcome cat, into a dull, persistent ache that sat upon my stomach. It had come to me only twice before, but I knew that the pain and fever were harbingers of what my mother, on the few occasions she ever mentioned it, called the monthly obstacle, the cloud upon the moon.

Should I have warned my cousin? I doubt he would have listened to any of my protests. Ought I to have struggled? Why, to save him from his own appetites? And anyway, he was older than I, heavier and stronger. From what I know now of men my resistance would have served only to whet the edge of his desire. As always, I did nothing. If he was surprised to find the parts between my legs that exerted such a hold upon him trussed in the small, tight garment I wore at such times he did not give voice to it, he simply used his hands instead of his feet, peeling the elasticated cotton from me. Was he concerned that, when he had spread and bent my legs into the required positions, the light of his new electric torch should reveal a piece of string emerging from the place where he had grown accustomed to pushing his fat fingers? I do not know, I remember only the gasp and the sensation of horror — it was really a tangible thrill, a shockwave that emanated from him — as he looked down upon the bloodied piece of wool he had pulled from me.

He was gone then in seconds. I waited until I felt sure that his hasty passing through the house had not disturbed my parents and then I went to the lavatory to wash myself and the sheet upon which the tampon had fallen.

Kenji was unwell the next day, I was told. He had been sick several times, and a doctor had been summoned. My aunt was telephoned and came down to us by the afternoon flight. She thought her son still too unwell to travel, but Kenji was adamant, he must be taken home. The doctor who came to see my cousin could find nothing wrong, and it was my aunt who diagnosed a sudden allergy. I suppose Kenji's allergy lasted for a long, long time because he married late, and I know that his complete lack of interest in girls caused my aunt to despair of his ever finding a suitable marriage partner. Indeed, perhaps her constantly expressed anxieties over this were simply the polite but necessary veils she drew about a far deeper concern for Kenji. Certainly there was much rejoicing when he did, at last, take a wife and so, at least publicly, maintain his family's honour, and it is the public view we care about more than anything else. But still I wonder why Kenji's wife always looks so sad.

Was it after that summer my father began driving me to and from school? It could not have been, for I was at senior high school when that happened. I cannot remember when exactly I was first told that my father would act as chauffeur. I remember only the smell inside the cars he drove, his smell, cigarettes and the cologne he had sprinkled on his suits uneasily mixed with naptha. I know I was not given a reason why I could no longer walk the short distance to my school. When I asked my mother she only said that I was not to question my father's decisions, that he was a good and kind man who cared only for me. Even then I knew what she said was untrue. My father cared only for my father.

I suppose it was to prevent me talking to boys. If it was, then my father's journeys were wasted for I was innocent in thought and deed of any such offence. I had no consciousness of the male sex, indeed, I had no consciousness of my own. Of course I had my friends, Akiko, Reiko, Setsuko, the girls in the volley-ball club, and I was aware of them as women, aware of their changing bodies, as I was aware of my own, but it was an innocent awareness, sensuous not sensual. I was deeply, deeply in love with my friends, and I will admit that I was deeply in love with myself. I needed ferocious, passionate attachments after my mother broke my heart and I found them in those girls and in myself.

In those high school years I wanted only to be with my friends, as once I had wanted only to be with my mother. I wanted only to hear the sweet, senseless chatter of their voices, like so many birds feasting upon the day's joyous crumbs, to touch the soft skin of their hands, to smell their hair. To this day I love the smell of young girls' hair; it is the fragrance of hope, and it sours all too soon.

If I could not be with my friends then I wanted no one, I wanted only solitude, I wanted myself. Our love for each other, for ourselves, was so pure. We were young, we were growing in every way. The fear that had clouded our earlier years had given way to curiosity and a shared trust, as the sun will break through the clouds of morning, illuminating the day. Did we do wrong, together or apart? I cannot believe it. I was fascinated by the changes taking place in myself and the others; I loved to see them naked when we bathed together, I loved to see myself. In that lonely house I was my own constant companion, and I stood for hours before the mirror in my room, naked, feasting wondering, questioning eyes upon my body. I watched my budding breasts and buttocks like an anxious gardener willing the seed to flower. I was half anxious, half fearful, because my breasts refused to grow, unlike the others'. Akiko had such breasts when she was still only a girl, and delighted in them. In the bath she would display them for us, only us, her trusted ones, her loved ones, and we, the chosen, would watch in awe the sway of them, the gentle displacement of the water about them as she lowered herself into the bath. Once, it was in the summer term, she let me put my hands beneath her cotton sailor's blouse and I almost swooned as my hands cupped the swollen globes, the warmth and weight of them, the softness. I kissed her then, I remember, utterly, utterly without passion, a kiss of trust and love.

Is it possible that my father sensed something of this, caught the scent of the delight I shared rising from my skin, like a perfume? But if he did, why should he have wished to smother it, wrapping me in the odour of his own dull life? I suppose I had about me then a radiance he could not tolerate, and so he must, and would, do his best to destroy it. He did not succeed, because he misinterpreted its source, and he misread its nature. It was a small victory for me, I knew it even then, but it was a victory and one I must remember now that I am finally defeated.

I was an innocent among innocents. What did we spend so much time speaking of, we girls? Oh, the things we did and would do, our work, our play, the universities where we would study, the men we would meet, the marriages we would make, the children we would bear. We thought we knew so much, and we were blessed in knowing so little. Ignorance is bliss, the English say, and they are right in this. Michael used to tell me that Japanese girls looked and behaved like children, and Japanese women looked and behaved like girls. I think he was right. At seventeen and eighteen my friends and I were children.

For a long time I had known that when I graduated from high school I should go to the University of the Blessed Martyr in Tokyo, although I did not really understand why my ambition had the force of certainty. It was an impulse that had been inside my heart for so many years it seemed a part of my nature, my destiny. It was something I wanted as I wanted to gaze upon myself in the mirror. On trips to Tokyo I always insisted that my mother take me to walk about the campus, and I loved and envied the freshmen and sophomores in their tailored suits and white blouses. I drank the sound of their laughter as it floated in the air, careless amidst the clipped lawns and pristine pathways, and the draught sustained me for weeks after we returned home.

My parents did nothing to support me in my ambition, but then again, they did nothing to hinder me either. It was assumed that I would go to university in Tokyo, and it was assumed that I would enter one of the great women's schools rather than a national university. Perhaps, in his way, my father actually approved of my plans for at the University of the Blessed Martyr I would be more severely chaperoned than I was at home. Until my junior year I must live either with a relative in Tokyo or in one of the university dormitories. I had no intention of sharing a house with my cousin Kenji again, and so it was evident that I would pass into the closed world of the dormitories. Here I required written permission from my father to leave the campus alone, and I must put out my light at nine o'clock each evening. Of course, I would be totally separated from boys.

What my father still did not know was that I had no desire to share the company of boys. I would not be alone at the Blessed Martyr, Reiko and Akiko would accompany me. We would be together as we had never been together before, and this thought thrilled me through the long hours of study which separated us as we approached the time of graduation from high school.

We made the journey north together to sit the entrance exams, and we travelled without our parents, each of us in school uniform as the regulations of our high school demanded, each carrying a small bag with our toiletries and changes of underwear. We were to stay in the capital overnight, all of us sharing a room at the house of Akiko's uncle in Denenchofu. It was cold and there was snow on the ground as our train moved through the suburbs towards Tokyo station, and we pulled our gloves on our hands, making ready to alight. We looked like daughters of the snow ourselves in our creamy woollen jerkins and berets. It was a strange sensation, girls of the south caught up in the wintry air.

Strange too walking the crowded streets, for we did not go at once to Akiko's uncle. He had, it seemed, wanted to meet us at the station, and it had taken all of Akiko's guile and even her tears to prevent it. Finally her father, and then her uncle, had relented, and so we were free for an hour or so to wander. We could not go far, but for us, tied to the narrow streets of our home town as we were, not far was far enough.

We walked to Nihonbashi and the Takashimaya store. There we fed our senses on the riches spread out before us:

the colours and the smells of cloth and perfume, wood and leather, of wealth. We envied the immaculate girls who worked in the store: the sales assistants in their pretty uniforms, and above all the elevator attendants, resplendent, elegant, aristocratic. They seemed so full of grace, those girls, the deft movements of their white-gloved hands preparations for the revelation of some mystery, and in the certainty of their knowledge they were secure guardians of their shrine as they moved it up and down the building, guiding people here and there, offering advice, bowing to the other girls who waited on the ground floor to shepherd more and still more customers into their momentary care. It was hard to leave that warm palace, and the stairway down into the subway seemed like steps into hell as we began, finally, unwillingly, the journey to Denenchofu.

Mr and Mrs Namekata, Akiko's aunt and uncle, were welcoming and very kind. We ate with them and then went early to our room; our examination was to begin at nine o'clock and we must make an early start, for the university was a long way from the Namekata's house. Reiko was asleep when I returned from the bath, but Akiko, who said she was too nervous to settle, wanted to talk. Quietly, with the light dimmed, we lay upon our mattresses like lovers, whispering our fears and our hopes for the morning as it drew ever closer.

I had never seen such crowds as there were in the stations and the trains. We were pushed and buffeted about, crushed, stepped upon, ignorant sticks borne along on a determinedly certain tide. In the carriages of the trains the heat from the bodies packed about us steamed the windows, and I could feel the clean undershirt I had put on begin to dampen as my sweat soaked into it. Then we were carried from the train by the rush of people and the air of the platform chilled me.

I had not been able to eat any of the breakfast Akiko's aunt had prepared, the steam from the soup and the smell of grilled fish touched my nostrils and nauseated me. I felt unwell again now from the terrible journey we had made and the fears that were swelling in my stomach as I knew that soon we must see the tower of the university rising above the trees that surround it. Then it would be but a few minutes' walk to the great wooden gates.

It was a misty morning, and colder still in the streets than the stations. My legs were bare for my school forbade the wearing of tights even on the most wintery of days and the cold wrapped itself eagerly about the exposed skin. We followed the twisting skein of the roadway from the station, past the silent pachinko parlours, the shuttered bars, stepping carefully to avoid the pools of spewed noodles and beer that marked the ended festivities of the night before. Soon we were in the quiet roads that surrounded the school, and then turned a corner to see the gates, the trees, the soaring tower.

Up to that moment we were still free, free to go on or turn away as we would, but when we entered the gates we no longer acted upon our own volition. We were caught in a swirl of notices, arrowed signs that led us always to the point at which we three friends must be separated. I remember seeking out Reiko's face as she was led away to her assigned classroom, and then Akiko, close to tears, was taken from me as well. I held my examination card and number firmly in my hand as I followed with my group the sophomore student in her grey suit, the waist tucked and disciplined, to a gymnasium and there at my small desk, among the strangers and the stacked mattresses and vaulting horses, the wall-bars and wired windows, I began to write when I was told to write and I stopped when I was told to stop. By midday it was all over.

There should perhaps have been some sense of liberation then, but there was none. I ate alone with Reiko, for Akiko had to hurry off across the city to sit another entrance examination at another university. We two that were left ate in silence, as if the sudden separation in the cold and mist of the early morning had been a final one. I felt I should never know again the love, the intimacy, I had shared with my friends, as I should never know again the sights and smells of school, the sensation of our skins touching, the smells and sudden hungers, the easy laughter that held us closer than blood held us. And I was sad. The food stayed tasteless in my mouth, all but impossible for me to swallow.

I went with Reiko to Ginza, but here, again, we separated, promising to meet at Tokyo station for the train back to Kyushu in the evening. Then she set off with the list of presents her parents had told her to buy, things equally available in our home town but which would have more appeal wrapped in the crested papers of the great Tokyo stores. I turned to cross the road towards the Kyukyodo building. My mother had provided me with a ticket to an afternoon performance at the Kabuki, but it was my intention to trade it in for something else. All my life I had longed to visit the Takarazuka theatre, all my life it had been forbidden to me. It was vulgar, my mother said, a frippery suited only to foolish girls and middle-aged women who ought to know better. I did not care what my mother said, I knew only that this was my first chance to see one of their performances, and I would risk everything for it.

I can still remember my excitement. It was the most thrilling experience of my life, the first time I had disobeyed my parents, and my transgression would not end with the exchange of the ticket for I knew I must lie to my mother when she asked about the performance she would expect me to have seen. The knowledge made my excitement at what I was doing all the keener.

I say I exchanged the ticket but that was not true, I sold it, sold it to a foreigner, a man, who stood perplexed before the ticket counter, uncertain what to do. I spoke to him in English, the first time I had ever been so near to a foreigner, the first time I had ever spoken to a foreigner. I don't know how I kept the strange English words moving from my brain to my tongue for his odour choked me at the back of my throat, but I did, I did it all, I was strong and I was brave.

I asked him if he wanted a ticket for the Kabuki, and when he said yes I told him I could sell him one. He did not even bother to ask when the performance began, or where the theatre was, he just pushed the money I asked for into my hand and left the shop, and I turned to the girl at the counter, begging fate that there would be a seat left at the Takarazuka, some seat, any seat. She said all the tickets for that afternoon's performance had been returned to the theatre and that I must try at the box office there. I was out of the building, running, before she had finished speaking, and when I got to the theatre, when I held the ticket in my hand, I could feel the sweat finding its way down my legs, and I trembled with excitement, with the pleasure of anticipation. I felt as if I was melting.

It was so wonderful. They performed *The Pirate*, the story of a Venetian nobleman, wrongfully accused of a crime and driven into exile, who becomes a pirate captain, a corsair, who wins back his good name, and the hand in marriage of the woman, to whom he had been betrothed before his disgrace, by an act of courage and chivalry.

It seems so silly now when I think of it: vulgar, even as my mother said, ridiculous, the girls pretending to be men with their short hair and implausible moustaches, the kisses that were not kisses, the dancing pirates, the pauses for songs. It was not silly or vulgar to me then, it was not ridiculous that a girl should kiss a girl. I envied those kisses then, I envy them when I go to the theatre now, after all the time that has passed, after all the things that have happened, the knowledge I have gained. I think I envy them more now than I did then. For still I go to the Takarazuka, and still it is a secret from my mother, perhaps the one innocuous secret I have from her. The only person I have ever shared that secret with, the only person I have ever willingly shared that place with, was Michael. He laughed at it all, and I was angry with him, hurt by him, so that my visits there became a secret again, even from him.

My head was swimming when the performance ended, and I was more breathless when I left the theatre than I had been when I entered it after my desperate run through the crowded streets. I could have walked to Tokyo station, but I did not trust my legs and so I went down into the subway with the crowds, dreaming of pirate ships and princesses, and dreaming, I missed the station where I needed to change, then panicked, became confused, lost my way entirely, and when I found it again, when I at last reached the entrance to the bullet train tracks, Reiko and Akiko were besides themselves with concern. We ran and had not got into our seats when the doors closed and the great train began to move away from the platform. It gathered speed, throwing us together, and together again, truly together again after the separateness of the day, we laughed and clung to one another.

It was then I noticed the peculiar dampness against my buttocks, and reaching around to feel it I discovered the slit in my skirt, so neat, so sharp it could have been done with the slash of a cutlass. I went to the lavatory and there, unsteady with the motion of the moving train, I slipped my skirt and underskirt from me and examined the slit which had gone through both garments. I began to feel afraid, thinking that the blade which had made those slashes must also have cut into my flesh, that the dampness I had felt was blood. I took off my undergarment, but it was unmarked except for a damp patch which showed white around the edge where it had begun to dry. I lifted the soiled material to my nose and smelt a sharp, almost salty odour unlike anything I had smelled before. I was too innocent then to understand what had happened and so I washed the stain through as once before my grandmother had done. When I put my panties on again, I felt a little uncomfortable but worried more about how I would explain the cuts in my clothing to my mother than the sensation of wet cotton against my skin.

I did not know then that in the crush of a subway train a man, probably a man like my father, a respectable man, probably a man with daughters of my own age, had cut my skirt, and in the crush had put himself against me, as close against me as he might without actually entering me, and this respectable man had caused his seed to flow onto me. In the crush I felt nothing, nothing at all.

I read once, in a book I was given, an English book, of a young woman's wedding night. She was innocent and her husband, when he was alone with her, when he had undressed her, laid her on the bed. She expected his kiss and his caresses, but instead he knelt over her and excited himself with his hand until his seed flowed, then, when it was done, he rubbed it upon her breasts and between her legs and told her he had christened her. Then he lay beside her and slept.

If I were writing the story of a life like mine, if I were writing the story of my life in the diary that I never kept, I might see what happened to me so long ago upon a crowded train as a christening, an awakening, an initiation, with semen instead of holy water. I might make it a moment of great significance in view of all that would come later. I might, but it would be an afterthought and therefore a lie, or at least a distorting of the truth. The truth was that then, and for such a long time after that unknown man had marked me with his seed, I felt nothing. I felt nothing.

FIVE

I often think of that girl straddled by her husband, his seed splashing her innocent skin, staining the wedding sheets. I think of her fear, and the power it gave to the man, her husband of so few hours. I shall think of her tonight as I lie on my own wedding sheets and wait for Mr Ueno.

Of course, he will not have the power of that man. In a way I almost wish he did, for a moment, have that strength, that cruel certainty. It might, at least, give me something to look forward to tonight, my wedding night, even if that something is only fear. Instead there will be his damp hands and dry, cracked lips, his hesitancy. I know he will sit trembling before me, wondering what he should do, how he should begin. Perhaps he will make an excuse, saying that he is tired, that we have both had a long day and there is an early journey to the airport tomorrow morning. His parents will accompany us to Narita, naturally. I am half-surprised they have not reserved a room in the hotel for tonight themselves. Mr Ueno's mother is jealous of the few hours I am to have alone with her son. I can tell. She is already savouring the time when she can make me pay for them. I know women like his mother. I know men like Mr Ueno.

I have been in this hotel before. At night, after the wedding parties have ended, I have walked through the lobby and seen the newly-married couples making their way to their rooms, their wedding sheets, their wedding nights.

Sometimes they are with a group of late-lingering friends, men from the husband's college or company perhaps, intent on dragging out the ritual's final moments, the last, weary piece of bawdy, the last, weary piece of horseplay.

If you look at the bride then she seems lost, her eyes glazed over by the surfeit of emotions: the sadness and fatigue, the boredom, a sense of distaste perhaps for what has gone and what is to come, the disappointment. She is apart in every sense. Look at the man and, if he has changed into a lounge suit, you will find it hard to discern the groom. He could be any one of them, and they could be any group of men. Push them out into the street, they would melt into the other groups of men making a wavering progress to the nearest station, their dignity swilled into the gutter with their vomit.

It is with the couples who are on their own that you see the truth, for then it is the men who seem set apart. They are. They are set apart from their idea of themselves. The uncertain progress these men make across the thick carpets towards the elevators is not because they are drunk. The men hold keys they know unlock the future as well as hotel bedrooms, and they look as if this knowledge frightens them. All the certainty of the courtship is gone, the strong demands and assertions.

These men understand that, for the first time in their lives, they must undress and lie with a woman they have not bought in quite the same way they might buy some little waitress in a pink bar; someone paid to offer her breasts, and not disturb the unsubtle fingers that crawl around between her legs; someone who will bow when the little extra intimacy is required and ask how it is to be charged.

Afterwards, perhaps when the honeymoon is over, perhaps as soon as the first tomorrow morning of all the tomorrow mornings the two of them will endure together, it will be different. The unknown moments will be gone, negotiated somehow, survived and so forgotten. When they are settled into the routine of the sort of days their mothers taught them to expect, they can become men again; men whose wives will get up in the grey hours to cook for them, to set out their underwear and shirts, their socks and ties, to clean shoes for them, and shake from their coats all the debris of the night before, the smells of beer and tobacco, the vomit, the blood sometimes, sometimes the perfume. To air out the other, invisible pollutions that accompany them, that list of pathetic indiscretions men are capable of convincing themselves they enjoy. Thus can they go out into the world again, these men, these husbands, certain that when they return late in the evening their wives will be waiting for them, not as my mother waited, waits, kneeling by the door, but waiting nevertheless, the meal cooked, the bath ready, the bed made. This is their power.

In a way I wish Mr Ueno had the power of that man who knelt over his terrified bride because I know he will never have that other power. Well, I know he will not have it over me. I know too that my wish is a foolish wish for I am sure Mr Ueno is a virgin. It is I who will have the power tonight. It is I who will sit across Mr Ueno's chest. I will do it, when he comes to bed, if he comes to bed, because I will give him his wedding night, I will give him the memory of that because I will give him nothing else.

How shall I do it? Shall I act like a waitress in a pink club? Or stand with my back to him so that he might pretend I am a schoolgirl on a train? Perhaps I should take him into the bathroom, put his hands upon my breasts as I soap his thin ribs, write the price of ecstasy with my finger in the steam that settles on the bathroom mirror. I will let him think that he has bought me. In a way he has. Well, my father sold me, so Mr Ueno must have bought me. Money was exchanged. Of course, Mr Ueno does not know the full extent of the bill, yet. Neither does my father. If I am treated like a whore I shall act like a whore. My father said I was a whore the day I told him I wanted to marry Michael. A foreigner's whore, that's what he called me. Yes, if I am treated like a whore, if I am called a whore, then I shall act like one. I know how to do it. I was taught by men.

Once I did not have this knowledge. Once — shall I say once upon a time? — I was innocent. Once upon a time I did not even know what it was some man had stained my underwear with. Once upon a time I was just a girl, an innocent girl, and a man, a stranger, put himself against me in a train and marked me with his seed. Once upon a time a man held his wife down on a bed and marked her with his seed. He said he had christened her and then he went to sleep. A stranger marked me and then went away. If I close my eyes I can feel myself swaying as I wash in the narrow cabin of the train, I can feel the cold water splashing, the damp cotton against my skin as I pull my undergarment on again. When I think back to that time I believe something died in me that day. Perhaps it was hope.

My imagination again, my inherent sentimentalism. Some hopes did die, but they were not that important, I suppose. The hope that I would go to university with Reiko and Akiko died. They both failed in the entrance examination for the Blessed Martyr. The following April I went alone through the great gates. No, that is not true either, I was accompanied by my mother.

She came with me to the dormitory where I was to stay. She came with me to the room that would be mine for the next year. She unpacked my clothes for me and laid my mattress and quilts upon the boards of the bed I would sleep in. She opened the window to admit the warm spring wind that seemed to sigh against the pane. During the entrance ceremony she sat with the other parents as, one by one, the names of the new entrants were called from the stage of the great hall and we stood, each of us in turn, each of us in our new grey costumes. I wore stockings for the first time in my life that day, and I can still remember the sensation of the sheer nylon upon my legs, the gentle hiss of the fabric as I stood.

Afterwards I went with my mother to the university shop where we bought a few necessities, and then it was time for her to leave. We walked back to the gates together and made our goodbyes there. My mother said I was to remember what she had told me when we left my aunt's house that morning. What she had told me was that I must not do anything to bring disgrace upon my father's name. We bowed and then I watched her as she walked away towards the station. She did not look back after she turned from me.

I was very lonely during that first year at the Blessed Martyr. The uniform I had coveted so as a schoolgirl did not bring me any happiness. Most of the girls in my year were rich and empty-headed. They talked about make-up and hairstyles, about fashion, and about men. The only classes they thought to be worthwhile were the classes their parents had obtained permission from the university authorities for them to attend outside the campus, classes in cookery and flower arranging, and the tea ceremony. These they considered useful because they would help them when the time came to meet the men they would marry and because, once beyond the grey cement walls of the university, they were free to meet the men they would not marry.

Many of the girls kept a spare set of clothes in a coin-locker at the station, and changed from their uniforms in the toilets. Others made friends quickly with seniors who lived in small apartments close to the campus, and stored their secret wardrobe there. I had come to university to learn and so my conversations in the first few days were short. Anyway, almost everyone in my year was from Tokyo, or at least from the Kanto district. I know they found my provincial accent amusing, and I am sure my provincial ideas amused them as well, but not for long, nothing amused those girls for long.

I quickly found that I was left alone. If I sat at a table in the students' coffee shop where there were others, then the others would stop their chatter and leave. I met a girl from Hokkaido and in the classes we took together we would share a desk, but she lived with a cousin of her mother's and his family in Ikebukuro and had to leave as soon as the bell went for the end of the last period. So I spent most of my evenings by myself, except for Tuesdays when the volley-ball club met. Even then I hardly spoke a word. The training was very hard, and as a freshman member I had menial tasks to perform when practice was over.

How did I survive the bitter ashes of my dream? In part, perhaps, survived because I was already used to disappointment. I remember when I was a child there was a certain coat I longed for. I had seen other girls from my junior high school wearing similar ones at the weekends. It was made of a heavy woollen fabric and had a hood, almost identical in design to what the English call a duffel coat. I think it was the hood I liked most about it. I was so jealous of my friends. I would pass the window of the largest store in the town on my way home in the evenings, making a lengthy detour just to gaze at the object of my desire. Whenever I could I would make an excuse to walk by the store with my mother and dawdle there, forcing her to look at the mannequin that wore the coat.

One night my father came home unusually early, for I had not yet finished eating. He was drunk, and perhaps the liquor had released a wave of sentimentality in him. It could only have been that, for we Japanese have no feelings, not as foreigners understand them, but we are prey to sentimentality, especially when drunk. Whatever the cause, something had prompted him to buy me a present because he had with him a large parcel which he set down on the table in front of me. I knew it was the coat as soon as I touched the paper and in my excitement I could not make my fingers loosen the string that bound the precious bundle. In the end I think it was my mother who unwrapped the coat, for I had been correct in my guess as to what the parcel contained. It was a coat, but not the coat. The coat the mannequin wore was dark blue, the coats of my friends were dark blue. Mine was a light brown, almost camel, colour.

I could not hide my disappointment, and though I mouthed the words of thanks my lack of gratitude penetrated even my father's spoiled brain. The coat was snatched from me and I was sent to bed. I never saw it again.

Am I making too much of this? Really, that first year was not so bad. I was not as alone as I sometimes would like to think I was. Akiko was also in Tokyo. She had failed to gain a place at the Blessed Martyr but succeeded in winning entry to Waseda. How she had done so was a mystery that we spent most of the winter vacation before going up to Tokyo talking about, that is, when we were not commiserating with poor Reiko. She, the brightest of all of us, had failed each of the examinations she had taken and was condemned to two years at the local junior college with Setsuko.

Akiko and I met on the first Saturday of the term at a coffee shop in Takadanobaba, and we continued to meet there on Saturdays whenever we were in Tokyo. We travelled home together as well at the beginning of each vacation, saving my father the price of two tickets on the bullet train, for he had told my mother that he did not want strangers, he meant of course men, sitting next to me on the journey. I think my father came to like Akiko, or at least the idea of Akiko, for he never met her. Perhaps he took over the feeling from me because I found myself liking Akiko less and less.

I am not certain why — no, that's not true — I am quite certain why. Akiko began to behave towards me as if I was no longer quite good enough to be her friend, and our meetings took on the air of being an act of charity on her part towards someone less fortunate than herself. It was as if, recovering from her bemusement at the piece of good fortune which had secured her a place at so important an institution as Waseda, she had decided that, after all, she was really rather bright. Too bright, certainly, to spend time with someone like me, someone at a mere finishing school for rich girls. Nothing was ever said, but then of course, with us, nothing is ever said, nothing ever needs to be said. We know, and that is enough.

I think Akiko was right about my university, it was a finishing school for rich girls. Where she erred was in thinking of Waseda as being any different. Oh, of course the atmosphere was different, the sense the students had about themselves was different. Perhaps it, and the other mixed universities, come closer to vacation villages than finishing schools. I remember taking a certain comfort from my sense that the girls at the Blessed Martyr had a certain style which, in spite of all their efforts to fabricate their peculiar hybrid air of American Ivy League and English Oxbridge, Waseda students never quite managed.

I suppose I sought refuge from my isolation in work, but it was my work that set me aside from my classmates more than anything else, more than my provincial accent, more than my lack of interest in men.

My work set me apart from the other girls and, I saw later, it set me apart from the teachers as well. Miss Sekiya was the teacher responsible for the seminar I joined in the first year. There were four such; they were meant to ensure that girls from the different subject streams got to know one another, but in practice it simply enabled me to be alone among a different set of classmates. I came to terms with this as I always did: I read the assigned books, I wrote the assigned papers. I was attentive in class and afterwards, sometimes, not often but sometimes, I would follow Miss Sekiya back to her room to ask questions, have her elaborate on this or that point.

I did this with most of my teachers, not because I was really interested in what they had to say. After three or four weeks of the term had passed I knew they had very little, if anything at all, to say, nor was I seeking to flatter them. I suppose I wanted them to feel that I, at least, was interested in their classes, that I, at least, cared about the subject at a level other than whether or not I would receive a passing grade. In the end my endeavour was driven by the desire that they like me. For a long time I thought Miss Sekiya did like me, in spite of the comments she wrote on my essays. It was only when I was older that I realized she did not, that actually she hated me.

I was used to disappointment from my home life, and the reality of existence at the Blessed Martyr was not so different. Perhaps, after all, our parents do prepare us well for the world we must live in after childhood, in our schools and universities, in our offices and factories. After childhood? I wonder if we Japanese ever really grow up. After all, we are a people who turn our children into living teddy bears, dressing them like furry little animals, and our animals into little humans. We never grow too old for dolls, men or women. We decorate our bank books and cash cards with cartoon creatures, Mickey and Minnie, Paddington Bear, Peter Rabbit. We have little use for beauty, but suck endlessly upon the pap of cuteness. In sickness we crave the foods that nourished our childhood, rice porridge and sweet custard and cake, granting them an efficacy far beyond the healing power of any drug.

Yet children can be the cruellest of all living creatures, and it should not be so surprising then how cruel we are to those over whom we have power. We exist in a continuum of violence, we own or we are owned, we bully or we are bullied, we beat or we are ourselves beaten. Living so, what can we know of liking, and what can we know of love?

Certainly, I knew nothing of love then, in any of its senses. To be truthful, I was not even aware that I knew nothing, so deep was my ignorance, my innocence. Sometimes I listened, a distant ear, to the conversations of the other girls, their endless talk of men, even, a little, of sex, but to me it was utterly without meaning. It was a subject I did not major in, at least, not at university. In a sense I received private lessons, although it was I, officially, who was the tutor.

In my final year I was engaged to teach English, Japanese literature and mathematics to the daughter of a prominent Tokyo lawyer. That he was an important man was evident the first time I went to his house. I travelled by train to the nearest station and then engaged a taxi for the rest of the journey. As soon as I gave the driver the address he said that the house was that of Mr Ebisawa and thereafter, whenever I visited the house, I always spoke my employer's name when I entered the taxi and within minutes was at my destination.

I still do not know why I agreed to take such a task on. Certainly it was not for money, although Mr Ebisawa offered me a fee that was more than generous. Perhaps it was the promise of contact with someone who might grow to like me. Perhaps I saw the possibility of a friendship, and a friendship not with the daughter alone but with the whole family. I was lonely, and I wanted company. I also wanted to please Miss Sekiya, and it was she who asked me to consider the position. I felt I had grown close to her in the time I had spent at the Blessed Martyr, I felt she liked me and, more importantly, that she trusted me in spite of all she said of my sentimentality, my overly personal involvements in the books I read. I wanted her to think me worthy of her trust and liking. I really think I was a little in love with her, and I knew I would accept as soon as she approached me, for I would have done anything for her, anything.

My pupil, her name was Mayumi, was fifteen when I first met her. She was not pretty, at least not in the ways we think of. Perhaps she was already too mature. We prefer, do we not, our pretty girls sugar-sweet, in froths of lace, with crooked smiles and innocent eyes? Mayumi's eyes were not innocent. The gaze she cast upon the world was a cold one, as if she had already fed upon the meat of experience. She had about her that sense of knowing I have since seen in other eyes, my own perhaps, when I have come to consciousness staring back at myself in the mirror, but at that time the things Mayumi knew were still a mystery to me.

I remember how sullen she was at our first meeting, standing by her father's chair as he made his long recitation of her failures at school, her social worthlessness. It was a litany in which I was already practised for I had heard it all before from my own father's mouth. Of course, habit and custom requires such expressions as shows of modesty, but when my father's words of disparagement fell upon my ears, usually when he had returned from drinking in the evening, bringing some friend or colleague home with him, they had about them a conviction which made me quite sure that, for once in his life, he meant exactly what he said. I had that same sense listening to Mr Ebisawa, and when I looked at Mayumi's face, I was confirmed in my understanding.

We accomplished little of any value on that first occasion. After her father had finished discounting his daughter's character and achievements, Mayumi's mother began to fuss around us, sweeping me off to the girl's room, where the lessons would take place, before serving tea and sweet cakes. Mayumi obviously had not inherited her taciturn demeanour from her mother, for the woman shrilled like a canary with the sun on its feathers. When I left the house, in a taxi impressively summoned with just the statement of the family name into the telephone, I was glad of the sudden silence, although I was filled with a sense of trepidation at what I had taken on. I was not sure that, had the family been

less celebrated, had Miss Sekiya not personally requested me
to undertake the tutoring of Mayumi, I should have returned
the following week. However, I did, and the task of education was begun.

At the start I thought of my pupil as an unhappy girl.
Certainly she had much to be unhappy about. Her father
had little time for her. She had failed him from the beginning
as I had failed mine, for she had been born a girl and, again
like me, there were no other children. For all that, Mr
Ebisawa nursed ambitions for his daughter: his hope was she
would follow him into the law department of Tokyo University and from there to the bar. Why this was so I could not
understand, for even after a brief acquaintance with Mayumi
it was obvious to me that she was not about to fulfil her
father's dreams. She could not study, or rather, she would
not study, and it was this fact which made me reconsider my
opinion of her, for Mayumi was not an unhappy girl; she was
surly and uncooperative, and she hated her home as much as
she hated her parents, but she was not unhappy.

I tried so hard to interest her in her studies. I tried because
I was being paid money to perform my task, and I knew that
I could not take the envelope Mrs Ebisawa's restless hand
proffered to me each week after the tea and sweet cakes, the
fifteen minutes of manic conversation, unless I felt I had
done my best. I tried as well because I enjoyed the sudden
sense of identity I found I had acquired. From the moment I
arrived at the taxi rank in front of the station I was known;
after two or three weeks the drivers did not even bother to
ask my destination but drove me straight to the Ebisawas'
house. I found myself defined by Mr Ebisawa's fame and
reputation. And also there was Mayumi. I tried because I
liked her, in spite of her moods and the occasional curtness of
her tongue. I was her tutor, but she treated me, in the
beginning, as if I were some intrusive housemaid.

In the beginning, in the beginning it was difficult between
us. I would set out the texts we were to study that night and
give Mayumi the exercises I had prepared, only for her to
turn away like a spoilt puppy denied its favourite food. I
spoke into the air for most of the time I was with her.

Mayumi would sprawl across her bed, her eyes open but seeing nothing. She would not answer my questions, she would not acknowledge my words. I talked and talked, filling each empty moment until the time came for our lesson to end. As I walked down to Mayumi's mother, with her tea and brittle English china cups, her tray of sweet cakes, her frantic words that never once openly gave voice to her fears, for her daughter, of her husband, as I walked down the stairs each step seemed to scream at the failure of my efforts.

This continued until I decided that I might catch Mayumi's interest if I focused less upon what I thought she should learn and more on the things she needed to know. The girl quickly responded to this new approach; the things Mayumi needed to know were the answers to her homework. Within a short time we had established a new routine: I would complete her school assignments, and she would read a magazine. So successful was this stratagem, and it was such since I was completely self-deceived as to its real effect, that I was requested by Mrs Ebisawa to attend her daughter on two evenings a week instead of just one.

I cannot pretend that my conscience was easy, particularly when, one Saturday after I returned to my dormitory after meeting Akiko for tea and condescension, I was summoned to the telephone to take a call from Mr Ebisawa. I had not seen him since the occasion of my first visit to the house, but he wished to thank me in person, or at least, as much in person as the telephone permitted. Thank me? What for? My mind, which had already decided he intended to relieve me of my post, could not quite take in his words. He wished, he said, to thank me for the effect of both my teaching and my example with regards to his daughter. Her grades had improved beyond all expectations. Her teachers, at first astonished, were now delighted. As his praise grew ever more fulsome I took the complete measure of my deception. There was nothing I could say other than to repeat the standard formulae of self-deprecation in which our language is so peculiarly rich, and acknowledge to myself with a tightening of the stomach that I would be found out as

I was bound to be when Mayumi failed her mid-term examinations.

In my room that night I asked myself why I had begun this subterfuge, and I answered that I had begun it from the best of intentions. Why, then, was I continuing it? Again, I pleaded in my own defence, my motives were honourable. I felt that, at some point, Mayumi might respond, might grow accustomed to the pleasures of academic success, and with that familiarity seek to extend its duration through her own effort and application.

I was not convinced but then, at our very next meeting, I felt that I was given a sign that she was, at last, responding to me. Just before I made to leave the room after finishing a set of calculus problems, she said she wondered if I might be free to meet her the following afternoon. When I asked why, she told me she had tickets for an art exhibition at one of the department stores in Shinjuku and wanted me to accompany her. I readily agreed and, later, as I took tea with her mother, it was my conversation which bounded frenetically among the plumped cushions and lace table-covers, for I was convinced I had received a sign that Mayumi wished to change.

We met in front of the store at about four-thirty. I arrived late, having come from a lecture. I half-expected that Mayumi would not be there but she was and we went straight to the gallery on the seventh floor. On the way she talked to me more than at any of the other times I had been with her. She told me how much she liked the work of the artist, but it was a painter of whom I was entirely ignorant and the name mattered little to me so I could not store it in my head. Nothing really mattered to me that afternoon other than the fact that, at last, the barrier between Mayumi and myself had broken down, the proof lay in the sheer torrent of words that poured from her. I was so happy and, as she talked, I found myself making plans for the future, plans for directing this new confidence, this sudden energy, into the correct channels.

When we entered the exhibition she took hold of my arm, pulling me past paintings so quickly they more or less blurred before my eyes. At last she found what I supposed she had been looking for. She let go of my arm and said yes, it is here. I hoped it would be. I can still remember the sensation of coming to rest before the painting Mayumi had sought. I can still remember the slow accretion of awareness as to just what it was I had been brought here to look at, and the shock with which that awareness was accompanied.

A woman was seated on a chair with a young girl across her lap, a child really, for she had ribbons in her hair. The girl's dress was raised and she was naked from the waist down, except for her knee socks and a pair of slippers.

As I looked more intently at the painting I saw that the woman had her hand between the girl's legs and the girl, the child, was pulling at the neck of the woman's dress, pulling it down to expose a small and pointed breast. With her other hand the woman held the girl's hair as if to keep her from raising her head, and yet there was no sense of violence in the painting. The child's face, with her half-closed eyes and the composure of her mouth, was serene, and the woman gazed down at her with love. On the floor in front of them was a guitar.

When, finally, I was able to look away I found I could not speak, and as I met Mayumi's eyes I felt myself grow suddenly hot. I do not know now exactly what my emotions were at that precise moment, perhaps I did not know what they were then. Perhaps I was confused by a mixture of feelings: shock, embarrassment certainly, anger. Was I angry? Was I offended? I recall that as soon as I found my voice I told Mayumi I was leaving. She asked me why, and I said that if she did not know why then there was little use my telling her. This response of mine startled me because it was one my mother frequently made to me when I had done something to displease her. I was — I would like to say I was horrified, but it was not so extreme a sentiment as that — I was disappointed that I should have allowed one of my mother's spiteful little phrases to exit my mouth. Was this why my resolve to leave softened under Mayumi's entreaties? Again, I cannot honestly remember, but perhaps it was so. Perhaps, as well, I wanted to stay.

When we had finished we went down to the tea-room and there made our way through the clouded conversations of women to a table by one of the tall windows that overlook the busy street below. Someone came to take our order almost immediately for it was getting late and the store would soon be closing. I asked for tea and a selection of cakes, although I was not in a mood for the cloying sweetness of chocolate and cream I knew we would be presented with. When the waitress had gone I fixed Mayumi with an angry stare and told her I wanted to know why she had brought me to the exhibition. I suppose my tone of voice was also quite severe.

If I had expected contrition I was mistaken because she returned my gaze without hesitation and in the end it was I who had to look away, down into the street, the people and the cars, the first uncertain flickerings of the lamps, the woken neon blinking in the closing light. When Mayumi spoke, her words were simple and straightforward. She said, 'I brought you here because I wanted you to see the paintings. I wanted you to know what I think about when you are with me.'

I was right about the cakes. When the waitress returned she set before us two oozing confections of chocolate and cream. I did not touch mine, and when I saw that Mayumi had finished hers and was looking hungrily at what was in front of me, I gestured her to take it. I did not even drink the tea I had poured for myself so carefully, for I did not want to show my companion the agitation she had caused me to feel.

Of course, I knew I could not continue to teach Mayumi, and that night, before I went to bed, I wrote a short letter to her parents resigning my position. I intended sending it by express post in the morning so that they might waste no time in finding another tutor for their daughter. After sealing the letter and setting the envelope on my desk, all I wished to do was obliviate the day and its disturbing events with sleep, but I dreamed that night.

I dreamed I was a child again and back in the hospital where I had been taken when I fell ill with rheumatic fever. My mother was with me, but dressed all in white. She looked like a nurse, except that she wore a bride's head-dress instead of the small white cap of a nurse; the front fold of it was so deep it covered her eyes. I was feverish and she bathed my face with a sponge she would dip from time to time in a deep, perfectly white pitcher of water. It was the most beautiful sensation I had ever known, and I wanted to tell her how much I enjoyed the touch of the sponge, the brief coursings of the water down my face, like rain upon a leaf, but because I could not see her eyes I was unable to speak. The words remained chained upon my tongue.

How long this lasted I cannot remember, but it seems to me now that it was something I did not want to end. It was almost as if I was conscious that I was dreaming and commanded the web of thoughts and desires my brain had spun to linger so that I might enjoy it to the limits of my pleasure. And then my mother appeared to tire in her task, interrupt the rhythm of her actions. Stooping to replenish the sponge she paused, and the hesitation was of intent as well as movement. When returned to me, the sponge seemed to shudder, so heavy was it with water. My mother brushed my sopping fringe across my forehead with her free hand and then pulled back the sheet which covered me. To my astonishment I was naked, and the body now revealed, although it was my body, was not that of a child's, for I had breasts; yet the area around the pubis was completely without its dark covering triangle and as white as it had been all those years ago.

My mother began to lay the sponge upon me again, lightly brushing my skin, setting streams of water to trickle down the gentle slope of my stomach to form a pool in my navel, before wiping it away and carrying the water back to the beginning of its little journey. I kept trying to find her eyes because it seemed to me now that it was terribly important for me to tell her how much I loved her, to say how precious was her touch to me, but still, I could not penetrate the shadow cast by the fold of her wedding cap.

I was looking into the shadow that masked her face when I felt the first drops of water fall between my legs, and the whispered presence of the sponge. I could not move my eyes then, although, somehow, as if I had suddenly become two persons, I could see what she was doing, and as I looked and did not look, I became aware that the sponge had been cast aside, the water it held already beginning to seep into the mattress by my buttocks, and my mother was running her fingers lightly between the fold of my sex.

As she caressed me she took hold of my hair with her other hand, pulling it quite strongly. I felt afraid then, and it became more and more important for me to tell her that I loved her, and I did love her, I loved her so much I knew I would endure anything for her, even this. But each time I tried to speak the words of love they vanished in the hollow of my mouth, which seemed to my watching self a place of shadows quite as deep as the shadow wherein my mother's eyes were hidden.

The more her fingers probed me the more I knew I must tell her of my love, but the more I tried to speak the more her hand pulled at my hair. I felt my love become a bird which beat its wings against the bars of its prison until they hung like bloodied flags, and still I could not speak. I rolled my head as if I were possessed, insensitive to my pulled hair, arching my back and thrusting my hips to meet my mother's fingers, seeking, it seemed, to show with my body what I could not say with my mouth. I found her hand with each thrust, greeting the intimate fingers again and then again until at last the poor bird flew from its cage. And as I lay, my love let go at last, she took the shadow from her eyes as if it were a blind man's bandage. I understood then that the white shrouded figure was not my mother at all, it was the demon in the garden, the one who rode upon the wind, the one my grandmother had told me would come for me.

I woke then and wondered, in the first moments of consciousness, where I was, if I was alone. It was early, and the greyness of the city dawn was thick in the room. My covers were all awry, and my first thought was to settle them around me again for I was, and am, subject to colds if I allow myself to become chilled. It was then, as I shifted in my bed, that I became aware of the wetness around my thighs. I put my hand down and the sense of horror that had started in my chest bloomed, like blossoms in a sudden spring. I had wet myself.

Distraught, I got up as quickly as I could. I remember the sense of relief, the gratitude I felt that I was no longer a freshman sharing a room with another girl. I meant to strip the sheet from my mattress, but as I did so I realized that it was quite dry, and the shameful stain I had expected to find was not there. Thinking I must have dreamed it all, I touched my nightdress: it too was dry, or at least, only a little damp. I held it up and touched between my legs. If I had been wet there then the wetness was drying fast, and only a faintly glutinous residue remained on the insides of my thighs. I was relieved and yet, for all that, there remained the first suspicion, the sense that I had, somehow, befouled myself.

I took off my nightdress and ran some hot water into the little sink with which my room was equipped. I washed myself, shoulders and breasts, my buttocks, between my legs. Washing, I shivered with the cold and with the memories my actions called back into my mind: memories of my cousin, and the unknown man in the train. For I knew the white-robed figure in my dream who had begun as my mother and turned into a demon was a man. The demons are, are they not, always men? If women have a supernatural existence it is as poor ghosts, pathetic shades that wrap themselves like wreaths of early morning mist around the places where their sad lives were lived, their sad deaths occurred.

When I was dry again I took from my drawer a pair of new pajamas sent to me from home just the week before. They were still in their wrappings and I recall thinking it was very important for me to wear something quite, quite clean and new.

It was after I had dressed in the pajamas that I dragged the sheet off my bed onto the floor and stripped the outer covering from the eiderdown I slept beneath. I got back into bed and the roughness of the mattress ticking, the brief, sheeny cold of the eiderdown, felt like one of the penances the nuns talked of in our Religious Studies class, and I was glad.

SIX

I did not post that letter I wrote to Mr Ebisawa. I had intended to. I marked the envelope for express delivery, and meant to purchase the necessary stamps from the university bookshop at lunchtime. However, on my way there, I met Miss Sekiya. She was talking in one of the corridors with a tall, elderly man. I bowed my head and made to pass them by, but she called me to her.

She said she wanted to introduce me to the man she was with. In fact I knew him by sight and reputation already. He was one of my heroes, perhaps the only one.

Professor Kobayashi was a celebrated man. He was a physicist, famous for his work throughout Japan. He had been a professor at Tokyo University and the National Institute of Research and Technology. He was nearing the end of his career now and, having retired from the national university system, had come to teach at the Blessed Martyr. But he was not only a scientist; he was, as well, a poet and a philosopher. I had all of his collections of verse and many of his other books. He was often to be seen on television and, if I was away from home when the programme was to be broadcast, I would telephone my mother and ask her to record it for me so that I might watch it during the vacation. From time to time I would even attend his classes, although I could not really follow what he was saying. Yet for all that,

I paid more attention than the handful of other, gently dozing girls gathered in the hot classroom.

I suppose I had a crush on him — I know I had a crush on him — but then I would not have tolerated the notion. Crushes were what other girls had. What I felt for Professor Kobayashi had nothing in common with such nonsense.

Yet for all that, when Miss Sekiya called me over, and I found myself standing so close to this man that I might have touched him, I was breathless and quite unable to speak. I bowed again, as my mother had taught me, and hoped that the action might disguise my emotions, my silence so loud it embarrassed me.

Miss Sekiya said that it was a happy coincidence I passed when I did, for she and Professor Kobayashi had been speaking of me. I looked up, amazement diluting my timidity. Miss Sekiya said that it was Professor Kobayashi who had first approached her to find a tutor for Mayumi. He was an old friend of the Ebisawa family, having played on the same baseball team at university as Mr Ebisawa's father.

Still I could not speak, and my silence deepened even further when Professor Kobayashi addressed me himself. He had seen Mayumi's father at the weekend and heard of the wonderful improvement, a transformation almost, that my teaching had brought about. He had come to see Miss Sekiya because he wanted to meet the young woman responsible for such a marvel so that he might express his own gratitude personally.

As I gazed dumbly at him I thought I saw a moment of clouded doubt in his eyes, as if he thought he recognized my face from somewhere. It was this that gave me back my voice, for if he did remember me from the occasional lectures I had attended, he would ask what I was doing sitting through classes in the science faculty. The last thing I wanted him to think of me as was some love-sick puppy, and that was what he would think, I knew it, in spite of any explanation I might offer. It was impossible that he had not encountered all this before, a man as distinguished as he was.

He was distinguished, and not only in his mind. His features had been blessed by age; time had run a gentle, softening hand across his face, as a potter will over the surface of the clay. On his great head was a crown, oh yes, literally a crown of hair, a silver crown. He stooped a little, but this too added to his appearance, diminishing his height, making him seem almost vulnerable. I had looked upon his face so often — the quiet eyes gazing into nothing from the photograph on the jackets of his books, the smile that so often attached itself to his lips when he spoke before the television cameras. I ought to have been used to it, but coming upon him now, standing so close, it was as if I faced the golden disc of the sun itself; the brilliance of his beauty scorched me, shrivelled away the bitterness and cynicism that had attached to me at the university, left me naked, purified and healed.

When, finally, I was released from my enchantment, given back the use of my arms, my legs by Miss Sekiya's words of dismissal, I knew that I could not post the letter I had written to Mr Ebisawa. The very paper seemed to burn through the pocket of my coat, a visible mark of my treachery.

I did not eat any lunch that day; instead I walked about the campus until the bell sounded for the beginning of the third period. I was thinking about Mayumi. If I had considered my task of teaching her important before, it was now so much more than that, it was sacred. I pictured myself clothed in armour, like one of the knights in the stories of the English king, Arthur, or like St Joan perhaps. My twice-weekly journeys to the Ebisawa family were transformed into a quest, a holy mission, and I resolved to do everything and anything I could to faithfully discharge the solemn duty I owed this great man. I would not disappoint him. I could not betray him. I went into my next class a quite different person from the one I had been. Every part of my former self was burnt away, incinerated in the all-consuming fire, the sudden conflagration that raged within my heart. If I had not been in love with Professor Kobayashi before today, and I thought that I had not, could not have been, then I was now.

I had looked into his eyes and known they were the eyes of my beloved.

When I saw Mayumi again she too seemed changed. The sulky, surly girl of our early meetings was quite gone. She was waiting for me in her room, lying across her bed. This was not, in itself, unusual, it was the position in which I had grown used to finding her. What was different was that today she seemed pleased to see me, as if my coming were an event she had anticipated with some eagerness.

I was cool to her in my greeting, because I could not allow what had happened at our previous meeting to divert me from my task. I had to show her that my determination to make her succeed as a scholar was stronger than her indifference, and I intended that this would be the whole extent of our lesson that day.

I had hoped the severity of my voice might have cautioned her that something was going to happen, something she would not enjoy, but it did not. She looked up as I came in and said she had something to show me. I waited while she hunted out whatever it was from the pile of magazines and comic books on the desk which her parents had placed in the room. I remember it was an exceptionally large desk, as if its size by itself was meant to instruct and admonish. In fact it did neither; for Mayumi the desk was simply another surface on which she might deposit the various pieces of trash with which she filled her life.

When she had found what it was she was looking for she brought it over to me. It was a magazine, a Japanese edition of a French photographic magazine. She opened it to show me a photograph. It was almost the same scene I had looked upon with such bewildered disgust at the exhibition. A woman sat with her legs apart, her skirt in her lap, upon a dishevelled bed. She held a younger girl, standing, close to her. The girl held a violin, as if a music lesson had been in progress, but her skirt was raised to reveal her naked backside above white, knee-length socks.

I looked from the photograph to Mayumi and closed the magazine. I asked her what she thought she was doing with such a magazine, why she should want to show it to me. She said I knew why and then, taking the magazine from me, she opened it again. Look, she said, look at this. There were photographs of women together, their blouses unbuttoned, breasts and bellies naked, the few pieces of clothing remaining on their bodies, stockings, shoes, a suspender belt, seemingly forgotten in the passionate impulse of the seduction. That these were photographs of seduction I was quite sure. That they were part of Mayumi's intended seduction of me, I was now equally sure.

I asked her again what she thought she was doing, and she replied, flatly, honestly, with an ability to see through the pretended ignorance of my words, that I knew exactly what she thought she was doing, and if I did not then she was not going to tell me. I felt the words I had spoken to her at our last meeting, my mother's words, had been thrown in my face like cold water.

She brushed one of the photographs with her fingers and said she wanted to be with me in that way.

I attempted to answer her with a rationale my own experience could not support, relying upon my age to carry the bluff. I began telling Mayumi the feelings she had for me were not in themselves wrong, simply misdirected, that one day she would find a young man who would inspire those same feelings, that he would return them and they would marry, but Mayumi was laughing at me before I could finish. Her voice, when she spoke, still held the laughter. She said I knew very well that she would marry the man her parents told her to marry, that marriage had nothing to do with any of this. This, she said, was completely different.

She looked straight at me and said she had been sleeping with men since she was fourteen, but had never done it with another girl. She thought, she said, it would be nice to try it with me.

My calm collapsed with my argument, undermined as much by the words she used, the utter lack of emotion with which she used them, as the meaning they carried. I could not answer her, I could only listen as she went on. Had I never wondered what it would be like with another woman? When my lover held me, did I not sometimes wish he had breasts for me to fondle, folds and cavities in the flesh where my fingers might explore as his explored mine? Did I not find the speed of a man's passion boring after a time? Had I not longed to hold someone whose passion might go on and on as mine did? I could only answer that I had no knowledge of such things, that I had no lover, that I had never made love with a man.

Now it was Mayumi who was shocked. She could not believe what I had said and when, finally, she did accept that I was not lying to her, she opened herself up to another assault upon her credulity. She asked if, when I caressed myself, I did not sometimes imagine my hands were those of another girl. I shook my head.

She said, well, then, a man, you must always imagine a man. I said I imagined no one. I said I had never once touched myself in the way she implied. And it was true, I had not.

Once, I cannot remember where or how, I had come upon the word masturbation, and not knowing what it meant I asked my mother. She froze me with such a look I ran from the house and dared not enter it again until the light began to fail in the garden. Only my greater fear of the night and the demons drove me back inside. I knew that I had pronounced something very ugly and dirty, a secret so foul that having uttered the word I had defiled the innocence of my mouth for ever. When, at last, I discovered what it was, this thing that I had said, I burned with shame and cast the word and the deed it named away from me.

From that moment Mayumi and I were committed to a struggle against one another, a struggle I increasingly came to understand I could not win, but one from which I could not now disengage. All the sudden beauty that had clouded about my teaching vanished. Where once I had gone gladly to her house, now I went in fear. It is not too strong a word. The girl did frighten me. Almost from the moment I entered her room she would begin telling me of her sexual exploits, her desires. She would have more photographs to show me, or she would read to me, her voice rising above my own until I was forced to cease my protests for fear that her mother would hear. She brushed aside my coldness, she ignored the determination with which I would set about her school work. When I told her that I would have to resign my position as her tutor she said she knew I could not. When I said her father would dismiss me if her grades deteriorated, or she failed her examinations, she told me he would not.

She told me of the men she went with, the things they did to her, the things she did to them. At the time I had no idea whether any of what she said was true, but now, now that I have my own stories to tell, I think perhaps it was, all of it.

In spite of myself I found I was being pulled into the web Mayumi spun. As hard as I tried I could not stop my ears to her stories, the endless repetitions of passion, in cars and darkened houses. In the beginning I tried to challenge the authenticity of what she said, not in the intricacies of lust that she described, for how, then, could I have judged truth from fiction? My challenges were to do with how she escaped the supervision of her parents on the nights, and listening to Mayumi talk they must have been many, when she ran from their house to the arms of her lovers.

I remember the first time I voiced my doubts she answered me by getting up from her bed and going to the window, which she opened. Then, with a grace of which I had not thought her capable, she somersaulted over the sill into the night. I rushed to where, a moment before, she had been, where now only the restless curtains moved in the cold wind. Mayumi stood looking up at me. Her eyes seemed to shine, darker than the darkness itself. She turned and ran to the back of the house. A few minutes later she came back into the bedroom, cursing, something I had never heard a girl do before, because she had pulled her tights on a shrub in the garden.

She put her leg on the edge of the chair where I had been sitting to examine the hole she had made and smooth the material of her tights. I could not help noticing how slim and firm her calf was. When she looked up she smiled at me.

She asked me if it was really true that I had never touched myself, and, when I nodded my head, she began to caress her leg, moving her hands along it. She said that the first time a man had done that to her she got wet so quickly she thought she had had an accident.

I had moved away from her, but she came towards me, insisting that it was really very nice, and then she put her hand beneath my skirt, just for a moment, just long enough for me to feel its presence and sense her intention before she stepped back and smiled.

She said I ought to try it myself because she thought I would like it. She thought I would like it a lot.

I remember that when she spoke of how she had almost wet herself she used the vulgar language of a child. I remember because it was the only time I ever heard her use words like that. Listening to her talk it was impossible to imagine that she had ever been a child at all.

The men she went with worked mainly in night-clubs or pink bars. Given the business they were in I suppose they were little better than gangsters. Some of them probably were gangsters.

She would leave her room in the way she had shown me at one in the morning and cycle to the station to catch the last train into Shinjuku. There she would either walk into Kabuki-cho or take a taxi to Roppongi, it depended upon whom she felt like seeing that night. She would return to the house by four-thirty or five o'clock and be in bed, feigning sleep, when her mother came to wake her for school at six. She said that her parents never woke; her mother took sedatives for her nerves and her father, when he slept at home, which was not that often during the week, was drunk.

I asked her how she coped without sleep and she took a phial of tablets from her schoolbag. One of her lovers kept her supplied with them, she said.

Whenever I tried to reason with Mayumi she would turn my argument aside with laughter or a logic of her own. She lived in a world that was farther from me than the moon. When I appealed to her with examples from the world we did share I felt I was pretending to values I did not believe in myself, and she smelt the hypocrisy as it poured from my mouth. Once, I even caught myself repeating the words my mother had admonished me with the day she had left me at the gates of the Blessed Martyr. When I had finished telling Mayumi that she should not do anything to disgrace her father she screwed her mouth up in disgust, and said that her family's honour was just another way to control her.

No man, she said, controlled her. It was quite the contrary, she controlled them. She began to shout at me, and I was terrified again that we should bring her mother into the room. When I voiced my fear, Mayumi told me that she did not care.

I knew I must get away from her. My hopes grew that Mayumi's mid-term examination results would be so bad that her father would release me in disgust, but she achieved marks quite in keeping with the grades I had been winning for her. When I asked how, she told me she knew that the school used the same papers, rotating them every two years, and so she had bought the ones she needed from a senior student. After that it had just been a matter of paying someone else to provide her with the answers.

She always had money. Mayumi was a careless girl and sometimes there would be money left around her room: on her desk, on her bed. Once I saw five 10,000 yen notes lying on the floor. When I asked her where she got it she replied frankly that she got it from men. She told me never to worry about money, that if I ever needed any she would give it to me, no matter how much. She said, money is everything, money is even better than sex. She said that if I didn't understand that, then I understood nothing.

She told me once that she could arrange for me to earn a great deal of money. I tried to ignore her, but she continued anyway. She said she had been talking about me to a friend of hers, a man. He was interested in me. He wanted to meet me.

She had told him that I was a student and he said he would give me 50,000 yen to let him sleep with me. When she told him I was a student at the Blessed Martyr he offered double what he had offered before. Then Mayumi said that I was still a virgin and at once he pulled out his wallet, emptying its contents on the table. Mayumi counted it, there was over 250,000 yen. It seemed the man did not even want me for the whole night, he would pay just to have me that first time. It would be easy, Mayumi said, because he never lasted more than two or three minutes, indeed, he would probably be too excited even to penetrate me properly. Mayumi said it was difficult for the men she knew to get girls from the Blessed Martyr, that these men willingly paid 20,000 yen just for the university year book. If I was interested she could get me more than a million yen for three, perhaps four hours, of my time.

I said I was not interested, expecting her to sulk, but she did not. Instead she told me I was a fool. That I could make a lot of money, especially as I had her to steer me to the right men. She said she had sold her virginity six or seven times, but that she had never been given as much as I was being offered, even though she could pass for twelve or thirteen at the most.

I was terrified when I walked from the station back to the campus that night. I wondered if Mayumi had given my name to this man. If she had he would have been certain to look for my photograph in the year book. I wondered if I was being followed. I was so frightened I turned back towards the noise and lights around the station, and took a taxi from there the short distance to the university. It was something I had never done before.

The last time I saw Mayumi was in January, three weeks before my final examinations. I had been home for the New Year, of course. It was the same as it always was, a seemingly endless succession of visits from people connected with my father's business: workers, suppliers, the contractors he employed to fit out his new shops. My mother and I spent most of the holiday in the kitchen, helping the maids prepare the food and wash the dishes. My father sat with his guests, getting progressively drunker and more difficult to please.

I was happy to take the train with Akiko back to Tokyo, and I smiled through her condescension, which gushed from her because she had learned from Reiko that I intended to apply for a place as a postgraduate student at the Blessed Martyr instead of somewhere more prestigious. Akiko had already applied to Tsuda College. I did not care. I wanted to stay at the Blessed Martyr. I looked upon it as more of a home than my real home, and it contained the only people I truly cared for in all the world, Miss Sekiya and Professor Kobayashi. Quite why I felt this way was hard for me to articulate, even to my own satisfaction. My room was nothing more than a tiny cell, and as for the people I told myself I loved, one I never saw and the other seemed to delight in criticizing me.

When I arrived at the Ebisawa's that evening I was taken up to Mayumi by her mother, who kept up her stream of talk from the moment I entered the house until Mayumi shut the bedroom door in her face. I had brought some small gifts for the family, a selection of special foods from Kyushu, and I could hear the half-demented stream of thanks drifting up the stairs as she went back down to the kitchen.

Mayumi had something to show me, of course. A photograph of a blond woman lying on a bed, an ecstatic crucifixion. The woman had no hair at that point between her legs, like the child in the painting. Mayumi asked me if I liked the photograph. I told her I did not, that it was offensive to me. She shrugged and went to stand by the window, dropping the photograph onto the floor.

She said she knew the man who had taken the picture, that he sometimes took pictures of her. He liked her because she looked so young, she said. She had been featured in several of the panty magazines — not her face, of course. She laughed then, saying her father might recognize her, he *might*. He would not recognize her panties, which was all that was shown in such magazines. The people who bought them were not interested in faces.

Once, she told me, she had waited at a station bookstall and watched a man buy one of the magazines in which she appeared.

He was just like her father, very respectable, she said, perhaps with a daughter of her age as well. He bought a newspaper, a respectable one, not some baseball sheet, and some cigarettes, candy, a health drink, anything he could think of. Then, as if it had slipped his mind and he had just remembered, he picked up the panty magazine as well. She said she had seen schoolboys buying condoms in the super-market with less fuss. The woman put everything into a bag, which was what he wanted really. Mayumi said she knew all about men like that.

She said she followed the man, even going so far as to sit next to him on the train. He took the magazine out as soon as he sat down and turned straight to her picture, which was not difficult as all the pictures were of her. She had earned a lot of money for them, a lot.

At first the man held the magazine so that other people could not see what he was reading, but he became very excited, she could tell, she said, because his face went red and he started sweating. Then he didn't really care anymore and he just held the magazine open on his knee. There was a woman sitting on the other side of him, but she did what women always do and pretended she could not see.

The thought of her photographs exciting a man like that made Mayumi excited herself, so much so she thought of telling him it was her he was looking at. She considered asking him if he wanted to see her panties in real life, but decided not to because she thought the real thing would probably have frightened him. Men like that, she said, preferred the pictures.

I asked her what she meant by men like that, and she answered that the man probably took his daughter's panties out of the laundry basket, if he had a daughter, and spied on her in the bath. She wanted to know whether my father behaved in such a way.

I remember I was very angry with Mayumi then, and told her I did not want to hear any more of her talk, but it had no effect. She simply laughed at me. I sat down in my usual place and took out the work I had prepared for that evening. I still prepared work, although I knew it was futile. It was as if I had to keep faith somehow with the idea of being her teacher, even if our lessons were a charade.

Mayumi had picked up the photograph of the blond woman again and was looking at it. She said she had been present in the studio at the time when the model was posing.

The girl was Italian, Mayumi said. She kept herself

shaved because she worked in Tokyo so often, and because many men preferred her that way, the photographer, for example. He had slept with her the night after he had taken that picture, and Mayumi asked him what it was like the next time she slept with him. He said the girl was not as good in bed as she looked from her photographs, but he enjoyed it anyway because she had no hair. He said it was like being with a schoolgirl. Mayumi was quite annoyed by this, but what he meant was a very young girl, one too young to have any hair there.

When she had finished she paused for a moment, and then asked whether I preferred women with or without hair.

I told her, as I so often did, that I had no idea what she was talking about. Mayumi smiled, as she always did, and answered me by saying that I knew exactly what she was talking about.

She always called me 'teacher' even in the lewdest of her monologues, and she did so now before she went on to tell me that she thought I did not always tell the truth even to myself.

I would not answer her, instead I began to talk about the holidays that had just passed. Mayumi told me of the presents she had received from her men friends and, as if to show me she could read the doubts I entertained at her descriptions of the extravagance of these gifts, she told me to open the drawer in her desk. It was filled with money, the notes carelessly littering the shallow space. As well, there were two watches, Rollexes. She said there had been others but she had already sold them.

There was a discernable air of resignation in her young voice as she complained of her admirers' lack of imagination when it came to giving presents.

She told me she had a present for me and I chided her, good-naturedly, for I was never truly able to make myself dislike Mayumi. I asked whether she had chosen her gift with imagination, or was it one of her superfluous Rollexes. She said I would soon see, but that before she could give me my present I must sit up straight in my chair like a good Japanese girl.

I still do not know quite how Mayumi accomplished what she did next, but she did. I expected her to reach behind her pillow or into some other hiding place for the present she had for me. She did not, instead it seemed as if she turned a pirouette to cross the room and land upon my lap, for suddenly she lay on her back across my thighs. And I, I was so startled I could do nothing but look down at my pupil who smiled at me, and then, slowly, began to draw up her skirt.

She wore nothing beneath it, and she had removed the hair from herself. She lifted her head for a moment as if to look down at what she had done, but then she turned her eyes to me and said she was my present.

I was utterly without motion. I do not believe I even drew breath for some moments, but then I moved my knees to one side so that Mayumi slipped to the floor. I suppose she may have hurt herself, if that was so she did not show it. She simply picked herself up and went over to her bed, falling upon it as she usually did. I began to pack up the things I had brought with me, the exercises, the pencils and notepads. When I had everything back in my briefcase, I stood and walked to the door.

As I opened it Mayumi called out to me, no one will ever give themselves to you as I would have given myself. They'll always take more, they'll always take more. You'll never be given something for nothing.

Downstairs I excused myself to Mrs Ebisawa. I said I had a headache, and so was obliged to leave early. She fussed, as I had known she would, forcing aspirin upon me, hot tea, but eventually I got away. I told her I would not be able to see Mayumi again for some time as my final examinations were due very soon, and after they were over I must return to my parents' house.

She already knew this, of course, it had been the topic of our last conversation before I left Tokyo at the New Year. What she did not know was that I had no intention of ever returning to her house. Somehow I would find a way, an excuse, for ending my association with the Ebisawa family. I was quite determined now.

And it was the last time I saw Mayumi. I was right about

that. However, that this was so was not of my doing. Mayumi's other life became known to her parents. Her class teacher sent a letter to Mr Ebisawa asking him to call at the school to discuss Mayumi's progress. Of course, her mother read the letter and made the journey herself. There she was informed that her daughter was keeping company with unsuitable companions. At first, poor Mrs Ebisawa could not decipher the subtle hieroglyphics of the teacher's words, but, and I can picture the depth of the embarrassment each woman must have shared, when at last she did understand, she could not believe it. Perhaps she dared not believe it.

How Mayumi's life in the neon streets and alleys came to the awareness of her teacher I never did discover, but perhaps it was because of jealousy. Mayumi talked about where she went at night, what she did, to her friends. Did one of them choose to repay these boasts by making the pool of schoolyard gossip eddy as far as a teacher's ears? I do not know.

Or perhaps it was jealousy of a more direct kind, for Mayumi told me, boasted to me, that she had, once or twice, involved herself with one of the male teachers. It began, she said, when she was with an older pupil, a boy, in one of the class-rooms. The teacher caught them and sent the boy home, saying he would punish him later. Mayumi's punishment was to follow more swiftly. He said, quite bluntly, that what she had been about to do with the boy she could do with him, and then he took her, there, on top of a desk.

Mayumi said it meant nothing to her, that it gave her power over the man, but perhaps it also put power, somehow, into the hands of someone else, the woman who was her class teacher. Perhaps this man was the object of her own teacher's affection, one of the deeply-buried loves that such women keep inside themselves, and somehow she discovered they had been together. I do not know.

What I do know is that when her mother returned to the house she had understood enough of what she had been told to search her daughter's room. Just by opening the door she would have found evidence enough to convince her that there was something in what the teacher had said, but as she sifted through the piles of magazines, the discarded, unwashed clothing, the make-up, she found the series of exercise books in which Mayumi kept a detailed account of her sexual adventures. I had seen some of these books myself; Mayumi enjoyed reading from them to me.

When Mayumi came back her father was waiting for her. His unexpected presence in the house must have told her at once what had happened and she did what I imagine she had always known she would do when this day arrived, for it could not have been entirely unexpected.

She ran. She ran to her lovers, the men who owned the night-clubs, the gangsters. She ran into the darkness, the narrow streets and secret places.

My poor little acrobat, how she must have twisted and turned in her flight from her parents. Yet, for all her agility, she could not, finally, escape them.

Once, when I had questioned her on the dangerous game she played, when I told her that, as her father's daughter, she must be known, and that if she was not picked up by the police and brought home then at the very least news of what she was doing would be reported to her parents, she laughed at me. She said she was a juggler who played with power and fear. The gangsters were afraid of her father, but the police were afraid of the gangsters, and her father, her father was afraid of her, of what an open acknowledgement that she was what she was might do to his career.

She was wrong. The equation of fear did not, after all, balance. It was the one sum she ever had to do alone, and she could not find the right answer. She was, after all, her father's daughter, and it was that which pulled her back to him, as if he had reached out into the night and caught the hem of her skirt. Her father claimed her, and the streets where she had enjoyed her pleasure gave her up. She was taken back, she was constrained. Her father caged her, in schools, in the law, in the family.

He held her until she was twenty and then he married her to a man thought to be suitable enough, and strong enough, to hold her when her father let her go. I understand she has children of her own now.

Whether in her existence as a wife she finds space for the pleasures she pursued as a daughter, I do not know. If she does I imagine it is with more circumspection than she was used to employ, and probably less joy.

SEVEN

I thought I had been away so long then, but it was only
moments. Mr Ueno's professor is still speaking. He seems
to be going through the lecture notes for every one of his
classes Mr Ueno attended. Everyone looks so bored. I don't
suppose he has noticed. I don't suppose this is so very
different from one of his classes, except that he wasn't able to
turn up here twenty minutes late.

Who was I thinking about then? Mayumi. Poor little
Mayumi. I wonder what sort of speech her teacher would
have given if he had been invited to her wedding? I mean the
man, of course. He probably wasn't invited. Still, he might
have been. It would not have been so unusual. There's far
more of that sort of thing going on than people imagine. Poor
Mayumi, when I think about things there was so much she
was right about, and it makes me sad that she should have
been so young and have had that sort of knowledge. I almost
wish she was here today, so that she could look at me and say
to me with her eyes, I told you so.

Last week I picked up a magazine, I can't even remember
which one it was now — *An An* or *Hanako* — something like
that. I don't usually buy such things. I suppose it was the
complete boredom of being so much in my mother's company that drove me to it. I found an article about weddings.
I was so shocked by the coincidence I actually read it. There
was information about the best hotels for weddings — I am

having my wedding in the best hotel, my father was right about that — places to go for the honeymoon, wedding dresses.

It even gave advice on how much each of the guests should hand over when they come in, friends 20,000 yen, relatives 50,000. We call it a congratulatory gift and dress it up in an elaborate envelope, tie the envelope with a ceremonial paper and cord; but, no matter how fancy the wrapping, still we mark the inner envelope with the figure of how much is contained inside. The money is what is important, and so, in spite of the glittery bows and the pretty paper, it seems like nothing more to me than the price of admission. When the ceremony is over there will be the settling of accounts, and my father's loudly proclaimed generosity in providing all this, all these moments of splendour, all these dreams come true for his daughter, will be returned to him. Knowing my father, he might even make a profit.

The wife of Mr Ueno's head of department is sitting beside me. Sometimes, when I turn slightly, I catch her eye and she tries to smile at me, but the smile never quite forms, as if it is a young bird unsure of its power to fly. She looks ill, she is so nervous. I don't know why, all she has to do is come with me when I leave the hall to change my dress. She does not even have to help me change, there are dressers provided by the hotel to see to that.

I didn't recognize her when I saw her today. I thought she was some aunt of Mr Ueno come up for an early look at the victim. I was quite rude to her, and I regret that now. So many of the others, in their black kimonos, look like vultures waiting to strip the flesh from me, but this woman doesn't look like that. She is thin and very tall, and she stoops all the time as if in constant apology for her height. The obi she is wearing has flattened her breasts so much she does not really look like a woman. She is more like a drawing someone thought better of, and tried to erase. She almost is not there. And beneath her nervousness is a terrible sadness.

I remember going to the zoo in Ueno Park one Saturday, because I had seen the show at the Takarazuka but desperately needed to get out of my room for an hour. It was

January and very cold. The wind off the lake in the park was from the north, and felt like ice. Yet the sun was shining, I remember that the bright light of the sun gave no warmth. The sun in winter never gives warmth, it is like us really. We Japanese, with all our manners, our politeness, are the coldest people on earth, even our passion is cold.

What was I thinking about then? Oh, the zoo, yes, there were a lot of people from the country there, people from the north. They were more like animals than the animals. I remember a crowd of them stood there throwing things, pieces of wood, stones, anything they could find, at the elephants. And there was a foreigner, a blond girl. These people from the north had never seen anyone like her before, she was as strange to them as the zoo animals, except that she was not in a cage. Some of the women were pulling at her hair, as if they could not believe that such a thing could exist. I hurried away, ashamed, a little frightened even.

I walked over to the far side of the zoo, to the smaller exhibits, because it looked quieter there. The animals seemed to cower in their cages. There was one poor creature all on its own in a very small enclosure. It was a fox of some sort, or a wolf.

At first I thought the cage was empty, because I could not see anything living inside. Then I saw it, I saw the eyes. Oh, the saddest eyes I have ever seen. The poor creature lay in a little hollow it had scraped in the dust, and as I looked I understood why I had not seen it before. It was not that its fur was camouflaged, it was much more that this animal was trying not to be seen. No, it was more than that. It was trying not to be. It was trying not to exist. Then, for a moment, just a moment, it looked at me and saw me. It really saw me. I had never looked at an animal like that before, never had the sense that this creature so completely other than myself, with whom I shared nothing except the fact of being alive, was trying to communicate with me. I felt the depth of the sorrow that had overwhelmed it, and I felt a sense of asserted sisterhood with it, as if the wolf wanted to warn me in case I shared its fate some day.

I wept then. I wept for the wolf in the dust and the frigid, sunlit air, and I wept for all the other creatures in the zoo, the sad apes, the elephants that danced beneath the barrage of trash and ignorance, and I wept for myself. I was not sure why, but perhaps I had a sense of the bars of my own prison tightening about me. It is the eyes of the woman sitting next to me which remind me of that day such a long time ago, and the wolf and her sorrow.

At last, Mr Ueno's professor has shut up. They let teachers attend these things without charge. Perhaps if they had to pay the same as the others they might be more worried about getting their money's worth of food and make their speeches shorter.

Miss Sekiya is to speak next. I suppose she will make at least one of her little jokes at my expense, or, at least for today, at my father's expense. She will talk about my passionate nature, I am sure, my incurable romanticism. They are things she knows about, after all. Just what exactly she will say about them I am less certain. She cannot, after all, tell people the truth, although I suspect she would like to. Apart from her impeccable manners she would be afraid to say the things she does know about me, afraid, because of the things I could say about her.

It is quite funny really, all that time I spent half in love with her, thinking that she, at least, liked me. I imagined we shared something, something based upon intelligence, the love of books, the pursuit of truth; things in which, of course, she led and I followed. But I thought we walked the same path through life.

It was only later, after so much else had happened, that she told me the truth, that she spoke to me as a woman instead of a teacher. Then I understood that we had shared nothing other than a certain aspect of fate, and what she felt for me was a curious stew of dislike and jealousy and, I suspect, pity.

Because, for all little Mayumi's talk and posturing it was not she who seduced me, it was this woman who is just getting up from her seat, this respectable woman with the slightly thickening waistline, and the expensive clothes that are, perhaps, ten years too young for her now, her hair, her manicure, her Fogal tights and Italian shoes, her jealous heart, her rejected, and forever-empty womb.

I despise her because she did not have the honesty to try and take me herself, she acted for someone else, she procured me for someone else, as if we were characters in some novel. That is the problem with teachers, is it not, they mix up art with life, and infect their students with the same confusion.

I remember a professor lecturing us on new writing in Japan. He criticized many of our younger novelists because they substituted misery for tragedy in their work, seemingly unable to distinguish between them. Now, of course, I know that the professor was wrong and the writers he attacked correct. They understood before I did that tragedy does not exist, except as a literary device, whereas misery does. Misery is real, it is a part of too many people's lives to be excluded from the pages of books. Perhaps I should have known it then as well, but, even if I had what could I have done? I was the student. He was the professor. I could not have questioned him. It is the way things are with us.

I sat the postgraduate entrance examination two weeks after finishing my finals. I knew I would pass even before I started writing the first answer. Even if I had been stupid the trustees would not have turned me down; they needed money, and they knew my father would provide them with some if I were to be admitted to the graduate school. It was not that he approved of his daughter continuing her education for so long, or that he had a strong commitment to learning. When my father was at university he spent all his time playing baseball and, as he continually reminds anyone who is close enough to hear him when he is drunk and remembering the past, preparing to sacrifice himself for his Emperor and his people. My father did, in the end, provide much of the money for the extension to the library. His name is inscribed on a bronze plaque attached to one of the walls. He considered that was good for business. Anyway, I am not stupid. I looked at the questions on the paper and knew I would pass.

I had an interview with the postgraduate committee two days later. Miss Sekiya was there. Afterwards, she walked out into the corridor with me. She said she wanted to tell me how impressed everyone had been with my paper. She did not say how impressed she had been, she would not go that far, but I felt she was trying hard to be nice to me and I truly loved her for that, for the effort I knew it must cost. As I made to leave her, she asked if I might be free to have dinner with her before she went away on holiday.

I remember exactly the expression she used, she indicated the distance between us still, she conveyed exactly the sense that this invitation did not come from her heart; but at the time, in that moment, I was too overwhelmed to think of the fine points of her phrasing. I was, if I tell the truth, taken aback at first because, since I had known her, she had never offered to move beyond the accepted parameters of our relationship. She had not, as some teachers did with their pupils, taken me for tea, she had not even enquired whether I might perhaps drink a cup of coffee in her office. Yet the shock, if it was so strong an effect as that, was quite washed away by the sense of happiness that swept across me.

I was to meet her in Ginza at Senbikiya, and from there we would go on to a private restaurant. The arrangements, at least, did not surprise me. It was what I would have expected from a woman of Miss Sekiya's tastes, perfectly in keeping with the clothes she wore, new outfits each season from Hanae Mori or Jun Ashida, in keeping, too, with the precise and simple elegance of her hair, the holidays she took in Italy each spring and, in the summer months, at her family's house in Karuizawa.

I imagined us dining together in a room of quiet refinement, surrounded by women just like my teacher, women of quality and independence. I imagined the food, it would be European of course, probably French. We would drink wine. We would talk. I prepared my conversation as carefully as if it was itself a meal, and each word a separate item on the menu I had made with love.

I saw to my appearance with equal care. I had told my mother of the invitation, of course. I was to have been at home by that time and I needed my parents' permission to stay on in Tokyo for the few extra days. My mother sent me money for clothes, which I spent at Hanae Mori. I had my hair cut at the same salon as Miss Sekiya used, I even made my appointment with the same stylist. When I looked at myself in the mirror before I set out that evening I found I was looking at a younger, rather less self-assured version of the woman I was going to meet. I did not know myself. I was very pleased.

I was half an hour early when I arrived at Senbikiya and so I walked along to the Yamaha record store and browsed self-consciously for twenty minutes before going back out into the street. I stood where I thought I could not be seen, and watched for my teacher to arrive. My mother had taught me my manners well enough for me to know that it would be extremely discourteous for me to arrive first and be waiting in the café. Miss Sekiya might be late, and we would both feel uncomfortable with the shift in status that must occur unless I were to follow her inside, allowing, of course, a few minutes for her to find a table and compose herself.

I waited, and she did not come. When I looked at my watch and saw that it was ten minutes after the appointed time I began to worry in case I had missed her while I was looking at records, and so I decided to go into the shop and up to the cafeteria on the second floor. She was not there. Then I truly found myself in a dilemma, and what little composure I had managed to carry from my clothes to my heart dissolved away, like a moth's wing in a flame. Should I return to the street, or should I wait at a table in case she had been delayed and telephoned to ask me to wait for her?

In the end I chose the latter course. I allowed myself to be led to a table by the waitress who had floated before me, my own apparent indecision infecting her. I gave my name with my order for tea, and asked if there was a message for me. There was none. I sipped my tea and waited.

Miss Sekiya still had not come when the café began to close. I paid my bill and, when I had returned my purse to my handbag, took out the piece of paper on which I had written the details of our appointment. I wondered whether I had perhaps, somehow, mistaken the time or date, even perhaps, the place. I was mistaken, but not over any of the details. It was the greater design that had eluded me.

I was preparing to leave when someone approached my table. I felt the presence of a man, the manager, I assumed, but, when I looked up, I saw that it was Professor Kobayashi. He asked if I remembered him, and then, when I said that I did, of course I did, asked if I was waiting for someone. I told him that I was, and I told him who. He looked worried suddenly, a cloud passed over his face as it had done that first time when Miss Sekiya introduced me to him. He said perhaps I should telephone to see if something was wrong. I replied that I could not, dare not, do such a thing. I laughed, I am afraid. I laughed because I was so nervous. He smiled upon me in such a kindly way I felt as if the sun had touched my cheek. And so I should for he was well practised in that sort of thing.

He said I was not to worry, that he would telephone for me. He was back in moments, saying that Miss Sekiya's mother had told him she had taken ill with a stomach infection. They had telephoned the cafeteria and left a message. I was only too eager to add to the fiction, and said that perhaps my own discomposure had confused the waitress and she had forgotten to ask whether or not there was a message for me, or, having asked, had omitted to pass it on to me. And then I laughed again, excusing everything that had happened as my own foolishness.

It was a fiction, of course, all of it. Miss Sekiya's absence was not due to illness, it was by design, just as Professor Kobayashi's presence was. It was all part of a play he and she had written, a play in which everyone was well-rehearsed and word-perfect. Everyone, that is, except myself. The role assigned to me was that of the innocent, and it was assumed, given such experienced fellow actors, that I would be able to make up my own lines with a little prompting. And I did.

The professor was so good that night. We walked out into the street and he began to talk about Mayumi. That was how I came to know what had happened to her. Not everything, of course, not that evening. There were to be other evenings when he would tell me other things about Mayumi. Then he told me only as much as our brief acquaintanceship required and allowed, but it was enough for me to understand that I would not see her again.

We had come to the entrance to the subway when he suggested that I accompany him to the restaurant where he was going to dine himself. He had called in at Senbikiya to buy some fruit for his wife from the shop on the first floor, and the smell of coffee drifting down the stairs had made him decide to take a cup before setting off on his journey again.

Yes, he was good. The mention of his wife came casually, naturally, and quite disarmed his proposal of any illicit intent. He was simply being kind to me. That I had been disappointed by Miss Sekiya was no reason for me to waste the whole evening, he said. In fact, as they were colleagues, it was his duty to make sure that I was not too inconvenienced by her sudden illness, he said. And I must not keep him from his duty, he said. He said. He said. He said.

And so I went with him, to a private restaurant where it was he, rather than Miss Sekiya, who was known.

I do not remember what we ate that night. I do not remember what we drank, other than the fact that it was wine. I remember thinking that this was the first time I had seen a man drink and still hold on to his dignity, his humanity. When the professor drank his face did not redden, as my father's did, his voice did not grow loud and coarse, as my father's did. He was a distinguished man, he was a gentleman, I told myself. I remember too his hands. His nails were manicured, and his fingers were quite free from the yellow stain of tobacco.

We talked, of course we talked. He asked me about my future, now that I had completed my degree. When I said I had applied for a place in the graduate school he seemed pleased, even a little surprised, although Miss Sekiya must already have told him that I had been successful or we would not have been where we were that night. He said I might need some help, a reference perhaps, when the time came for me to look for an apartment, assuming that I was to become a postgraduate student. He said he had friends who owned property, and that he would be delighted to give me an introduction to them, and a reference should I decide to rent something.

I was grateful. As a graduate student I must live off campus and I had worried that my parents might force me to stay with my aunt Mie and the awful Kenji. However, if I could take my parents to see an apartment recommended by someone as highly regarded as Professor Kobayashi, then I might be permitted to live alone. He seemed eager that I accept his offer of help, and I did.

When the meal was over, and he indicated that it was time for us to go, I imagined myself the happiest girl in the world. I had quite forgotten Miss Sekiya and her illness. When I was put into a taxi, and saw the fare given to the driver with my destination, I was even happier. It was such a perfect gesture, and so perfectly accomplished. I was driven off into the night as if I were a princess handed into a silver coach by a prince. It did not matter to me that my prince was older than my father. It did not matter to me at all. And yet, my head was not so entirely in the clouds that I told my mother what had happened when I saw her the next day. Something made me keep the truth of my evening a secret. It was the first of all my secrets.

I was at home for the whole of the holiday. My father declined to award my work at the Blessed Martyr with a trip abroad as it was becoming fashionable for fathers to do. Akiko was in the United States, making her way across the country from California to New York. I received a series of post cards from her, one would arrive every ten days or so. She had nothing, really, to say to me, yet I could imagine the malicious delight with which she must be writing to me, each card a reminder of how much further in life she had progressed than I.

In October she was to take up a scholarship to study in England, having failed the entrance examination for graduate work at Tsuda. My father had arranged it for her through the awards committee of the International Friendship Circle. For me, he had arranged nothing more than a course of instruction at a driving school in which he had a financial interest.

It was quite clear to me from the very first lesson that I was utterly hopeless. By the third day of my tuition I could tell that my instructor had formed the same opinion. I found it difficult to coordinate my feet and hands when I did not know why I must depress the clutch, or why I must change into second gear, and the unhappy young man who had been assigned to teach me could not or perhaps would not answer any of the questions I put to him. I think he understood that his future with the company depended upon my passing the test, and so he became increasingly morose and less inclined than before to say anything to me at all that was not absolutely necessary.

One day, after the first week of lessons, my father came to the school. With him watching I was even more incompetent than usual and somehow managed to drive into the side of another car. My father was furious and left without speaking to me. I went to bed early that night purposely to avoid him, but I could hear him shouting at my mother when he came in. He was very drunk. I fell asleep as I had done when I was a child, afraid of the darkness, and my father's anger.

The times I was not crying over a steering wheel, I spent with Reiko and Setsuko. When we were together it seemed to me that nothing had really changed in the years since we had left school, but it had, everything had changed. Setsuko had worked in a bank since leaving junior college. She said she enjoyed it, in spite of the long hours, but she had been introduced to a young man by her tea ceremony teacher. Her parents approved of the young man and he and Setsuko were informally engaged now. When they married Setsuko must leave her work as it was against the bank's policy to employ married women.

Reiko also worked. She had decided that two years of junior college were enough for her, and she had not sat the examinations to transfer to a degree course at a university, although I know she could have. She was always the cleverest of us all. Reiko's future was as certain as Setsuko's. She helped out in the afternoons at her father's company. She was the only child, her parents were growing old and Reiko accepted that she must look after them in their last years. She must marry a suitable man, and her husband would take over the family firm when Reiko's father retired. Reiko was so beautiful, so clever, but these things did not matter except inasmuch as they were commodities to add to the other things, property and a little wealth, that would be traded when the son her parents had not borne was brought into the family through marriage.

The world was pulling us apart, I knew it. I knew that the life I would have would not be lived in the same way as theirs. My friends knew it as well. They would joke with me about the things I did in Tokyo, the glamorous and exciting times I must have there. I do not think they envied me. There was nothing for them to envy really, my life was neither glamorous nor exciting, and I said nothing that would have led them to think it was.

I spoke only of my life at the Blessed Martyr, which, after all, was my life. I kept my visits to the Takarazuka a secret, and I said nothing of anything else. Their assertions to the contrary regarding my behaviour when I was in Tokyo were simply to tease me, and they teased me, I believe, to mask the sadness we all of us felt. For we knew these few weeks when winter died in the arms of spring, when the soiled blossom of the plum trees still littered the ground and the breeze that nursed the first of the cherry's flowers carried the petals of the peach through the warming air, would be the last of our time together. Afterwards so much would intrude, husbands and children, the necessary routines of the old, and we would never again be as we were now. It was passing, it was passing. The world was pulling us apart.

In the second week of March I went with my mother to Tokyo for my graduation. We walked together through the great gates, as we had almost four years before. I wore my uniform, as I had then. My mother wore the same kimono. Even the distance between us was the same. Afterwards we joined my father. He had come to Tokyo with us, but had gone straight from the station to a business meeting instead of to his daughter's graduation. We sat around the table in Maxim's with nothing to say to one another. My father did not like French cooking at all, and had only chosen Maxim's because he had been told how expensive the food was. In fact my father disliked any food that did not taste like Kyushu food. That night he sent back almost every plate untouched. What he did like was the wine.

My father has almost no tolerance for alcohol, but that has never stopped him drinking. One glass, no matter what it is, and his face flushes with blood, he begins to perspire, and his voice grows loud and coarse. That night he drank two bottles of wine. Of course, they were the most expensive bottles the restaurant had to offer, but the effect was the same as if he had been drinking the cheapest. He began one of his monologues about how unkindly life had dealt with him, how he had fought for his country, how he had never surrendered, the work he had done to build the new Japan. Now, he told all those who could do nothing else but hear him, he had so much money he could pay for all their meals and nothing to spend it on except a wife who could not even follow his conversations and a daughter who had graduated from university but was too stupid to learn to drive a car.

There were many other things as well, but time has taken the memory of most of them from me. Even then I tried hard not to hear. I filled my head with thoughts of another restaurant and another man, a gentle man, a gentleman, not this drunken lout who by some ridiculous accident was my father.

My father seemed to take my lack of progress in learning to drive as some kind of disobedience on my part, as if I was deliberately failing in order to spite him. Perhaps he was right. The driving lessons were his graduation present to me and in not mastering them I was, in a sense, refusing a gift from him for the second time. But he was determined he would not be beaten. When we returned home I was told that I must spend the afternoons as well as the mornings at the driving school.

This extra, enforced tuition must have had some effect because I passed the preliminary test and was licensed to go out of the school compound with my instructor and onto the public highway. I was now being taught by the school's senior teacher, a man of about the same age as my father. I had not seen the nervous young man since the day of my accident. We drove the highways that led from the town to the east. They were lined with short-stay hotels, places where couples could rent a room by the hour, places where necessity and fantasy combined.

Of course, now I know all about love hotels, but then I did not. I knew only that they were the sort of place where no respectable person went. As we passed them my instructor would leeringly enquire whether I wanted to practise making a turn into one of the driveways. He told me an hour with him in such a place would be worth more than a week of ordinary lessons. I would glare at him then, and he would have to tell me to keep my eyes on the road. I would wrench the wheel, slewing the car back into a straight line.

I found this man increasingly distasteful to be with. His language became progressively more suggestive with each new lesson, until it seemed to me even the simplest of his instructions was heavy with sensual innuendo. When I complained to my father he told me that the sooner I passed my test the sooner I would be rid of the instructor.

I did pass my test. The week before I was due to take it I began driving a new route. It was one I was to come to know well over the next few days. It was also the one I was taken on during the test itself. When I returned to the school from the police station, having passed the official written part of the examination, and had my eyes checked and my blood pressure taken, the principal of the school ordered one of his mechanics to drive me home. He said he had already telephoned my father and told him that although I now had a license I should under no circumstances be allowed behind the wheel of a car again.

My father was furious. I had taken the test in the morning, and was home by lunch-time. My father was waiting for me. He told me that after lunch I was to come with him to his office because he had several errands that needed to be done and there was no one he could spare from work to do them. I could do something for him for a change. I could go on these errands. When I asked how he told me I could drive his car.

The terror I ought to have felt upon finding myself alone

in a car was almost obliterated by the fury in my heart towards my father. When I got into the car and had switched on the ignition I could think only that I actually wanted to be killed, that death was preferable to continuing my life as this man's daughter. I pulled away in a cloud of exhaust fumes and tyre smoke, the rear wheels showering grit against the glass doors of his office.

I had three calls to make, but I got no farther than the first of them. I was to go to Kurume, to the home of one of my father's workers. The man had injured himself slightly the day before and my father wanted me to take a basket of fruit to him. It was a way of showing the company's regret and compassion. This would be underlined were the fruit to be delivered by no less a person than the boss's daughter.

My father is famous for the care he takes of his workers. Had he ever shown even a little of the concern to my mother and me that he shows to his beloved workers we might both have been happier. As it was, only the anger he felt towards me because of the humiliation I had contrived to heap upon him by my abysmal performance at the driving school saved my mother from making the long journey by public transport instead.

Oh yes, my father is famous for the care he takes of his workers. I remember once, when I was still in high school, a girl, a girl about my age, who was working as a part-timer in one of the shops, was very badly hurt. Somehow the fat in one of the open fryers exploded, scalding her on the face and arms. She was a very beautiful girl, but the accident disfigured her. Of course the company paid. The family was contacted by one of the local gangs while the girl was in hospital and they sent some men to shout at my father. It made no difference to the company, my father would have paid anyway, but for the family it meant that, in the end, they received almost nothing. The gangsters took it all.

My father was so upset by this that he sent my mother to the girl's home to offer a personal apology, and then, when the girl was recovered and it became clear that her beautiful face could never be restored, he took other measures. The disfigurement was permanent, in spite of everything the doctors did. She was sent to the best cosmetic surgeon in Tokyo, but her case could not be treated.

Of course it meant that all chances of marriage were gone. Even had the doctors been able to give her the loveliest face of men's imaginings the very knowledge of the disfigurement beneath the surface, the shadow below the bought patina of skin, would have deterred any prospective suitors for fear that somehow the spoiled flesh might appear in her children.

It is a fear that haunts us, the sense of the hidden monster emerging into the sunlight, revealing the past we have thought shut in some dark cupboard. That is why we order the detectives to search for evidence of corruption in the families we consider matching our children with. What we fear is far less often moral or even criminal, it is corruption of the blood: Korean, or our own untouchables, and anyone, anyone who might, through the genes of parents or grand-parents, carry in them some distant memory of those brilliant flashes of light so long ago in the skies above Hiroshima and Nagasaki.

Well, understanding this, my father knew what he must do. He could not allow that innocent to live out her life alone, and so he ordered the young manager of the shop, who was unmarried, to be the husband no one else would be. The wedding took place within six months, with my father acting as their go-between.

The drive to Kurume was like one of the dreams I had been having ever since beginning my lessons. I was not, in any real sense, in control of the car, and each time I had to brake it seemed to me as if I would slide inexorably into the vehicle in front of me. There were moments when I actually had my eyes closed, and others when I was so utterly blinded by my tears that I might as well have had them closed.

The man whose home I was to visit lived on the outskirts of the town, thankfully. I managed to get to the house without hitting anything, although at one point I did drive some two hundred metres along a one-way street in the face of the oncoming traffic. By the time I had stopped the car and got the basket of fruit to the door I was close to collapse.

I was plied with tea and politeness by the wife — in spite

of his illness her husband was out somewhere or other — but, as much as I wanted to stay, I knew that if I did not get back into the car as quickly as possible I never would, I would walk away and leave it there. Perhaps that is what I should have done.

The wife came with me to the door and then followed me outside. I had pulled the car up awkwardly, slewed at an angle and with the front end half inside the small car-port, which was built on at the side of the house. My troubles began as soon as I switched on the ignition, for I had forgotten to check that the gears were disengaged. I had already released the handbrake and so the car shot forward, banging the wing on the left side into the wall of the house.

I could hear the woman outside jabbering that it was all right, it was all right, but I had no idea what she was talking about. What was all right? The car, the house, what?

Of course the engine was stalled, and as I tried to start it again the car rolled back, but it stopped before I could get the handbrake on.

Somehow I got back in control, I started the engine, found the reverse gear, released the handbrake. Nothing happened. My father's employee's wife was still shouting that it was all right, and when I put my foot down again on the accelerator I was glad that the roar of the engine drowned her voice. Still nothing was happening, and I was utterly confused, wondering what it was now that I had forgotten to do. I was still revving the engine when I heard a terrible groaning sound. I had no idea what it might be, but the car did seem to be moving at last so I pressed my foot down even harder.

Suddenly I was rushing backwards at a terrible speed. I felt the back wheels bump up and over something, and then the steering wheel pulled itself free of my hands and the car seemed to be spinning around on its own. The windows were showered with dirt, and it was some moments before I realized that I had driven onto the small garden at the side of the house. I stopped when I ran into one of the shrubs which divided this house from the one next door. The shrub sat in a heavy stone container, and, correctly speaking, it was this that halted the car's backward progress.

The engine was stalled again, I turned off the ignition and got out, setting my heels upon the freshly turned earth of what had once been a garden. The moss had been chewed up by the wheels of my father's car, and I had destroyed most of the little trees with which the garden had been planted. Very quickly I understood just what had taken place.

The groaning sound I had heard was the wing of the car being torn off. What had stopped me rolling backwards out of the car-port was that the wing, already damaged against the house wall, had got itself caught against one of the poles supporting the plastic corrugated sheeting which formed the roof.

The woman was holding the torn piece of metal, still telling me that everything was all right. When I got up to her she began to apologize for having caused so much trouble by building the car-port in the first place, and then for the garden and the additional problems its siting had caused. She seemed as if she would have been only too happy to have supervised me while I undertook the complete destruction of her property, but I felt I had done enough. I told her that I would leave the car where it was and go home by train. I would ensure that someone else came to collect the car in the morning. When I offered her my apology for what I had done she insisted that it was all her and her husband's fault. I left her still holding the misshapen wing of my father's car and calling after me how sorry she was, but that I was not to worry, everything was all right.

I learned later that her sick husband drove the car back to my father's office himself. I learned this from my mother. When my father came in that night his breath was clean for the first time since I had returned from Tokyo. He had called my mother from the office telling her to expect him early and what he wanted for his evening meal. He ate alone and in complete silence. He went to bed early, and without speaking either to my mother or to me.

EIGHT

I have dreamt the car dream ever since that time when I was learning to drive. Always the same, it is always the same, the powerlessness, the inability to prevent the disaster, the inevitability of destruction. I turn the wheel but the car does not answer, I press down upon the brakes but the car does not stop. In the dream I can no more stop the car than in life I can stop this wedding. I had the dream again last night. Well, of course I did. This wedding is just another event over which I have no control. The whole of my life has been like that, no control. Even when I have tried to take control I have found that I cannot. When I have thought I have had control I find that I have not, in the end. In the end I have been the one controlled. I am not stupid. I know what has happened and how I have lived. I have tried to stop it. I have tried to be strong. It is just that there has always been someone stronger. I turn the wheel but the car does not answer, I press down upon the brakes but the car does not stop.

I returned to Tokyo one week before the start of the new academic year. I was with my mother. She came to choose an apartment for me. It was part of a compromise about where I was to live during my postgraduate course. My father had assumed I would simply move in with my aunt Mie. When I said I did not want to, he ordered my mother to find me what he called 'suitable accommodation'. He shouted this out one morning when he was eating his breakfast. I wiped the grains of rice his breath had spattered upon the table as I helped the maid clear his bowls away.

He had said nothing over what I had done to his car, and my contradiction of his wishes concerning the place I would live for the next two years must have added to his feelings towards me. I knew what was within him, as if his anger were a fire upon which I had thrown wet wood. It smoked and steamed, and the flames burned red within the pile. yet he did not show that anger to me directly. I think perhaps he dared not. Had he done so he might, he really might, have beaten me. At the time he told my mother she was to accompany me to Tokyo I imagined my father had compromised with me, but I was wrong. He made his compromise, if it was a compromise, with his anger, not his daughter.

We stayed, my mother and I, at the New Otani. My father's secretary made the reservation. It was a small punishment. Normally, when we came to Tokyo and did not sleep at the house of a relative, we put up at the Hotel Okura.

And we shared a room. I found this particularly unpleasant. As I grew older the love I had once felt so strongly for my mother had turned to repugnance, so that I could not bear any physical closeness at all. Of course, there was not much of that. There never had been. I cannot remember my mother holding me when I was a child. In my times of illness she never embraced me, never touched me unless it was a thing of necessity. Even her words were stiff. From the age of three or four she ceased to address me as 'dear Sachiko'; when she spoke my name, which was not often, she would add the more formal suffix, as if I were one of the women who worked for her, rather than her daughter. My friends, Setsuko and Reiko, even Akiko, thought my mother refined. I thought her cold, and I envied them the warm familiarities of their own families.

The sense of loss I had slowly grew, and the love that was within me congealed, altered. I came to despise my mother. Whenever she was near I was repelled by her presence. Her smell, which, once upon a time, I had hunted as if it were a friendly ghost, could now cause me to retch like the foulest odour.

That period when I was with her in the New Otani was a torture to me. I remember, even now, the sensation of distaste at our enforced intimacy. The first morning, after we had checked in and I understood what my father had done, I bought a packet of antiseptic tissues, the sort of thing middle-aged women carry with them in case they should find themselves faced with having to use a western lavatory and must sanitize the seat. I cleaned the bathroom with them after my mother had finished. I would go in, holding my breath for as long as I could, and rub down every conceivable surface she might have touched; not just the toilet, but the washbasin, the bath, shelving, even the floor. And still I could not bring myself to bathe, the thought of my body lying where she had lain made my skin crawl.

The time after Michael left me, when I thought I might have his child, when I wanted to have his child, I made a promise to myself that I would not go back to my parents' house to have it, even if they would let me go there. I could not, I did not want her near me. But then, in the New Otani, there was no child, there was no Michael, there was simply the room, and there was my desire.

I went with my mother to all the agencies; I looked at the rooms they showed us. None of them pleased me. How could they? I knew the room I would take. I did not know where it was. I did not know what it looked like. I knew only the person who would show it to me. That person was not my mother.

At the end of the week my mother returned to Kyushu. My father allowed me five more days at the New Otani in which to find something he would approve of. He was coming to Tokyo himself then. If I had nothing he would take me to my aunt's house, and I would stay there for the next two years. I went with my mother to the station. As soon as I had watched her train leave I found a telephone and I called the number Professor Kobayashi had given me. He answered himself, and when I heard his voice I felt I wanted to cry.

Everything was settled by the time my father arrived. What I had was not an apartment, of course, not in the English sense of the word. It was a reasonably large room, six tatami mats, with a smaller, western-style room attached, a corridor, containing a sink and a gas-ring, and a small bathroom. It had been added on, as an afterthought perhaps, to a larger house, occupied by an elderly widow. Her husband had once been a colleague of Professor Kobayashi's. She had no children, and, by letting out the small apartment, she acquired, I suppose, a sense of companionship.

The apartment was in a quiet neighbourhood some thirty minutes by train from the university and fifteen minutes' walk from the nearest station, so in a sense it was not entirely convenient. At least, it was not entirely convenient for me. But it was for Professor Kobayashi. He could visit me there easily and safely. I knew from the moment I picked up the telephone to call him that day in the Tokyo station what it was I was doing. My convenience was the least of the things I intended to surrender to him.

My father approved of the place in which I proposed to live, although he seemed a little suspicious that I should have found it on my own initiative. Before he left me he made arrangements for a telephone to be installed in his name, and stipulated that an itemized bill be sent to him every month. When he was gone, and I was quite sure he would not come back, I ran out to a convenience store not too far away and bought enough food for a meal, the first meal I would prepare in my own home.

It was my own home, but it was one I intended to share. I set about furnishing it with money my father had put into my account. At first I had thought of putting a carpet down over the matting, buying a desk and table, a sofa perhaps, of casting aside the paper screens in front of the windows in favour of curtains. And, I thought, I would buy a bed, for the smaller room.

I did not. Professor Kobayashi advised me to use the smaller room as my study. He arranged for workmen to refurbish the window screens, and I had new matting installed on the floor. Together we chose a suitable table. I asked my mother to send me the scrolls that had hung in my room in Kyushu, changing with the seasons. Professor Kobayashi presented me with a beautiful vase, austere in its lines and the simplicity of the glazing. I bought bedding: mattresses and down-filled comforters. Everything was ready by the first Saturday, and I telephoned Professor Kobayashi to ask if he might eat with me in the evening. He could not. His wife was expecting him. He came to me on the following Monday.

When I think about it now I cannot believe how easily I slipped into this new life, or how suddenly. But I can understand. I loved, and, in turn, I imagined I was loved. I am sure I did not know the exact implications of my actions. What I knew was that I wanted to be with this man as I wanted to be with no one else. I wanted to be with him as I had never wanted to be with anyone before. I knew, as well, that I wanted him to teach me. Being with me, I knew, he would teach me. I knew that these two things were inseparable. And I knew that his being with me was something I must never speak of. I knew this without being told. I knew this the first night when we were together in the restaurant.

And there was so much for him to teach me. I ordered the food I served to him in my room. I had to for I could not have cooked it myself. All my life I had been used to others cooking for me, the maids in my father's house, the cooks at the Blessed Martyr. After we had eaten as he was about to leave, he told me how much he enjoyed French cooking and that perhaps, the next time he came to visit me, I would prepare the meal for him myself. I was so happy, happy that he had found this place for me, happy that he had visited me here, happy that there would be another time when we would be together, there was nothing I would not have done for him. I confessed the reason why I had given him the meal I had, expecting him to laugh, at the least to laugh. He did not. Instead, he said he would speak with someone he knew, someone who was the principal of a cookery school. He mentioned the name. I knew it, it was the most exclusive school in Japan. Students were not even accepted for night classes unless they were recommended. He said he would recommend me.

He left, telling me he would be in touch. The next day he sent me roses. They were yellow, ten, perfect yellow roses. I put them in my study and the petals seemed to change the light in the room, turning it golden. I felt the golden light dance about me, illuminating my life, driving away the darkness and the demons. A week later he wrote to say that I had been accepted by the cookery school and that, if I so wished, I might join a class the following Tuesday. Enclosed in the letter was a receipt. The fees had already been paid.

I went to the cookery class and it marked the beginning of a new life for me. I joined other classes, for flower arranging, Japanese cookery, the tea ceremony, a course of elegant English conversation with the wife of the head of the British Council in Japan. So many courses, so much I had to learn. Increasingly my life outside of the university began to assume a greater and greater importance to me. I did almost no work for my university classes, just the minimum that was needed to pass them. The time from my getting up in the morning until I went to my evening classes seemed to pass in a kind of dream. I lived through it because it was necessary to do so. The moment when I walked out of the gates of the Blessed Martyr was a moment of release.

And I lived through my cooking and my flower arranging because these things brought me closer to another meeting with the wonderful man who cared to spend his time, his precious time, with me. I did not see him that often, perhaps two or three times a month. That did not matter. All I cared was that he came back to me. Each time he came I was able to show him how much I was learning, and I was able to show him that I was learning all these things for him, only for him.

Yes, it really was a new life but, of course, the old life was not gone entirely. Its shadows still intruded into the golden world. The telephone my father had installed for me was black. Each morning at seven o'clock it would ring and wake me. My mother would tell me what time it was, although, after a few days, I knew what time it was. Then she would tell me to get up. In the evenings she would call me again, at seven, unless I had previously said I would be out at the cinema or the theatre. At eleven the black telephone would ring again. This was done to make certain that I was behaving myself. That, as my mother would say, I was not doing anything to bring disgrace upon my father's name.

There was no other reason. My mother had nothing to say to me; on the few occasions, at the very beginning, when she attempted a normal conversation we were both embarrassed by the little there was to say to each other. Afterwards, the pretence that the phone-calls were anything other than what they so obviously were was abandoned. My father never spoke, although it was his honour that was being secured. As with his care for his workers the practical aspects fell to my mother.

How she sought to encircle me, casting about me her ropes of manners and convention: letters I must write, visits I must make, birthdays, weddings, graduations, all of which I must acknowledge; a birth to celebrate, a death to mourn. And then, at least twice a week, she would send a parcel to me. Eventually I began to marvel at the fertility of her imagination that she could so constantly find things to pack. I suppose it was easier to buy me things than to speak to me.

It is always this way with us, isn't it? I remember that once I went with her on a short tour, organized by one of the department stores in our city. It was a rather exclusive tour, by invitation only. The wives of those customers who had spent most during the previous year were asked to participate. My father understood it to be an acknowledgement of his position that my mother was one of those who received an invitation, and so he insisted upon her going. He also insisted that I accompany her, although I did not want to. Of course, we had to pay.

The tour was to a number of craft centres on Honshu. At each centre we were guided, eventually, inevitably, to a showroom and there we were presented with certain 'special offers', examples of the work we had just seen at prices which seemed, to me at least, far from special. Each time, my mother and the other women would pledge themselves to buy whatever it was, pottery or lacquer ware, the cost being added to their accounts at the department store. It was easier than saying no to the refined importunings of our guide.

The parcels my mother sent served the same end as everything else. She used one of the private carriers rather than the postal service, and so she was able to check whether or not I was at home when the parcel arrived. If I was not, and my landlady had taken it, she would want to know where I had been, who I was with and what I had been doing.

Quite what my parents imagined I might be doing I did not know. I was seeing an older, married man. I was seeing him in secret — very quickly it became established that, with few exceptions, I could never meet Professor Kobayashi outside of my apartment, I could not talk to him at the university, I could only call him on the number he had given me, it was for a telephone in his study which no one else but he would answer — why it was secret I was not quite sure. Apart from its secrecy our friendship was entirely innocent.

The pattern that had been established during the first visit was repeated with only minor variations. Professor Kobayashi would arrive at seven o'clock. I would greet him and lead him along the narrow corridor to the main room. After he was seated, I would make him a drink. At first, I prepared him whisky and water. It was the only drink I knew how to make. It was the drink my mother made for my father when he was at home. On other evenings I concocted martinis, Tom Collinses, all manner of things. Professor Kobayashi taught me. He was a good teacher. I was a good student, always.

Then I would listen while he talked, telling me about his work, what had happened since our last meeting, his plans for the future. We always began our meal at seven-thirty. By nine o'clock he was gone. Where he went I never knew, home perhaps, to a club. I never knew because I never asked. I did not think I had the right.

In all of the times we were together in those first weeks he never once touched me. I waited, I waited for his touch. I did not know how it would come, I only thought that it would. I wanted it to. I watched for it. The suggestion of a movement. There was nothing. I did not expect the crude, almost pathetic enthusiasm of Mayumi, but in the end even that would have been welcome. Instead there was nothing.

Ah, Mayumi. It was not true that she failed to seduce me. It was not true. Her touch found me out. That moment when her fingers brushed my skin woke something in me, something Kenji's clumsy hands had looked for but not found. She had known where it was hiding. She brought it out. I had begun to find it by myself. She had even known my dreams, dreams I had not dreamed myself. Now, in my quiet times, in my secret times, my fingers were her fingers, and my dreams were her dreams. It was not enough. Even at the beginning it was not enough. I wanted him as well.

I stayed in Tokyo during the summer, returning to my father's house only during the holiday for Obon. I told my mother I was too busy with my work to be at home. It was hardly true. I was not working. I was only pretending to work. I sat through the days and nights of heat in the city, waiting for September's rain to wash the streets, and cleanse the tired gardens. I did nothing. Sometimes in the afternoon I would go to the cinema, never in the evenings. In the evenings I sat and let the heavy stillness of the night close about me until the ringing of the telephone at eleven eddied the air of my room as a pebble tossed by a spiteful child disturbs the still surface of the pool.

I saw less of Professor Kobayashi. When I did see him I kept my silence, I never questioned him as to why the spaces between his visits had grown longer. Time seemed like a net drawn tight, the diamonds of the mesh expanded. I did not ask because I understood, somehow, that I should not, and because, somehow, I dared not. I was so afraid my words might tear the net, rend the tenuous filaments and let go the little silver fishes of my love. He came when he came, and that was all there was to know.

The summer passed. The rain came again, and then the warm, dry days of October. The new term began. I knew I would have to work now, not for the degree, that was assured, my father's money, the promise of my father's money, had already paid for it. I knew I would have to work for myself. I stayed late at the library, and when I walked from the station to my room I enjoyed the darkness of the autumn nights, the warm air that held the sudden scents of close-leafed gardens, the pools of light along the road where late moths danced.

As I disappeared into the night each narrow street closed behind me like a gate, and I carried in my ears the mournful clanging of the bell at the crossing next to the station until, at last, I turned the corner by my house and heard it no more, except in my memory. And the nights I had spent with Professor Kobayashi faded too, except in my memory. He did not come, and I did not look for him.

I am being romantic again, it must be the effect of Miss Sekiya's speech. I must stop treating my life as if it were one of my translations — lonely little rich girl Sachiko Miura had everything she wanted except love. When a handsome, learned older man came into her life she was swept off her feet, but was this what she was looking for? He was old enough to be her father (he was older than her father); he was married. Was this the love she had yearned for? Was it even love?

He telephoned me early one Saturday in November. I remember the date. It was the fifteenth, the day the children are taken to shrines to celebrate their survival through the difficult years, seven and three for the girls, five and three for the boys. Grandmother Miura took me when I was seven, dressed in a kimono like a little doll. I screamed and screamed as we approached the gateway to the shrine. I thought she was taking me there so that she could give me to the demons.

I was asleep when he called, and I picked up the receiver expecting to hear my mother's voice. Instead it was his. I had prepared myself for this. I had steeped myself in sorrow and disappointment, in tears, and a returning, keener sense of loneliness. I was ready to say no to him. I was ready to say to him what he had not had the courage to say to me, I was ready to tell him goodbye.

But he spoke and his voice washed it all away. The sorrow and disappointment, the loneliness, even the tears. With them went my determination, and the sounds which formed the word farewell. He wanted to see me again. He wanted to see me that night. I said he could, of course I did. I was to wait for him where I had waited before, but not, knowingly, for him. We were to have dinner. He would be bringing someone with him he said, a former student returned to Japan for a short time from the United States. He wanted me to act as his hostess. When I put the telephone down I bowed my head to it. I was his. I was his for as long as he wanted me, as long as he would have me.

I dressed myself in the clothes I had worn on that first occasion, and I was as punctual as I had been that first time. As I climbed the stairs to the coffee shop I knew he was already there, for I had watched him go in a little while before. I made my own entrance with all the practiced poise of an actress.

The former student was a man, perhaps four or five years older than myself, called Mr Matsuda. He had been supervised by Professor Kobayashi as a postgraduate researcher at the National Institute of Technology. He had gone from there to Los Angeles and was now studying at the California Institute of Technology. I did not like Mr Matsuda. He wore clothes, American clothes, more suitable, it seemed to me, for a teenager than someone in his late twenties. His hair was untidy and in need of cutting. When he spoke he peppered his conversation with American idioms which I found offensive. I smiled for him only because I felt Professor Kobayashi wished me to.

We had dinner at the same private restaurant as before. Mr Matsuda drank his soup as if he were standing in front of a noodle counter, and cut his meat into small pieces which he then pushed into his mouth with his fork held in his right hand. He had drunk vodka mixed with some dark liqueur before the meal, and before he had finished his first glass of wine it was evident that he was drunk.

Yet, Professor Kobayashi continued to praise him throughout the meal, and to disparage himself. Mr Matsuda, he said, was the future. A bright young Japanese who could meet the outside world on his own terms, without the sense of inferiority those who had lived through the war felt in the presence of foreigners. Mr Matsuda was the new Japan, one of the golden youths who would carry our nation into the coming century.

To me Mr Matsuda seemed more like an ill-mannered boy. I remembered the golden light the yellow roses had cast upon my room. I remembered the kindness in the eyes of the man who had sent them, his gentility, his wisdom. I looked at that noble head with its mane of silver hair. So much preciousness. So much silver, so much gold.

When we left the restaurant the two men saw me into a taxi. As I said my goodbyes I heard Professor Kobayashi telling Mr Matsuda that he was far too old to be taking up the time of a young girl like me, that I needed the company of someone younger. He suggested to Mr Matsuda that he should spend a little of the time he had left in Japan with me. Horrified, I accepted the business card that an uncertain hand held out to me. Horrified, I responded with my own. When I got to my room that night I found I could not sleep, and it seemed, when at last I did sleep, that I had hardly closed my eyes when my mother telephoned, wanting to know why I had not been in when she called the night before. I lied and then slept again.

I did not wake until two in the afternoon. I washed and put my clothes on, thinking that although I had missed my morning class I might still be able to get to the university by three o'clock for my tutorial with Miss Sekiya. Afterwards I intended to work in the library. I wished to be at home as little as possible over the next few days. In this way I hoped to avoid any unpleasantness that might be involved with turning down the invitation I now expected from Mr Matsuda.

As I prepared to leave the telephone rang. I hesitated before answering it, but finally picked up the receiver. I thought it might have been Professor Kobayashi, and I could not deny myself his voice, not after so long a silence. It was not the professor, it was his student. I heard him asking me if he might see me that evening, and I heard myself saying yes. When he had rung off I sat down. By the time I had come to my senses again it was too late to go out, and so I undressed and got back into bed.

I met Mr Matsuda that night, and then again the next evening. He had only those two days left in Tokyo before he went to see his family in Nigata. He was to spend a week there and then travel directly to the airport at Narita for the return flight to America.

I did not like Mr Matsuda very much. His conversation was full of America, and from his conversation I found I liked America rather less than I liked Mr Matsuda. Nothing in Japan seemed to please him anymore. Japan, he said, was tied to the past, while America held the reins of the future. The metaphor is mine. Mr Matsuda's mind was rather more prosaic. He was full of his life there, the freedom he had found, the food, his car, days at the beach. He talked about the beach a great deal. The beach, he said, was the place to be, the place to meet people. I think he meant that the beach was the place to meet women. He talked about women a great deal as well.

He said that American women were different. They were free. Free was a favourite word with him, free in the sense of being liberated from the code of moral values that we lived by in Japan. Perhaps it was more even than that. For him, being free was an act of will. For Americans, for American women, it was their natural state of being. I think that he meant by this was that it was very easy to sleep with women in America. Poor Mr Matsuda, for all his efforts he was still so Japanese. The sense of the American woman as the supreme deity of sex is very strong. I have often heard my father say that he wished he could be a Moslem; then he would have a French wife to cook for him, an American wife to sleep with him, and a Japanese wife to do everything else. He says this sort of thing when he is drunk, or when my mother has displeased him in some way.

The first time I met Mr Matsuda he took me to Harajuku. The evenings were still warm and so we sat at a table in an open-air cafe. When the waiter came Mr Matsuda made a point of ordering an 'American' espresso. It came and I asked him how it differed from an Italian espresso. He stirred his spoon in the thick, dark liquid and raised a sliver of something that I could not quite make out. He told me it was lemon peel and seemed pleased that I had asked the question.

Mr Matsuda told me that he only went to the more international areas of Tokyo: here, Roppongi, places where he could escape from what he called the noodle mentality of Japan. I smiled and recalled the way he had drunk his soup. Of course, Harajuku is international, I suppose. At least there are foreigners who go there, perhaps not as many as Mr Matsuda would have liked, but enough. There were some at a table near us, and I could not help noticing the fact that, whenever one of them passed by us on the way to the toilet, Mr Matsuda would raise his voice and speak to me in English, saying things in his coarse American accent that had nothing to do with the conversation we had been having in Japanese.

I told him I must be home by ten-thirty and he looked at me with an expression that seemed to say I had just confirmed everything he had been telling me all evening, but he did not question me. I think he believed I lived with my family. Certainly he could not have known otherwise, unless he had asked Professor Kobayashi about me. I thought that unlikely as Mr Matsuda seemed possessed of interest in no one save himself. He walked with me to the subway and asked if he might see me again the following night. I hesitated before agreeing, but in the end I did say yes. Even now I cannot understand why.

He telephoned me quite early the next morning. He intended hiring a car for his journey to Nigata and had decided he would use it on his last day in Tokyo as well. He wanted to know how to find where I lived so that he might collect me in the evening. I had no intention of letting Mr Matsuda see where I lived, and so I told him, quite firmly I think, that I would meet him at some more mutually convenient place. He accepted this without question.

We drove to Yokohama. Mr Matsuda knew of a good

Chinese restaurant there. The food, he said, was just like Chinese food in America. It turned out to be a comparison I could not have made even if I had been to the United States myself because the restaurant was closed when we got to it. Instead, we drove back towards Tokyo, until Mr Matsuda decided to pull off the highway because he had seen the sign of one of those Japanese restaurants which serve an approximation of American food in an approximation of an American environment, Skylark or Jonathan's, I cannot remember the names. There were obviously many others in Japan who shared Mr Matsuda's tastes for things American because the large carpark was full and we had to drive around it twice before coming across a space about to be vacated.

Mr Matsuda did not enjoy his food, but we stayed a long time in the restaurant. When ten o'clock came and I saw that I could not possibly reach my room in time to take my mother's telephone call, I made an excuse and went to the toilet. There was a public telephone there and I was able to talk to my mother. I told her I was out with Miss Sekiya and would probably stay with her that night. I said I would speak to her again in the morning. It was a dangerous story to tell. My mother was not on friendly terms with my teacher's family, yet I knew that would not stop her from asking them to speak to their daughter. If she did I would be discovered in my deception, unless Miss Sekiya understood what was happening and supported my story. Somehow, I did not think she would. On the way back to Mr Matsuda I began to worry.

It was very late when we left the restaurant. The number of cars in the carpark had lessened, but there were obviously still many people who enjoyed the American way of life enough to want to stay up drinking coffee all night. I did not. I was tired. I wanted to get back to Tokyo. I knew it would be difficult finding a taxi at that time, but I was determined Mr Matsuda should not drive me home.

Mr Matsuda seemed not to have had a very good time. He was quiet in the car. He put the key into the ignition, but then just sat there, staring out into the darkness. I asked him if he was all right, and he seemed not to hear. I asked again, was he all right? Was something the matter? I touched his arm. Only then did he turn to me, taking my hand, pulling me across the seat towards him. He was saying something to me, in English I think, but I could not understand him and then I was being kissed.

I was shocked more by the sensation than the action itself. I had never had anyone's lips fastened upon my face before, except once, once when Akiko and I had kissed, and that had not been anything like this. There was a violence in Mr Matsuda which frightened me. It seemed as if he wanted to eat my face, and the smell of his skin, the texture of it, was unpleasant to me. When he put his tongue between my lips my first reaction was to bite it, but I did not. For, mixed in with all my feelings of revulsion, was the sensation of doing something that had been forbidden to me all of my life, that was forbidden to me still, and with that came the idea, the realization that this kiss was but the prelude to something else, something I would allow to happen to me simply because — because at that moment it was what I had decided. I was caught in that moment.

I cannot pretend that I had any real pleasure from what followed. Certainly it was not the pleasure I had become accustomed to finding with myself. In that sense there was no pleasure at all. I was frightened for much of the time it took, and when I was not frightened I was disgusted. And yet, and yet, there was something, something I have never had since with a man, not even with Michael. I remember I kept telling myself, in a moment I will stop him. We cannot do this here. But I did not, I could not. I suppose, as well, I would not.

Afterwards, a long time afterwards, when I was alone again in my room, I thought about what had happened. That it was a little like a visit to the dentist really; I mean the same mixture of wanting and not wanting, the effort to resist the progress of something I had, if not actually set in motion, then at least acquiesced in. And I remembered the sensations, how the violence of that kiss at the beginning had grown in the man until it seemed he was fighting me, did actually wish to hurt me, to force from me cries of pain and terror.

I remembered what it was like with him inside me, how strange it was to have a piece of living flesh inside my body and yet not be able to know what it was experiencing, not to know the feelings of the thing that I could feel.

The force of his passion, when it came, surprised me, the power of it. Now I know men, I believe that time with me may have been his first. It frightened me, the first shock of his spasm, and I did cry out then, in fear. I felt the breath driven from me, and the bruising of my flesh.

Above all, I had about me then a sense of having surrendered myself in the most complete and final way, and I thought of myself as violated, even though it was an act in which I myself had been a willing accomplice. I felt like someone who had assisted in her own murder. I carried that sense with me for days afterwards, and it was quite precise and physical in its location. It was between my legs.

The truly strange thing, the thing that now makes me go cold when I think of it, is that I did not once wonder if I might be pregnant. I am quite sure he did not use anything, there was no time. If he had stopped at all I should have got out of the car. I think even he knew that. As long as his desire was in full force I was willing to let it carry me along, as a stick thrown into a swollen stream. I suppose I was very lucky. At the time the possibility of conception never entered my head. A few days later I had my regular bleeding. The flow of blood seemed particularly strong that month. I looked upon it as a cleansing, a washing away of filth.

Do I mean any of that? There are times when I do not know myself. Really, it was nothing, nothing at all. I let a man have me in a car parked behind a restaurant one night. It meant nothing, in the long run, nothing at all. The only thing I honestly remember thinking of then, when it happened and afterwards as well, was that scene in *Madame Bovary* where Emma goes with Rodolphe in the carriage. Perhaps that is why I did what I did. I was reading it in Miss Sekiya's class at the time.

Anyway, what happened with Matsuda was nothing. He

was more upset than I was, afterwards. He cried. I comforted him, like a baby. When we arrived back in Tokyo I got out of the car and into a taxi. That was it. Of course, I never saw him again. I have not even thought of him in years. What happened with him was taken from my mind by something else, something that seemed much more important at the time. Professor Kobayashi telephoned me.

When was it? A week later? He came to see me the same evening and it was as if nothing had happened. I had thought that, when he looked at me, he would know what I had done, he would be angry and go away and I should never see him again. But everything was the same as before. I made him his drink, and then I cooked for him. It was just an omelette with rice and salad, because I did not have time to think about the meal, but it did not matter. Afterwards, after the meal, we listened to the radio. It was an orchestral concert, the Sibelius violin concerto.

There was an interval before the next piece and I went out into the kitchen to make him coffee. He only drank Blue Mountain blend, and I kept some especially for him. I never drank coffee then myself, I found it made me nervous.

When I took it in to him he had turned the radio off. He seemed a little nervous himself, and I thought that, after all, he did know, but then he asked me to go away with him that weekend. What he actually said was that he had decided to go away for a few days, to a hotel near Lake Kawaguchi and that he would be honoured and delighted if I would consent to accompany him. From his tongue the words seemed so innocent, and it seemed to me that he grew younger as he spoke, the years falling from him before my eyes. Honoured. And delighted.

In fact, the language he used was so polite, I was not entirely sure what he intended, and it was only when he had completed the registration card at the hotel and received the key to our room that I knew for certain I was to share it with him. It was a twin room, which confused the sudden certainty I had felt, but that night, when I came from the bath, he beckoned me to the bed in which he lay and we became lovers. It all seemed very simple and, for a little while, it was.

He was kind to me the next morning. I woke him, and while he drank the tea I had prepared for him, asked whether I should prefer to take breakfast in the room rather than go downstairs. I appreciated his gesture, his thoughtfulness and caring, but I could not see the need to hide. I did not feel that the sudden transition in our friendship — he always called it our friendship — would be obvious to those who had seen us arrive together the night before. Indeed, I was sure they would either have assumed that I was his daughter or that I was already his mistress. The only people I was afraid of being seen by were members of my family, and I could not believe that fate should deal so unkindly with me as to have my mother and father taking breakfast in the main dining room of the Hotel Fuji View when I entered with my lover.

We had arrived on the Friday evening. The hotel was almost empty then, but it began to fill up with guests as Saturday advanced. In the morning, when we ate our breakfast together, we were alone, except for a solitary family of Europeans, who seemed uncertain and cowed by the surroundings in which they found themselves. Professor Kobayashi took me walking after we had finished eating. He was a keen amateur ornithologist, and every few minutes he would pause to show me some bird or other. We had lunch at twelve-thirty, and then he suggested that we retire to our room. I expected we would make love again, but in fact he wanted to sleep. He smiled upon me before he closed his eyes, and said he really was as old as he looked. I watched him as he slept and then, when I was certain that my leaving the room would not disturb him, took the book I had brought with me to read in one of the lounges.

I found a comfortable chair near a window and ordered tea. I felt so completely happy, looking out into the wintered garden, the trees bound against the coming cold, the yellow, fading grass. Some people came into the lounge, two couples. The men were Americans, from one of the military bases I supposed. The girls were Japanese, and dressed in a very vulgar fashion, like bar-girls.

These newcomers made a lot of noise, laughing and shouting. They were drinking, although it was still early in the afternoon. I could not read because of the noise, and so I found myself watching them. The men kept touching the girls, but not in a way that might be termed affectionate. They kept taking hold of their arms, their faces, as if, yes, as if asserting ownership. That is what I thought, those men owned the girls they were with. They had bought them and they wanted to show that they had bought them. I could not finish my tea. Instead I walked out into the gardens, relishing the coldness of the air.

I returned to the room a little after four o'clock. Professor Kobayashi was just waking up. I prepared tea for him, and then he said he would go to the public bath. I read for a while, then I bathed myself, in our own bathroom, in readiness for dinner. I was dressed and had done my hair by the time he returned.

We sat in the bar for half an hour before dinner. He had his Tom Collins, it was what he was drinking then. When we were taken to our table for dinner I noted how crowded the dining room was, but it was only when I sat down and looked about me that I saw almost all of the people eating were couples, couples like ourselves. The room was filled with old men and young girls, as if it were some sort of club outing for adulterous geriatrics.

I did not taste my food that night. I could not. I could only watch the old men with the young girls, showing them the good things of life: which knife and fork to use with which dish, the correct wine for fish, for game. They were educating them, as I was being educated. I stared at the man I was with and I think my eyes saw him for the first time. He owned me just as much as those Americans owned their girls. He was as proud of it as they were. The only difference was that he preferred to show me off in a way they did not, could not perhaps. And I began to wonder then why this had not happened before. Why he had not taken me before. I wondered about Matsuda, why we had been brought together; for we had been brought together, of that I was quite certain now. Had the man sitting opposite me determined that someone else should take my virginity because it was against his own scruples to do so? Or beyond him, physically? Had he given me to a younger man to wear me in, as if I were a pair of shoes?

There was a bitterness in my mouth. I remembered Mayumi, and what she had said to me, that I would never be given something for nothing. I thought then that I could understand her, at last I could understand. I even felt a certain respect for the men she had gone with. At least they had been willing to pay for her. The Americans I had seen had been willing to pay.

When we returned to our room I got into my own bed and said that I was feeling a little unwell, that I would go straight to sleep. He did not seem to mind. We returned to Tokyo the next day, and when I said goodbye I was determined never to see him again. I telephoned my mother and told her I wanted to come home a little earlier than usual for the New Year. I set out for Kyushu on the Monday. I did not inform anyone about where I was going. In the weeks of the holiday I thought I had shaken myself free of what I knew was something terribly wrong, but when I went back to my apartment in the second week of January there was a letter waiting for me. I think I had known there would be. I read it. When he telephoned and asked if he might see me again I said yes. I continued to say yes for the next seven years.

NINE

He called me Dolly. Professor Kobayashi called me Dolly. It was his name for me. His special name, the one only he used. He liked to play the piano with me, pieces for four hands. When my piano came the first piece that we played together was 'Dolly'. That is how he gave me the name.

I cannot remember when he first proposed that he should buy me a piano. I suppose we had been to a recital, and he asked me whether I could play. I remember only that I was somewhat surprised by his question. Playing the piano is one of those accomplishments with which all Japanese girls are equipped by our adoring parents, is it not? Every one of us plays the piano, at least after a fashion. In fact, I am quite good. Was quite good. I haven't played for such a long time. Then I was good, almost as good as he was.

He wanted to buy me a piano so that we could play together, but of course I could not let him. It would not have been proper, and anyway I had enough trouble as it was hiding all the other things he had given me whenever my mother came to Tokyo: the books, the records, the little pieces of jewellery, the clothes. I could hardly have pushed a piano into one of the cupboards along with everything else.

I have never really thought about it before, but it strikes me now that the reason we have so many cupboards in our houses is that we are a people who constantly, consistently, hide things. We are by nature deceitful, it is bred into us and it is taught to us and practised by us.

My mother and I would go through an ornate little ritual each time she visited. During one of her telephone calls she would inform me of her intention to come to Tokyo in two or three days' time. I would spend this period of grace desperately cleaning my apartment, washing sheets and covers, polishing, moving things out of the way — I mean, of course, moving my lover's things out of my mother's way.

I had to erase all traces of his presence, or at least, I had to make the effort to do so. It was a game, and I think we both understood the rules by which it had to be played, although, of course, nothing was ever said. With us, nothing is ever said, but I knew that, if I did my part, my mother would do hers.

As long as I hid the things Professor Kobayashi had bought for me I felt that my mother would not go looking into any of my cupboards to find them. I thought she might not go looking into any of my cupboards because she knew she might find something if she did.

I was quite certain she had a strong suspicion that I was seeing someone. I could tell from our telephone conversations, the questions she asked and the questions she did not ask. I was also quite certain that she did not want her suspicions confirmed and would do nothing herself to confirm them unless I forced her.

Yes, our cupboards are very important to us, in our homes and in our lives, without them we could not live, there would be too much — too much unpleasantness about us; too many things we would rather not see. Even marriage is a cupboard, with us. My parents are putting me away in it so I will not cause them any further embarrassment, so they will not have to see me anymore. They have tidied me up, like a doll left on the floor by a negligent child.

What was I thinking of? Dolls? Dolly, yes, yes, he called me Dolly. It was his name for me. And the piano, yes, well, of course I could not take a piano from him. My mother would have known at once.

Yet it was his wish that I have a piano and so, in the end, I asked to have my own piano sent up to Tokyo from my parents' house. I remember it arrived on a Thursday afternoon, and the tuner came the following morning. When Professor Kobayashi next visited me it was ready. It looked completely out of place in my room, of course, but he was pleased that I had done what he wanted.

I played for him — that Mozart piece every child knows, 'Ah, vous dirai-je, maman', the one to which English children sing the funny song about the star.

When I had finished I cooked his meal and afterwards, after he had eaten, he took the sheet music for the Fauré from his briefcase and we played together. It was then, when we had played it, that he said he would always call me Dolly.

I never knew when I would see him, or for how long. Usually, if he intended to visit me, he would telephone an hour or so beforehand, and I would just have time to shop for the food I would serve to him. If he was able to stay we would not eat until quite late. He would drink his whisky cocktail and talk to me. Afterwards, when we had eaten, he might read to me, or we would sit together, with a game of chess perhaps.

After the piano came we would play something together, or if he was too tired, I would play for him. Once he criticized my technique and the next day I asked one of the girls at the university to introduce me to her piano teacher. The teacher was small and very fat, and she gave me a short practise piece to do, a test to see whether or not I was acceptable as a pupil. I was. When she said she would take me her manner seemed to suggest that I should consider myself honoured.

And so I added music lessons to the classes in cookery and flower-arrangement I already attended. A few weeks later, after he found out what I was doing, he put the money for the piano tutor into the account he had opened for me, along with my other allowances.

He had begun giving me money by that time. Perhaps it was to make up for the fact that we so seldom went out together. He told me that it was difficult. When we did go out it would be to an amateur performance of the Noh drama perhaps, or a concert recital in one of the smaller halls. Afterwards we would have dinner at his club, or one of the restaurants where he was a known and valued customer, places he could trust with the secret of his passion, if it was a passion.

I wondered then and I wonder now, for we almost never made love. In all the years before he told me he no longer wished to see me we slept together, in the literal sense of the words, only twice, when he took me away with him to that hotel where he had taken me the first time, and then to Nikko one weekend, which was the last weekend for us. Sometimes he would want me when he came to my apartment, but it was not often.

It was not that our coming together, when it happened, was unfulfilling. It is true that it was difficult for him to begin, but when he was ready he would come to his pleasure surely enough, in the slow progression that is the way of elderly men.

It was difficult for him to begin physically, but he was, as well, a shy man in such matters, and he found it embarrassing to approach me to speak of his desire. We developed a little code between ourselves to spare him this. If, when he telephoned me to say that he would be visiting, he called me by my proper name, then I understood that I was to prepare my bed and have everything in readiness to take him into it when he arrived. If he called me Dolly I knew I was to prepare only his food. Usually he called me Dolly.

More and more I think that those times when we were lovers in the physical sense were simply acts of possession, as if he felt he had, from time to time, to reassert his hold upon me. The poor man, I was never really his after that first night, when he had me at the Fuji View Hotel.

How did I pass them, the days and months of years of what was then my life? I waited for him, and I wrote letters; I unpacked the parcels from my mother, and I waited for him. I answered the telephone, always thinking it would be him. I slept and I woke, and I waited for him. I laughed and I wept, and I waited for him. I lived my life waiting for him. Why? I still cannot answer myself. Why?

Well, there were other things, it was not all like that, in fact it was not at all like that. I wrote my dissertation on the novels of Jean Rhys. She was quite an appropriate choice I felt, at the time. I did almost no work at all during the time I was in the graduate school. How could I have done any? I was too busy learning to cook, going to flower-arranging classes, piano lessons, having my hair cut, shopping for clothes. I wrote my thesis in three weeks, and during that time I did not sleep. I ate a proper meal only every two or three days, when I would send out to a nearby restaurant for food. The rest of the time I survived on rice crackers and tea.

Of course, I knew I would be given the degree as long as I completed my dissertation, because my father had pledged a large amount of money to the college, but in fact what I wrote was quite brilliant, brilliant enough for my ideas to be stolen from me later. And afterwards, even though she had not approved of my work, Miss Sekiya arranged for me to become a part-time teacher at one of the colleges where she had connections. I accepted the post because my father made me accept it. He said I could only learn the value of money if I had to earn some myself. One of the few things my father knows about is the value of money.

I was at my parents' house the day Miss Sekiya telephoned me with the offer. When my mother told my father he grew so agitated with me because I had not said yes there and then that I feared he might not be intending to continue my allowance, and I should be forced to join all the other women scraping the bits and pieces of a life together with a class here, a class there. I knew who they were. I had sat before them in lecture halls, and seen them sleeping on trains. They had an air about them that was made up of more than cheap clothes and scent, the pallor of their skin; it was defeat. You saw it in their eyes, the acceptance that life would never be any better for them than it was at that moment. Yet I worried myself for nothing, my father's histrionics were caused by the drink he had in him when he came back to the house. The money was in my account the next time I went to the bank. When I saw the numbers on the credit slip I almost felt grateful to him.

What else did I do? I moved. I took a place more conveniently situated for the journey I must make each Tuesday to the college. And I began, at my parents' insistence, going to meetings, carefully arranged and chaperoned meetings, with eligible young men in the hope, my parents' hope, that I would agree to marry one of them. And I became the lover of Satoshi Mizuno. And I slept with other men, sometimes. Perhaps five or six of them. I suppose if I were to tell the truth about what I did while I waited for Professor Kobayashi I should have to say that I became a slut.

The meetings with all those prospective bridegrooms were supervised by my mother. I was twenty-four when they began. I suppose my father thought it was time I married and made my mother do something about it. She used a marriage broker in Tokyo, a fat woman who looked so much like my piano teacher I thought the differing threads of my life had fallen from my fingers and become entangled when I first saw her. I gasped, and the blood fell from my cheeks as she came to greet us across the lobby of the Hotel Okura. I was there with my mother to have my picture taken in the photographic studio attached to the hotel. It was considered the correct thing to do at the time, although now I believe that families tend to exchange rather less formal portraits, and the very chic even go so far as to send snapshots.

We used a broker in Tokyo because my father had no intention at that time of giving me away to someone from Kyushu. Later on he changed his mind, and in the end, of course, he took whatever he could get, but then he wanted an alliance with a metropolitan family, an old family with a tradition of sending their men into one of the professions. Quite why he felt the daughter of Kyushu's fried chicken king would be attractive as a marriage partner for the son of such a family I do not know. Perhaps he thought his money could disperse the smell of cooking oil. Perhaps he was right, certainly I did not lack for would-be husbands. What I lacked was any enthusiasm for such a match myself.

They were an ordeal for me, those meetings. My mother would receive the information about the man's family and decide the clothes I should wear. Sometimes, if she felt it was appropriate, we would both be at the beauty shop two hours beforehand to be strapped into a kimono. Or, if Western clothes had been decided on, my mother would send the dress I was to wear, together with the accessories she had chosen for me, from Kyushu a few days before, so that I might hang things up and let the creases fall from them.

We always met the other party in the foyer of some hotel, usually the Okura, occasionally the New Otani, where we would have tea before going on to the cinema or theatre. Afterwards, there was the meal, at one or the other of those exclusive little restaurants where my father had an account. At first, I remember, I worried that we might some day go to a restaurant where I was known from visits with my lover, but then, thinking about it, I decided it was very unlikely my father's tastes would ever coincide with Professor Kobayashi's. Besides, even had such an unfortunate coincidence occurred, I am sure the staff would have been far too discreet to allow themselves any public manifestation of recognition.

I was an extremely popular girl. Each of the men I met indicated that their family would approve of a marriage with me. It was I who never seemed able to approve of a marriage with them. My parents said nothing to me when I expressed my disinclination each time, but they did not need to. I felt their displeasure. Displeasure is not quite the word I want. My father's anger eddied from him, filling the room with heat and violence, like the coming of a storm in summer.

My mother and father lacked entirely my own distinctions of taste. That they approved of the men they arranged for me to meet was self-evident: each one was viewed as being more than acceptable, they would not have had me meet with them had this not been so. They would not have approved of Satoshi Mizuno. His own marriage would have immediately disqualified him in their eyes.

It is funny how I can say that name now. When I was with him I could not bring myself to use it. Before Michael the most familiar I became with anyone was to address them as mister, or, most often, as teacher. Why? Why could I never call these men by their names? They were men who undressed me, who spent themselves within me, men I held naked, with their head upon my lap, yet I could not, I could not speak their names. Satoshi Mizuno I called teacher.

He was forty when I was first introduced to him. He was an assistant professor of English at the college where I taught, and I met him because we both happened to be there on the same day. I remember being taken into the teachers' room on that first morning and the line of faces that I was put before. His was one of them, but later I had no recollection of ever having seen him before. Before? Before what? Before I saw him again.

It was a Saturday afternoon and I was walking towards the subway from the Maruzen store in Nihonbashi. He saw me there and followed me, calling to me just as I made to go down the stairway into the station. I had no idea who he was until he introduced himself, and the annoyance I felt must have been apparent in some way for when he offered me tea I felt it was done as a kind of apology for his having spoken in the first place.

We went into Fugetsudo, and he seemed nervous when he gave our order to the waitress. While we waited for the tea to come he kept pushing his hair back from his forehead, like a young girl. I was not nervous at all, and I felt in command of things, of whatever it was that would happen between us, as if I were possessed of a power. I think I knew in those first few minutes that he wanted to sleep with me. The power I imagined I had was my knowledge that he would get what he wanted. I began to make conversation, to put him at his ease. I began to talk to him about his book.

I did not know him, but I knew of him. He had enjoyed a few moments of celebrity when he had published a book while still a post-graduate student. It had helped that the material was sensational enough to be taken up by the baseball sheets as well as the more serious newspapers, and he had been a constant guest on late-night television for a year or so. I had read the book when I was a student. It was called *The Messiahs of the Senses* and was about the work of foreign writers such as D.H. Lawrence and Henry Miller, Krafft-Ebbing and Wilhelm Reich. In other words, it was a book about sex, and its subject had ensured it would be a best-seller, one whose scurrilous nature might be excused by the author's presumed scholarly intent.

Of course, what really made the book sell was that Satoshi Mizuno had translated those passages from the work of his chosen authors that their official translators had thought it better not to, or had rendered into prose of such a densely poetic nature as to be all but incomprehensible. Once this information percolated through the reviews and into the newspapers and television shows, the book's fame was assured.

I myself had been unimpressed, but then I had not read the book, as Satoshi Mizuno later told me so many others had, holding it in my left hand and with my trousers about my ankles. Of course, I did not tell him that I had been unimpressed. I lied, for the sake of charity and good manners. I said he had helped me to understand the psycho-sexual background of the period I myself had written about for my master's thesis.

When I spoke I addressed him as 'teacher'. I watched him relax, watched the tension fall from his arms and shoulders as if his body were a suit of clothes my mother had sent for one of my marriage dates, shaken out and put upon a hanger.

In his mind he had begun to preen himself, like a caged songbird before its mirror. Japanese men always react in this way, I have learned, when women say the right words to them. Then, I was only unsure just what it was I had said to achieve this effect: was it the word 'sexual', tumbling from my presumably innocent lips to fall upon his eager ears quite detached from the root I had given it, or was it instead my precise articulation of 'teacher'? Still, I do not know.

We talked through an hour and two cups of tea. He expressed an interest in reading my dissertation. I, coyly, said that I had a copy of it in my house and that if he really, really wished to look at my work, worthless as it was, then I should be honoured. Inevitably, when we walked together to the subway it was to catch the same train.

I was living in Tokiwadai then. Land has always been

cheaper along the Tobu-Tojo line, and for the same rental I had been paying for my old apartment I had found a small house in a quiet street of anonymous, grey-walled gardens, where housewives in white aprons swept the road outside their gates each morning and evening. Professor Kobayashi had visited the agent with me and, although he did not altogether approve of the location, for it meant he must travel a farther distance along a disagreeable route to see me, he appreciated the fact that he was unlikely to meet anyone with whom he was acquainted in such an area, and so might maintain his reputation entirely secure.

I loved the house. I first saw it on a dark afternoon in late June. It had rained heavily, and the dark massing of clouds above the glossily-tiled roofs indicated that more rain was to come. The agent who was to show me the house opened the gate and I followed him along a path made narrow by the luxuriance of the hydrangea bushes lining it on either side. The green of the garden was as heavy as the grey of the sky, and the blue heads of the hydrangea blossoms, a blue that seemed like bruises on the body of all that greenness, were almost threatening, as if they were sentries challenging my intrusion. I ignored the challenge and, as I walked across the uneven slabs of stone which formed the path, I let my hand brush the full and nodding flowers, soaking my fingers.

I had four rooms in that house: a large kitchen, big enough to put a dining table and four chairs in, with a bathroom just beyond behind sliding doors of pebbled glass, and then another, Japanese, room, across a narrow corridor, and upstairs two more rooms. There was so much space, and I did not care that the agent seemed disapproving when I said that I was not married and lived alone. The first night I spent in the house I danced from room to room across the dark wooden floors.

As I led Satoshi Mizuno through the gate that day I was already wet between my legs, for I knew I would be naked with him in a few minutes. I think what made me so excited was the certainty of my knowledge, when he could only wonder.

He was clumsy and nervous in the house, and when I told

him that the dissertation was in my bedroom he glanced about him as if he wanted a way out. I still cannot explain my behaviour that day, and thinking of it now, here in this place where my marriage is being celebrated, I am both appalled and exhilarated by the memory of him coming behind me up the steep and narrow stairs. At the top I turned to him and said that he could have the book, that he could have me as well, if he wanted. The look on his face then was almost worth everything that came afterwards.

I have no remembrance of how we came together after that, only of the passion I had upon me. It was like a shroud. I saw nothing. I heard nothing. I felt nothing. There was only a blackness which cleared for me to find myself upon the small bed my parents had chosen for the bedroom, my legs up on the shoulders of a man whose face was, for those first moments of returning consciousness, utterly unknown to me. He said something but I did not understand, and he had to repeat that he was near to his moment and would need assistance. I interpreted the precise vagueness of his words and reached behind me to the little box where I kept the contraceptive sheaths Professor Kobayashi used, but before I could take one out the telephone rang and, automatically, I answered it. It was my lover, my other lover.

I heard my name, my proper name, pronounced with the somewhat phlegmy tone that he had so often in those days and I felt as if I had conjured him from the air, my lover, my other lover. He spoke my name, not Dolly, but my name, and his voice and his manner of calling, and this other man inside me brought on my excitement again so that I moved my hips.

Satoshi Mizuno tried to pull away, but I held him tight within me, and closed my calves around his neck. I held them both, both those men, one with my legs, one with my voice. I do not think I had ever spoken to Professor Kobayashi for as long on the telephone as I did then. I was inspired, finding some new thing to say, some fresh comment to make, each time it seemed he was about to bring our conversation to an end. I suppose I had a madness in me, but it was a very fine madness, and I wanted it to go on, to go on and go deeper. It ended, the madness, the conversation and everything else when I heard Satoshi Mizuno whimper and then the telephone receiver was jolted from my grasp as he spent himself within me, the force of his impertinent ecstasy banging my shoulders against the wooden headboard of the bed.

He was gone minutes afterwards, but I knew he would be back, like a dog who has sniffed a bitch in heat, he would want more. I knew it, and I wanted his appetite. I had less than an hour to prepare for my second visitor, and though I stripped the stained sheet from the mattress I did not have time to wash myself and I took that old man into me while I was still wet with a younger man's seed. I was sure he would know that I had been with someone else, and my certainty seemed somehow to add to the power of my passion. It was very great that time, and that time, the sole occasion when it happened with that old man, I went to the limits of my passion, and went there with such a fury I saw his eyes glazed with fearfulness when I had done. Professor Kobayashi did not touch me again in that way for almost a year.

That night, when I was alone again, I knew a fear myself, that I might have conceived a stranger's child. I wept and wept, and I worried for two long weeks until I bled, but then, when the blood came I had something else to grieve over. I came to the knowledge that I was now the lover of Satoshi Mizuno, and that I had delivered myself into the hands of a demon.

The next time Satoshi Mizuno came to my house he pushed through the door as I opened it to him, and began beating me with his open hands about the head and shoulders. I fled before him into the Japanese room, and there he held me down upon the matting with his hands at my throat until I told him the name of the man, he knew it was a man, I had spoken to on the telephone. When I told him the name he became quiet, the anger gone from him, and he was caring towards me, wiping the bloodied snot from my upper lip, fetching water for me from the kitchen.

After these kindnesses, he took my underclothing from me and had me upon the floor, ignoring my plea that he wait for a moment until I should fetch him the thing he had asked for before. He would not, and when I felt him stiffen for his moment of climax I pulled myself away from him so that he spilled his seed upon my thigh. He cursed my name as he did, and when he could he struck me across my ear with the palm of his hand, so hard I could not hear properly for an hour. He took me again, later on, but more gently that time, in my bed. He was considerate of me, coming away from me for a moment so that I might place a sheath upon his member before he was finished with me.

Afterwards he sought to explain his violence, telling me that he was a man who could not contain any of the emotions that were natural to him. He said he had conceived a great and noble passion for me the day he had first seen me, and meeting me in the bookshop, it seemed to him as if the fates had confirmed it. So, when he heard me speaking to another man in such familiar tones even as he lay with me, his anger and jealousy had flared, like a fire when spirit is thrown upon it.

I listened with my eyes lowered, and did not enquire how he had withheld so violent a conflagration for a whole week. Then he began to question me about my other lover. He did not seem to be jealous then, merely possessed of an insatiable curiosity, and whenever I wavered or seemed unwilling to answer him, he would threaten me with his fist.

He left me late in the evening, and as soon as he was gone, I dragged myself to the mirror in the bathroom. My face was red and already puffy where he had hit me. The next morning I was so ill I could not get out of bed for a long time, and when I did, and I saw myself in the mirror again, I could not recognize myself. My bruised and swollen face seemed to laugh at me and continued to do so for the next four days. I did not go to my classes that week, and, on those occasions when necessity forced me to leave the house, went into the street with a scarf over my head, and dark glasses to hide my eyes.

He was at my house again on the following Saturday. I saw him come through the gate and along the path between the hydrangea bushes. At first I would not answer his ringing. I hid myself in the cupboard where I kept my heavy coats so that he might not hear the terror in my breathing. Yet he knew I was at home and began to shout and kick the door until, fearing the disturbance would cause the neighbours to complain to my landlord, I ran from the cupboard and begged him to leave. When he would not I let him in.

He wept when he saw my face. He took one of the knives I used in my cookery classes and told me that if I said for him to do it, he would plunge the blade into his thigh, he would cut his face. I asked him to put the knife back where he had taken it from, but he would not until I begged him to, mixing tears with my supplications, kissing his own tears from his face. He threw the knife into the sink and took me in his arms. Soon he had me on the kitchen table, my underthings about my ankles, all the time telling me how much he loved me, how he could kill himself for having hurt me. As he moved within me two thoughts kept running through my head: whether or not he had damaged the delicate edge of the knife when he threw it into the sink, and what I would do when he came to the climax of his passion. I did not, at that time, keep any sheaths in the kitchen, later I did, for Satoshi Mizuno proved to experience many moments of spontaneous desire for my body there. Indeed, it got to the point where I took to keeping a cushion on one of the kitchen chairs as well, for I grew weary of having him bang my head on the hard wood of the table.

As it turned out, I need not have feared that he would leave his seed in me. Such was his passion that day, spurred, no doubt, by remorse at what he had done to me, that he grew more and more athletic as his time approached. When the spasm took him he jerked his member quite out of me and lay in a quivering, whimpering heap, his head upon my breast, as he emptied himself into the folds of my skirt.

I surrendered something to Satoshi Mizuno that day. I ceded control of what was between us to him. He was utterly, utterly obsessed with me, and for a little while his obsession flattered me enough to hide the truth of what had happened. It did not, however, hide it for very long.

He told me we must work towards total honesty between ourselves. He told me that he was, himself, a totally honest person, that he had spent his life hunting down the lies which are about us. He said that there were as many lies in our loins as in our heads, and we must eliminate them, each and every one. What he meant by this was that he wanted to have me in as many different ways as possible. I believe he had a list of such things, or a programme of action perhaps. Anyway, each time he came to me there was a new lie for us to eliminate. The kitchen table, it seemed, had simply been the first item on the agenda. His next was to spend his seed in my mouth.

I had never done that before, and I found myself choking. It could not have been pleasant for him either. The first time he had me in this way I grazed him quite severely with my teeth. As for me, I vomited it all back up as soon as he left.

He would not give up the task, however, and he would not let me give it up either. In the end I bought a book on the subject of sexual skills, and practised with a banana. With my new proficiency I was able to hold his seed in my mouth and spit it into a handkerchief, but this angered him when I did it, and he struck me about the head and shoulders. The next time I made as if to kiss him afterwards, and emptied the semen into his mouth. I thought this would earn me another blow, but my action had so surprised him he swallowed it down and then, when he had understood what it was he had taken into his stomach, rushed to the lavatory to vomit himself. When he had finished he was too weak to do me harm and went home. We did not practise that particular perversion again.

He used to hit me a lot, usually whenever I showed resistance to one of his ideas. The night he buggered me, he beat me almost senseless first. When it was over, all of it, the beating and the sex, he held me and spoke to me as if I was a child. He said that what he was trying to do was free me from the power of sex by breaking the shackles of my inhibitions. He said he was educating me in the best way, leading me out of myself, he said, and when my education was complete I would be free in the truest and most meaningful sense of the word.

But the worse thing, truly the worst thing, was when he told me we must also immerse ourselves in our own wastes. He forced me to go with him into the lavatory and hold him as he passed water. When that was done, he dropped his clothes and sat upon the pedestal. It was odd, because I remember thinking how he had ridiculed the fact that I used a western-style lavatory, but had I not he would have been unable to keep me in there with him as he did then. I will never, ever, forget the stench that came up into my face, the hot stink of his motion. At other times with him I had thought I might die. At that moment, I truly wished for death. I had to wipe the mess from between his buttocks after he had emptied his bowels. He told me that, henceforward, our souls would be as naked to one another as our bodies were. Obviously this had been effected without his having to endure the same ordeal I had.

Only once before had I ever been so close to another person's dung. My grandmother, in her dotage, took to leaving parcels of her excrement in corners of the house. I found the first of them. It was neatly bundled up in a number of bank notes. I did not realize what it was until I had lifted the package up, and the smell came into my face.

I dropped the terrible thing back onto the floor and ran to find my mother. My father, when my mother told him what had happened, was furious because she had thrown both the parcel and its wrapping of bank notes into the rubbish. He made her go out into the night with a flashlight and retrieve the money which, when she had cleaned it, he told her to take to the bank and deposit in the automated teller.

He was married. Satoshi Mizuno was married. Well, of course, he was. They all are. As he came to spend more and more time with me during that winter he had to find excuses to be away from his wife. I have never really understood why most Japanese women acquiesce in their husbands' infidelities. They ignore them as best they can; they put the knowledge of what their husbands are doing into a little cupboard and slide the door shut. Satoshi Mizuno, however, was evidently afraid of his wife, for one reason or another.

In order to see me he bought a dog. Each time he left the house at night, or in the afternoon if he came at the weekend, he took the dog with him, telling his wife that he was giving the animal some necessary exercise. It was a large dog, of a foreign breed, and suffered from a personality disorder. It would change in a moment from the most vicious, savage mood — it bit Satoshi Mizuno on at least five occasions — to one that was outright maudlin.

At first, he would bring it to my house with him, but this was not a success. I admit that when I first saw the beast I imagined it was to play a part in the freeing of my soul, well, we had done almost everything else, so some form of congress with an animal seemed inevitable. In fact, this animal inhibited his master's activities rather than facilitated them. If he brought the dog into the house it would set about the wholesale destruction of whichever room it was left in. The time we left it in the kitchen it sank its teeth into my table, chewing one of the legs almost through. If we kept it in the garden it would set up the most melancholic howling until it was comforted.

In the end, Satoshi Mizuno took to tying the animal up outside of the station where he caught the train to come and see me. Perhaps he imagined that one day he would write it all down in a book; he insisted that he had another book, a novel, in him, and that I was a necessary part of the process by which his creative genius would be released. Perhaps he imagined that, after his book, the good people of his district would celebrate the writer and the dog by setting up a statue to the faithful animal, like the one to the dog Hachiko in Shibuya.

It was not to be, the fourth or fifth time he left the dog tied in this way he arrived back to find that someone had stolen the animal, and fearing that the thief might be a member of the local gangster organization who had taken it to train as a fighter, dared not report the theft to the police. He said that he told his wife the dog had pulled free of its leash and run away. I did not see Satoshi Mizuno for three weeks after that, and when I learned why I thought of going to the dog shrine at Ningyocho to give thanks.

He bought running shoes and a tracksuit then, telling his wife that he had decided to take up jogging; but she grew suspicious, he said, when his first three runs lasted for four or five hours each time. So he joined a gymnasium, which he would actually attend for an hour before coming to me. He had been prescribed a course of weight training, but he found the regime so exhausting he had no energy for anything else. He dared not allow his membership of the health club to lapse, however, for fear that his wife might telephone, asking if he had been there that night. He made up the time difference between leaving the gym and arriving home, by saying that he had first to set off on a training run, and then eat at a special restaurant frequented by the other men who trained with him.

It was his exhaustion that finally freed me from my fear of sex because it freed me, more or less, from sex with him. Yet when he could not sleep with me he insisted on talking to me. What he mostly wanted to talk about was Professor Koba-yashi.

He made me tell him everything about our relationship, and if I would not, if I even hesitated, he would threaten me with his hand. He was never too tired, it seemed, to hit me. He wanted to know how often we saw one another, what we did, what we talked about. Most of all, he wanted to know about the sex: when and where, how, how often, what was it like, what did it feel like for me. Usually I lied. I enjoyed feeding his jealousy. Unlike him, this was a creature which thrived on exercise and red meat. I made certain it received plenty of both.

He had a strange attitude to my other lover. In part he admired him and took a certain pride in the knowledge that he was sleeping with the same woman as someone whose name had been mentioned as a possible candidate for the Nobel prize in both science and the arts. At the same time he was caught in an agonizing frenzy of jealousy, and it was made worse by the fact that he knew he could not, even he could not, make me end the association, for he was afraid of this elderly man, and the power he had.

In fact, I seldom saw the professor at that period. Once each month perhaps, sometimes not even then. When I did see him he seemed always so tired, too tired even to play 'Dolly' with me. I wondered if, in fact, he was simply tired of me. After all, he could easily have replaced me, and I was no longer the girl he had taken so much care with, overseeing her grooming and education.

I had dropped all my classes. I told him. I had to, for I could not have continued to accept the money he allowed me for the tuition. He said it did not matter, that he would continue to pay for I might, one day, wish to resume them. I no longer had my hair cut in the way he liked. I no longer had my hair cut at all. It had grown long and ragged, and I had asked a local hairdresser to give me a perm so that I did not have to trouble with brushing it every day. My hair had grown long, and I had grown careless, of my clothes, of everything. Once or twice I caught him looking at the bruises Satoshi Mizuno had given me. He never said anything, but he must have known. I would make excuses then, that I had fallen downstairs, or walked into a door I had left open by mistake. He would murmur only that I should be more careful of myself.

Oh, I should, I should have been more careful of myself. More careful in all those years with him and with Satoshi Mizuno. I wanted to break from them, from them both, and yet I could not. I suppose I was like that dog, when I was inside the house I bit anything I could see, I bit until my own mouth ran red with blood; when I was outside, I howled for my master, the person I hated most in all the world.

Of all the men I have known I do believe I hated Satoshi Mizuno most. I hated him almost as much as I hate my father. And I did try to break from him, but he would not let me go. Once I told him I would not see him anymore, and although he beat me when I told him, when he was outside of my house I would not let him in again. Then he took to following me. I had resigned from the college, where he was a lecturer, after the first year. I could not stand the pretensions of the teachers and the stupidity of the students, the rows of smirking boys, undressing me with their eyes, the pathetic, petrified faces of the girls. I was working then for the translation agency, working in an office three days a week from ten o'clock in the morning until six o'clock at night. Sometimes I stayed until later. Sometimes I took work home with me. My father was extremely angry when my mother told him that I had given up all thought of becoming a teacher and was to work in an office instead. I think it was his anger that finally convinced me to take the job, just to spite him.

I have forgotten what I was thinking about again. It is this woman sitting beside me. She keeps looking at me with her frightened eyes and I forget my thoughts. She keeps pulling me back to this wedding, reminding me that it is my wedding, that it is not a dream. My thoughts are the dream. My life is the dream. My life is over and that is why I want to go back to it, because as bad as it was, remembering it is better than what is happening now. What was I thinking about? I was thinking about Satoshi Mizuno and what he did when I tried to leave him. Yes, when I tried to leave him he began following me. That's it, that's what I was thinking about. Satoshi Mizuno began following me.

He would be waiting for me outside the station when I arrived on the way home from my days at the office. And at the weekends, if I went out somewhere, he would appear. I would catch sight of him in the crowd, or see him reflected in a store window. In the beginning, when this first started, I would scream at him, shaming him in the street, but it had no effect. He simply took to following me at a greater distance. Even when I went out with other men, and I did, eventually, go out with other men, he would be there.

Once I found him hiding in my garden when I opened the door to let out a man who had been to visit me, who had been in my bed with me. When I saw the face of Satoshi Mizuno among the withered stalks of the hydrangea bushes I knew he had been watching, standing there with his head turned up towards my bedroom window where the light still burned. I grew very angry then and told him that now, now he was in for a beating himself. He ran away, falling on the path in his panic to escape the blows he imagined my outraged lover would let fall upon his head. He should have waited, for then he would have seen the man I had been with look at me as if to say he had no intention of beating anyone. He might have saved his breath, and the knees of his trousers.

I never saw the man I had slept with again. I saw Satoshi Mizuno again the following day as I walked towards a coffee shop in Shibuya.

Because I could not free myself of Satoshi Mizuno I decided I would make him as unhappy as he made me. I was unhappy. I lost my lovely house because of what had been going on. The neighbours complained to the landlord's agent, and I was asked to leave. When I first received the letter telling me I must vacate the house, I was terrified that my parents might be told why I had to go, but they were not.

I moved to a tiny place in Mejiro. I had to send my piano back to my parents' house because there was no room for it. Looking back, I suppose it was a sign that things were coming to an end. At the time, it seemed as if things were simply getting worse. The day I moved Satoshi Mizuno followed the truck carrying my things to the new apartment. No, that is not it, I followed the truck, in a taxi. Satoshi Mizuno followed the taxi on a bicycle he had taken to having with him whenever I saw him. I learned later that it was his latest excuse for leaving the house. He told his wife it was part of his preparations for becoming a triathlon competitor. Of course, it was also useful for following me.

By the time we all arrived in Mejiro he was exhausted and red-faced. He stood in the roadway, watching the men move my things in. When they had gone he was still there. I could see him standing, holding his bicycle, in the roadway. I went down and brought him in with me.

I knew he would want a passionate reconciliation, and I encouraged him. I flirted with him, I led him on. As he was about to mount me, I told him I was bleeding and that, anyway, I was expecting Professor Kobayashi in a few minutes' time. This last piece of information was true.

Satoshi Mizuno would, I know, have hit me had he dared. That he dared not was due to the power of Professor Kobayashi's name.

I looked up into Satoshi Mizuno's face and I said to him that if he ever dared to strike me again I would tell Professor Kobayashi what he had done. It was enough. I watched as the fear passed from his eyes to his penis, shrivelling it as the sun will shrivel a grape into a raisin. He pulled on his trousers and left without another word. I knew he would stand somewhere to see whether I was lying or not. I wanted him to. I wanted him to see the man who would visit me. I wanted his fear made manifest.

That was the beginning of a very bad time for him. Whenever he came to me I would shout at him, telling him that if he wished to go on seeing me he must get a divorce. He said he wanted to, wanted to marry me, but his wife, and his children, what would become of them? I laughed in his face. I had no intention of marrying a man like Satoshi Mizuno. I told him so. I said I wanted him to divorce his wife simply so that we could be equals, he and I. I knew he would not, could not, do what I said. I spoke thus only to make his life unbearable. I understood that his passion for me was not something he could help, that he must see me. I simply intended that his passion become his misery as well.

I began to frequent the bars in Shinjuku where university teachers went, especially those who flattered themselves with the notion that they were writers. I went there looking for men who knew Satoshi Mizuno. If I found one, and it was not often, I would let him sleep with me. It was a sort of revenge, a silent, secret revenge.

I wanted revenge on him. I wanted him single. I wanted him humiliated. I wanted him unhappy. I wanted him like me. I wanted him as unhappy as I was. I wanted us, both of us, prisoners in the same hell.

TEN

Prisoners in the same hell? That seems a little too much, even for me. My imagination is running away with me again. I think I understand why this poor woman at my side keeps on looking at me. I think she can read my thoughts. No, it isn't that. In a few moments I have to leave to change from my bridal gown into a disgusting froth of satin and lace, my costume for the candle ceremony. Mr Ueno's mother chose it. She was supposed only to help me choose it, because it was my father's money that paid for the thing, as it has paid for all the rest. Still, she made such a fuss when we were looking for the second dress because I turned my nose up, as the English say, at the one she liked, the one I am soon going to wear, that my mother very forcibly said I should take it. I did.

So, I am to wear the dress Mr Ueno's mother chose but did not pay for. It is completely unbecoming, of a pink so deep it is almost scarlet. I do not know whether my future mother-in-law — and I take immense comfort from the fact that this woman will not actually be any relation to me until after the civil contract registering the marriage is signed — is utterly lacking in taste, or whether the dress is a calculated insult, a marker for the future when she will be able to abuse me more freely. On the other hand, perhaps she thinks the colour more suited to my character than the unblemished white of my wedding gown.

I look ridiculous in it, of course, but I must admit to finding the prospect of my re-entry rather appealing. I am looking forward to watching the insincerity drip from all those faces as they murmur their pat little phrases telling me how lovely I am, how the dress, the colour, the cut and style of it, becomes me. I shall smile, shyly; with a little luck I might even manage a tear for one or two of the older aunts on Mr Ueno's side. Yes, the music has started, everyone is standing, looking at me, applauding me. I must bow and make my exit, the sad-faced wife of Mr Ueno's head of department in attendance.

We are going to a small dressing room, just across the corridor. There the women who put me into my bridal gown are waiting to pull it from me. Then they will dress me in the frills and froths of shocking pink Mr Ueno's mother affected to admire. The skirt is so puffed up with layers of lace the hem almost touches my armpits, and with the white stockings on my legs I shall probably resemble some sort of giant peony.

My hair is to be dressed again as well. The blossoms I am wearing now will be taken out, for they could not compete with the immense petals of my skirt. In their place I am to wear the largest, most vulgar tiara imaginable. It is valued at 45 million yen. My father is renting it for the day. My father is renting it, but I chose it. I chose it quite deliberately. My mother suggested I might wear a tiara because my father told her I was to wear one. Apart from the money he has paid for everything it is his one practical contribution to the day's events. He told my mother that I was to wear a tiara because he attended the wedding of one of his workers last year where the bride wore a rented tiara. At first I refused, but then, having seen the dress Mr Ueno's mother had decided to inflict on me, I agreed to the idea. My father went with me to the jewellers. I believe it was the first time that he and I had ever been out together in public without my mother since I was a child. I was almost moved.

In the jewellery shop I solved the problem of which piece to choose by immediately asking to see the most expensive thing they had on the premises. It was, of course, exactly what I had imagined it would be, and I insisted on being fitted with it at once. My father was so pleased he took me to tea.

They will take photographs of us, of Mr Ueno and I, as we light the candles. He and his mother will no doubt insist on using one of them for the cards we send out, after our return from Europe, announcing our new address. It is very popular to do so, amongst a certain type of person. Well, it is popular to do so among people like the Uenos. Akiko sent ones like that, at least she did for her Japanese wedding. She was actually married in England, of course. To her Stephen. I haven't seen her for such a long time. She comes back to Japan every year, but I do not see her. I hear about her from Reiko and Setsuko. She always makes a point of visiting them. She tells them how well she is, and shows off her children. The last time I spoke with Reiko she said the New Year would not be the same without a visit from Akiko and the children. I do not know if Stephen comes with her. No one ever mentions him.

I remember I was very upset when I heard that Akiko had married. I took it personally, as if it were an insult. In a sense, a very particular sense, it was. Well, the way she chose to tell me about it was insulting. I received a post card from her after what, eighteen months without a word? It was postmarked London, and at the bottom, after all the non-sense about the weather and the books she was reading and her new dress, she wrote in English, 'By the way, I was married last month — to a foreigner.'

I think now, after my own experiences, that only her family knew, and they, I am sure, were not told until after the event had taken place. They, in turn, told no one, I suppose, because they were so appalled at what she had done. They were appalled, whatever face they put upon the matter later. Reiko and Setsuko both said Akiko told them her mother had threatened to kill herself when she heard what her daughter had done. It must have been like that or else her mother would have been boasting of it all over the town and finally it would have come to my father for him to throw in my face, just like the Christmas cake he threw at me that year when everything was forgiven and Akiko brought her foreign husband home for their Japanese wedding and I lost both my lovers. Both of them. And my self-respect. All of it. Oh, yes, all of that.

I was with Satoshi Mizuno still. I had taken him back. I was in love, I suppose. I was not in love with Satoshi Mizuno, that was not why I had taken him back. I was in love with misery. Oh, that is not true either. It was nothing so dramatic. I took Satoshi Mizuno back because it was easier than not taking him back.

That I would not let him see me for so long, and when I did, at last, allow him to see me again and tried to make his life as unhappy as he made mine, did not alter the fact that Satoshi Mizuno treated me as if I were a practical research project through which he might prove those theories he had set out in the book he had published when he was young. Still, at least he stopped hitting me, more or less.

I continued to see my other lover as well. Not often, and almost never, now, as a lover, but I did see him. There were other men as well, men I would allow to sleep with me for a night or two, never more. I was not interested in more. To be truthful, I was not interested in the one or two nights really. I had those other men because I wanted to use them to hurt Satoshi Mizuno. I wanted my revenge. Sleeping with other men and then telling him about it, really telling him, all the details, seemed like a good revenge. Certainly it made him cry. He always used to say he did not believe me, but he always cried.

When he was not crying, he was urging me to try something new with him, although, with him, the something new always came down to the same thing, which was not really new at all. One day he began talking about what it would be like to bring someone else into our relationship. I said I had already brought quite a lot of other people into our relationship. He did not mean that, he meant a woman. He meant a woman who would join us in sex. I knew what he meant, but I said yes, someone else would be interesting, and it might stimulate me more to have two men at the same time. I might, I said, even have an orgasm. I used words like that with him then. Not so very long before I had not even known what an orgasm was.

I thought he might lift his hand to me for a moment, but he did not. He told me he had meant another woman, but then he cancelled his thoughts, saying it would be too difficult to arrange.

He did not speak of it again. I knew he would not. He lacked entirely the courage for that sort of thing. I, however, would not let it go. I had grown to be like that, daring him, taunting his cowardice, telling him his imagination out-stripped his capacities for action. One evening, I had been drinking, I said that if he still wanted another woman to be with us then he should telephone his wife and invite her to come over. He said nothing, but I would not let it go.

Then, I was out late one evening, with one of the other men. We passed through the subway station at Nagatacho and the public telephones there were covered with the business cards of those girls who work in the pink world. I stopped and took some of them, perhaps ten or twelve, I do not know, but enough. The man who was with me was obviously embarrassed by this and walked away, standing some distance from me as if he were on his own. Yet later, when I was in bed with him, he was extremely passionate towards me, and he said that what I had done in the subway had so aroused him he had not known how to contain himself. I remember thinking how things might be if only such a simple action could have a similar result for me.

When I was alone again I took the cards from my handbag and looked through them. Many were written in a sort of English, I suppose because of the proximity of the large international hotels. I already knew I would call one of the numbers given on the cards. In the end I selected that of a Miss Yumi, who said that she wanted, if I remember correctly, 'to have sexy plays with foreigners often'.

Why I chose her card from all the others I am less certain, perhaps it was the flavour of internationalism that was so in vogue then. Those were the days when our then prime minister, he who had served so bravely in the naval pay corps along with my father, was urging us all, men, women and children, to go out and purchase two items of foreign manufacture in order that the balance of trade figures might be somewhat less embarrassingly in our favour. The big stores in Ginza and Shibuya rallied valiantly to his call, declaring a 'Foreign Goods Week'. Market stalls were set up in the streets offering all sorts of things that no one really wanted, yet bought out of a sense of patriotic duty. I did not buy anything. I telephoned Miss Yumi, who proved to be quite amenable to my request.

Satoshi Mizuno was terrified when I introduced her to him. It was quite evident what she was, what she did to live. She was not pretty. Her eyes were very far apart, and round, as if she had had the operation to remove the first lid. Poor girl, she would have been better advised to spend her money on a good orthodontist, for her teeth were crooked and overlapped at one side of her mouth: devil's teeth. Her clothes were expensive, but unbecoming to her. When she took off her dress, she was wearing the ridiculous garments that men are supposed to find erotic, although she looked sad to me, a far journey from desire, with her blotchy, white skin and thin ribs, the bow of her right leg.

Of course, it did not really matter what she looked like, had she been a star plucked from heaven and given a woman's form, with skin of gold and hair dark as the raven's wing — in fact it was her hair that was gold, and of a very unconvincing shade — Satoshi Mizuno would not have noticed. His fear had made him blind.

Satoshi Mizuno was like many of the men I have known: in their minds they want so much, they have such hunger, but when what they hunger for is given to them, their appetite is gone. Then they gorge on terror, their own terror. Men, I spit on them.

So, Satoshi Mizuno had his two women, and he sat there trembling before them, before us. Finally, because he evidently was not going to do it himself, Miss Yumi suggested that we should both undress him. When we got his undershirt off I thought I could see his heart moving below the surface of the skin, behind the thin slats of his ribs.

He was not ready, for either of us, but I have to say that

Miss Yumi was skilled in the ways of her calling and, in the end, was able to coax him into a semblance of arousal. She straddled him as he lay beneath her on the floor. I sat and watched. In spite of her cries of passion it was not a particularly interesting performance. I had expected more. Nor was it a very long one. When he could, with Miss Yumi feigning exhaustion, Satoshi Mizuno took his clothes and told me he had to leave.

Miss Yumi did not leave. It was a Saturday afternoon and she did not usually work during the daytime, she said. Her next appointment was not until eight o'clock that evening. She told me she felt she had not provided all of the services for which she had contracted. Her peculiar little face seemed sad as she spoke. I suppose it was her sense of pride in her profession. I knew what she was suggesting in her round-about way, but, frankly, I was not interested. I offered a suggestion of my own, tea, and when it was ready we drank it together.

We must have made an interesting sight for anyone who had happened to see us then, me in my underwear and Miss Yumi naked, except for the ridiculous brassière thing she kept upon her thin chest even though it left her nipples exposed. Yet we were comfortable together, I think, and it was almost cosy, the two of us drinking tea in the warm room, safe against the cold greyness of the day outside. We talked; I began to ask Miss Yumi about herself, about her work. It was the most interesting conversation I had had for years.

It was a little after six when she left. I suppose Satoshi Mizuno had been hiding somewhere close by, for no sooner was the door closed than he began to knock upon it. I thought it must be Miss Yumi, that she had forgotten something. I slipped the latch, and he pushed in past me, pulling me after him by the hair.

I fought him then, for the first time, I fought him. I really thought he would kill me and so I fought for my life. He got me on the floor and had his hands about my throat. I truly thought I was dying, and yet all I could think of was that, only a little while before, he had been the one on the floor, and I wondered then how this man who was so weak could be doing this to me.

Of course, he did not kill me. He raped me instead, repeatedly. How many times? Once, twice, three times? I do not know. Perhaps it was only once. I only know he violated every part of me, my mouth, my hair, my backside, every part of me. It took a long time. It seemed to take a long time. It seemed to take the whole of my lifetime. Perhaps it was only minutes. I do not know. I was not there. I was somewhere else. I was floating, just as I am floating here, floating through this wedding. I just remember getting up from the floor and feeling so cold, because Satoshi Mizuno had left the door to my apartment open when he went out again. I do not know how long I had lain there after his leaving, lain there in the cold wind from outside, and stared at the hidden sky, the stars that shone somewhere above the risen clouds of the city's filth.

It was December. I wanted it to snow. I wanted it to snow and cover the streets with a blanket of the purest white so that I might lie beneath it to hide my shame. It did not snow, of course. It was much too early.

Did any of that really happen? I do not know, really. I think it did. I believe it did. If we tell a lie for long enough, persistently enough, and especially if we tell it to ourselves, it becomes the truth. No, it must have happened, but even then, even in those first few minutes after I returned to myself I could not entirely be sure.

And what did I do then? I got up from the floor, shut out the cold and went to wash myself. Afterwards, when I had sluiced him from me, I got into bed and worried before I fell asleep; worried, not whether he might have impregnated me, but about the finger marks he had left upon my neck. I worried that my make-up would not cover the bruising, for I had to work on the Monday.

I did work, not just then but through all of what had gone on, I did work. It seems incredible to me now, but I went to my office, I brought translations home with me. I answered my mother's telephone calls. I unpacked her parcels. I wrote her letters. I shopped and I cooked. I washed and ironed my clothes. I cleaned. I vacuumed the carpets, and I scrubbed the kitchen floor. I dusted. I dusted. How strange it is that in our language we have the same word for dust as honour. Having lost my honour, I attended to my dust. And that night, that night before I went to sleep, that night as I lay fretting over the marks Satoshi Mizuno's fingers had left upon my neck, I did something else, I decided to get out, to escape, before he, or some other man, killed me.

I thought of asking my father to help me. He had helped Akiko with her scholarship. I thought of asking him, but I did not; I knew he would do nothing for me. It would be as much as I might hope for, getting his permission to go abroad. That was my plan, my means of escape, I would go abroad for a period of foreign study. I would go as soon as possible and as far away as I could, and if my father would not help me then there was someone else who would. As I woke the next morning I telephoned Professor Kobayashi.

He did not answer, of course. I had not really expected that he would, and anyway, I was to see him in a few days time. We had arranged a meeting; it was to be for something special, I would ask him then. My telephone call was simply a symbolic gesture, an affirmation of what I had already decided. When I left for the office on the Monday I did not even bother to put anything on my neck, not even a scarf. I wore the bruises like a lover's necklace, which, in a sense, they were.

I am wearing a necklace today, of rubies. It is a gift from my father, bought for me, not hired. I quite like the necklace because the colour is so immodest. I caught the look of disapproval Mr Ueno's mother gave me when I saw her just before I stood in front of the minister with her son, and it warmed my heart. My heart needed warming. My poor heart, the bruises that were around my neck are now around my heart, and no one can see them, not even these women, stripping me so eagerly of my wedding dress.

I am feeling sorry for myself. I am feeling sad. I must not. I must not do this. I hate myself for it. I despise myself. Sadness is for others. Self-pity is for others. I must stop or I shall weep and then they will all think that I am weeping for this wedding, this ridiculous charade. I have to be strong. I have to look at these women who are with me now. I have to look at them, look at their hands. I have to look at them and think about the past. I have to tell myself my story. I have to remember the past because the past is better than now. The past is better than now because the past is over. I have to remember and I have to tell myself what I remember because there is no one else. There is no one else to listen. I have to think and remember. Already I have remembered so much. Now I have to remember Mr Camley.

Mr Camley was the Englishman. Mr Camley was Professor Kobayashi's friend. Mr Camley was very fat and his hair was very strange. It was like the steel pads the maids in my grandmother's kitchen used to scour the pots with. Mr Camley had very blue eyes. His jaw was dark. Mr Camley smoked a pipe. I have to remember.

Mr Camley smoked a pipe, and he was very famous. Perhaps he was even more famous than Professor Kobayashi. Mr Camley smoked a pipe and was very famous. My dress is on now, and the women are taking the flowers from my hair. Mr Camley was very famous and smoked a pipe. I shall have to go back in soon. Mr Camley was very famous and smoked a pipe, and had once been a teacher in Japan. Mr Camley was very famous and smoked a pipe, and he told me I was the most beautiful girl he had ever seen. Mr Camley was a poet. Mr Camley was a professor at Cambridge University. Mr Camley was Professor Kobayashi's friend, and I was to meet him.

I was to meet him. Professor Kobayashi had arranged for me to have dinner with them both and then to act as a guide for the Englishman. I remember now. I can go on now. It had been arranged over the telephone and I was very nervous. I was nervous because I had never been close to a foreigner before. I had never spoken to a foreigner before. Of course, of course, I had been to classes with foreign teachers, but that was different. I was not required to speak with them. I was required to speak with Mr Camley. I knew that, and so I was nervous. I had not spoken to a foreigner, really spoken, since the day I took the entrance examination for the

Blessed Martyr, the day I sold the ticket my mother had given me for the Kabuki so that I might see the girls at the Takarazuka.

Also, I was nervous because I had to tell Professor Kobayashi that I wanted to go away. I had to ask him to help me.

I met them in the lobby of the Imperial Hotel, and when I was introduced to Mr Camley I said I was very pleased to meet him. He took the hand I had offered him, which alarmed me for I was unused to being touched in this way and had never felt the skin of a foreigner before. Then Mr Camley replied that he was sure I was very pleased to meet him. I did not understand what he meant, and I did not understand why he and Professor Kobayashi both laughed.

We walked to Professor Kobayashi's dinner club. I cannot remember very much of what I ate, if I ate anything at all, for I was seated next to Mr Camley and the closeness of him, the closeness of that strange skin and hair, the peculiar smell of him, made me retch into my handkerchief. Mr Camley and Professor Kobayashi were talking together then and did not notice my discomfort.

Mr Camley talked a great deal, but I could not understand much of what he said. Most of what I learned came from Professor Kobayashi, who would speak to me in Japanese from time to time. Mr Camley had come to Japan from Australia, where he had been teaching for two months, and now he was on his way back to England for Christmas. He had come to Japan because he and Professor Kobayashi were to work on a book of translations from Japanese into English, poems.

What stands out most clearly in my memory is my surprise that Professor Kobayashi could speak English. It had never occurred to me that he would have such facility with another tongue. I remember also that I said nothing.

After the meal we were to go to the offices of the British Council in Jimbocho where Mr Camley was giving a lecture. The room in which he spoke was quite large and it was crowded with people, professors of English from many of the great universities in Tokyo. Miss Sekiya was there. Satoshi

Mizuno was there. I saw him as we entered the room, and I am sure he would have come over to me but for the fact that I was with Professor Kobayashi.

I think the lecture was on the poetry of Philip Larkin, but I cannot really remember. What I recall most strongly was afterwards when people were drinking together. Many of the professors called Mr Camley 'teacher' when they spoke to him.

Mr Camley seemed very happy and laughed if he was asked about the purpose of his visit. He told everyone he spoke to that he had come to Japan again because the girls were so pretty. When he said that he would put his arm around me and pull me close to him, telling everyone that he had found the prettiest girl in Japan to be his guide. Then he would say that he had left England because all of the girls in his classes there were very ugly, only to find that the girls in his classes in Australia were even uglier.

He kept saying the girls in Australia were so ugly he always took one or two of them with him when he went into the desert so that he would not be bothered by the flies. When he said this he would laugh and pull me close to him again.

The party at the British Council finished at nine o'clock, but Professor Kobayashi took a group of ten or fifteen people to a bar in Kanda where he was known. When I tried to say goodnight he seemed a little annoyed and told me that I should stay with him and Mr Camley. In the bar I was made to sit next to Mr Camley, who immediately put his arm around me.

Everyone was drinking whisky, I remember that I must have poured almost a whole bottle into Mr Camley's glass by the time I left. The more Mr Camley drank, the louder his voice became and the tighter he held me to him. He told Professor Kobayashi that he had not been with a woman since he left England, and he asked if he could borrow me for the night. Everyone laughed, but I did not think Mr Camley was trying to be funny.

At last I said to Professor Kobayashi that I must go, and he went with me to find a taxi. Outside the bar, in the street's cold darkness, I explained my decision to leave Japan and asked this man who was my lover for his help. I could not see his face, but he did not seem to be angry or upset, he said only that it was something we might discuss after Mr Camley had gone back to England. When I got into the taxi he turned from me and went into the bar again.

I am ready now. My dress is on, the tiara sits amongst the curls the hotel hairdresser set for me. We shall go back into the room and I will take Mr Ueno's hand again for the candle ceremony. A few moments ago I did not think that I would be able to do it, but everything is all right now. Everything is all right because I can remember again. I can remember Mr Camley. Someone is knocking at the door. It is time to go, but it does not matter now because I can remember Mr Camley.

Nothing matters. I move in the pink dress across the hall. The door opens and music is playing. What is it? It is certainly not the musicians from the Tokyo Philharmonic. Of course, I know now. It is a record. It is Mr Ueno's favourite record, a song called 'Lady in Red'. His mother told him about my dress and he said he thought it might be appropriate to have this music playing as we moved from table to table lighting the candles. I am almost pleasantly surprised, and can forgive him the discrepancy in the colours for I was expecting something far worse. When his sister married they had a Lionel Richie song playing. I know because I was forced to endure the video tape of the wedding on the two occasions I visited Mr Ueno's home after our engagement. At one point he even expressed a desire to use 'Strangers in the Night' because that is his departmental song, the one they sing at parties after the preparations for the budget statement are over each year. Mr Ueno once went so far as to confide that when he has sung this song he feels able to do almost anything. Yes, I think I am rather glad it is 'Lady in Red' we are having and not 'Strangers in the Night'.

The candle is lit, finally. I could feel the sweat break through Mr Ueno's glove when it would not catch the first time. These idiots are applauding already. We make a suitably slow and romantic progress to the first table, light the candle, smile at the smiles that greet us and move away as if we were the happiest couple in the world. Actually, poor Mr Ueno is so nervous his facial contortions are more suggestive of a recent stroke than happiness, but never mind, I shall smile for him and so perform the first of my wifely duties. We will make our unsteady progress about the room, from table to table, until only one candle is left unlit, the largest candle, the one protruding from that heap of ribbon and flowers near the wedding cake. When that is burning we shall sit down and the speeches will begin again: speeches from my friends, speeches from Mr Ueno's friends. On and on the wedding will go, but I shall not be here. I shall be with Mr Camley.

I saw Mr Camley again the next day. It had been arranged that I should be his guide to Tokyo as Professor Kobayashi was busy for most of the morning and afternoon. Again, I met him in the lobby of the Imperial Hotel. He was late, and when he did arrive it was to say that he had overslept and had not yet breakfasted, so we went to the hotel coffee shop where he took tea and a great number of sweet cakes. I had nothing; I was very nervous sitting alone with this foreigner and besides I have never enjoyed Western food in the morning.

He was very quiet, not at all as he had been the evening before. Indeed, when he had finished his breakfast his first words were ones of apology for the way he had behaved towards me then.

It was cold in the street outside the hotel, but we decided to walk back towards Ginza and begin our journey from there. I took him first to the great temple at Asakusa. I am certain that he must have seen it before, but he said nothing. Indeed, he said little about any of the places I took him to, or the things we saw there. When he did speak I had great trouble understanding him. I had thought my English was good, not as good as my French, but good. I made my living using it: well, I lived off the money my father allowed me but the money I earned myself I earned through English. It was just that I seemed unable to actually speak it with this foreigner, this Englishman.

When he spoke to me I could not hear the words properly, and I found myself staring at his mouth. When I wanted to speak to him I could not make my tongue move to form the words. In the end I bought a note pad and pencil, and we communicated through writing. He made a joke out of it and I suddenly found myself liking him more than I thought I could ever have. I left him in the lobby of his hotel, where I had waited for him that morning, where I had met him the night before. When he said goodbye he kissed me on the cheek, and I became embarrassed again, fumbling the words of farewell I had been silently rehearsing all the way back from the station.

I talked with Professor Kobayashi the following morning on the telephone. He called me at eight o'clock. I suppose it was a good time for him, a quiet time, for whenever there was something important for us to discuss he would telephone me at that time. He thanked me for taking care of Mr Camley, and said that I had made a great impression on him. He told me that Mr Camley was an important man, a poet and critic, a teacher, but that his personal circumstances were unhappy. He said that Mr Camley told him I had brought a little joy into his life. Then, when these preliminaries were over, Professor Kobayashi asked me how he might be of assistance to me.

I felt hurt that he offered his help so abruptly. It seemed as if he wanted me to go, as if he wanted to be rid of me so much that he was pleased to help me on my way. I had not expected this. I had expected sadness, regret, questioning. I wanted him to ask me why. He did not, he asked how I thought he might help. I mentioned scholarships. He asked when I thought of leaving. I wanted to shock him, to hurt him and so I gave a date in January. He said only that it might be difficult to do anything at such short notice, but he would try. He told me he would telephone again after the New Year holiday, when I had returned to Tokyo, and then he rang off. For the first time in all the time I had known him, I wept at the silence that remained when his voice was gone from the humming wires.

Of course, I was to go back to my parents' house for the holiday. It is what we do, is it not? We go home. Not that I went home, in the sense that everyone else did. I never went home. I went to my parents' house. And I always went well before the New Year, at my father's insistence, so that I might avoid the crush of year-end travellers on the trains. Even my father realized I could not keep an empty seat beside me at that time. Usually, I would leave Tokyo on the twenty-third or twenty-fourth each year, spending Christmas Day with my mother.

It is not a special day with us, Christmas Day, in spite of the department stores' desperate attempt to establish a tradition. All this nonsense of young men and women buying one another gifts they neither want nor can properly afford. I remember the Christmas I was with Michael, the Christmas I did not go back to Kyushu; we were in a restaurant and there were couples at all the other tables, young couples, well, at least, they were younger than we were. I remember the couple seated next to our table, so young, in their early twenties perhaps, perhaps even still at university. They were dressed like models in some fashion magazine, but sat uneasily in their clothes almost as if they were unwilling participants in this not-quite-ritual they were enacting. The boy seemed afraid of the waiters, the girl would not touch the wine that had been bought so expensively for her.

At last the boy produced his gift; the flurry of bows and golden cords with which the box was tied revealed a ring he had bought. Even from where I sat, I could see it was so obviously a ring. His girl unwrapped it, almost petulantly, and looked with disappointed eyes upon the diamond she set to sparkle in the candlelight. She gave him a wristwatch, an expensive wristwatch, which evoked as much enthusiasm in the boy as the ring had in her.

We gave no gifts that Christmas, Michael and I, and my family gave no gifts. We never did. My family never did. If we had a tradition it was that my father would arrive home early on Christmas Eve with a cake, a Christmas cake, and we would share it before going to bed.

That Christmas, that Christmas Akiko came back with her foreign husband, and her family held a ceremony and reception for her at a rather grander hotel than I had imagined they could afford. I was not invited, but the wedding intruded into my life as if it and not I were the unwanted guest.

I had not known that Akiko was back with her parents before I returned to Kyushu, but I was told as soon as I got off the train. My mother said how angry and ashamed my father was that Akiko had a husband, even if he was a foreigner, and I was still without so much as the prospect of one. I, in turn, informed my mother of my decision to leave Japan as soon as possible, and I asked her to speak of it to my father for me. My mother told me it must wait until after the holiday, that my father was too annoyed even to be approached with such a request until then when the four days of eating and drinking might have softened his temper a little.

I remember that on Christmas Eve my mother and I watched a play on television while we waited for my father to return. It was a drama set in Tokyo just after the war, a favourite period for our television writers. It enables them to celebrate the sorrows of defeat, while at the same time avoiding entirely the events that led to it. Thus we can enjoy the spectacle of ourselves as victims, bombed and burned and humiliated by a callous and seemingly unprovoked alien world beyond the seas. It is part of the carefully inculcated amnesia we Japanese suffer from.

The drama lasted until ten o'clock, and still my father had not returned. To be truthful, his absence was not marked until after the television was switched off. I went to the bathroom to wash the tears from my cheeks, leaving my mother to go out into the kitchen and make tea, complaining, for she would never admit to having such common things as emotions, that she had the beginnings of a cold upon her. It was only as we sat in the kitchen with the last of the tea, more than an hour later, that she made a remark about my father's lateness.

In fact, it was almost two o'clock in the morning when he came. He was obviously drunk, for he beat against the door with his fists, and then seemed to fall upon it. I rushed to let him in for fear that he would wake the neighbours.

My father was not alone. There were three women with him, and even had one of them not been a Filipina, I should have known at once, by their dyed and curling hair, that they were hostesses. One of them began to apologize to me for their presence, but said that my father had insisted on their accompanying him to his house. I told her it was all right, that I understood, and I thanked them for making sure that he arrived safely back with his family.

I was polite to these women for I could see that they really wanted no part of this and were deeply embarrassed, for themselves, for my father and for me. They began to make their goodnights and edge away towards the street. My father, reeling into the light from the darkness of the garden, stopped them. They were, he said, his friends, his guests, and he would drink with them in his house. He made to enter, but I stepped in front of him, barring the way.

I told him I would not allow this. I told him I did not care that he had no shame for himself, or for these women, but I would not let him humiliate my mother in this way. He is a small man, my father, and because I was standing on the step the advantage of my height was even more than usual, yet he glared at me so intensely with those black eyes of his that my courage dissolved and I stood back. He told the three women to enter the house, and when they would not, took hold of the Filipina and threw her inside. Then my mother came to see what was happening and why I had been away so long.

There is so much that I hate my father for, and it is true that I do not love my mother, but that night I could have wept for her; not the tears of sentiment I had shed for that nonsense on television, but real tears, tears of anguish and shame. My father made my mother kneel to those women that night; he made her offer them slippers so that they might enter the house, her house, and in the kitchen he made her boil water for the tea she was to serve to them. My father made my mother a servant to whores.

He had not forgotten that it was Christmas. He had the cake with him, and my mother was required to set it out upon a plate and carry the plate to the table. When he saw it, the cold white softness of the icing, the words 'Merry Christmas' as slurred upon the top as they slurred upon his breath, it seemed to agitate him. He began to shake his little fist about, the fist that had held the sword he had never surrendered, the fist that beckoned and dismissed, that ordered his world and everyone in it to do his bidding. He shook his little fist and he shook it, I realized at last, at me.

He indicated me to the three women, and pronounced that I was his daughter. His only daughter. His only child. He opened his fingers for a moment, to make a gesture of wiping me away as if I were a word marked in chalk that displeased him. He pointed to my mother, standing by the stove, standing, for she would not sit with these women. She would, at least, not do that. He pointed to my mother and pronounced that all she could give him was a daughter, and then the fingers returned to me, and he said the words again, all my mother could give him was a daughter.

His pig eyes bulged in his forehead and I assumed he was again engaged in the effort to force speech from his mouth. It was too much for him and so instead he brought his hand down into the richness of the Christmas cake. Then, very slowly, and without looking at me, he told the women my age. He said I was thirty. He was wrong. I was then twenty-nine. He began to weep, with the loud, self-pitying wails of a drunken man. I was thirty and I was not married. I was worthless to him. I was worth less to him than the Christmas cake. I was left on the shelf. No one would have me now, and so he would not even be given a grandson.

It was then that my mother spoke for the first time. She told him, very quietly, to shut up. And, with my father blubbering into his chest, she asked the three women to leave, saying that she was sorry they had been troubled in this way so late into the night. The women heard her words and were gone like ghosts.

I sat watching my father. I enjoyed it, the complete ungraciousness of his self-pitying wallow. Yet, at some point, he must have looked up and seen the contempt I had for him in my eyes, for he threw a handful of the cake he had destroyed at me, hitting me with it across the side of my face, and spattering the shoulder of my dress. I got to my feet very slowly wiping the mess from my cheek and left him without speaking, but never once letting go of him with my eyes.

Surprisingly, my mother spoke to him for me soon afterwards. Perhaps she felt his behaviour that night had given her the advantage. On New Year's Eve, as we completed the last of the cleaning we would do that year, she told me of my father's decision. I could go when I liked, where I liked, and he would pay my expenses as well as continuing my allowance, but I must find a place as a student in some respectable institution, and I must stay no longer than a year. When I returned I was to marry as soon as possible. I agreed, in spite of the last condition. It seemed to me a year was a very long time.

I saw Akiko and her husband on the last day of the holiday. I had been with Reiko and Setsuko the previous afternoon and we had arranged, the three of us, to visit her. I was surprised to find Akiko wearing a kimono and I asked her if she had just returned from visiting one of the shrines. She answered me in English, saying she had done that on New Year's Day, and then laughed as if her wearing a kimono in the house was the most natural thing in the world.

It was quite difficult to talk with Akiko because she was all the time with Stephen, and he would insist on joining in the conversation. Reiko and Setsuko spoke no English at all, and in spite of my recent practise with Mr Camley, I still felt uncomfortable using the language. Yet, in the end, it fell to me to do most of the talking, for Akiko would not speak to us in Japanese, as if she had renounced her own language. It was odd that she would not, for both she and Stephen knelt on the floor throughout our visit, which made me, sitting with Reiko and Setsuko on the sofa, feel ill at ease.

Yet, Stephen seemed to be a nice man. He was very tall, and very thin, with a hunched-up, awkward shape to him, and I could not understand why he and Akiko sat so persistently and uncomfortably on the floor when there were three perfectly serviceable chairs in the room which were unoccupied. Stephen seemed content with discomfort, however, choosing green tea in preference to Indian when Akiko's mother came in to us from the kitchen with the tray. I assumed that as this was his first visit to his wife's family, he wanted to impress upon them his interest in their country and traditions.

They had arrived two weeks before Christmas, and immediately after their Japanese wedding, had gone to Kyoto. There were of course photographs of the wedding, of the trip to Kyoto and Nara. I was shocked that Stephen had dressed in Japanese clothes for the marriage ceremony, and was shocked again that they had gone through a Shinto ritual. It seemed to me an unnecessarily accommodating gesture. Besides, Stephen looked funny in the clothes because the best the rental agency had seemed able to find were for a reasonably tall fat man, while Stephen was a very tall thin man.

I can still hear myself, asking Stephen inane questions in my high school English voice. How did he find Japan? Did he eat Japanese food? Could he use chop-sticks? He answered me very patiently, and even seemed enthusiastic about the things he had seen, the things he had done. All the while, Akiko knelt by him, gazing at his long face. I supposed it was love. It was not something I had seen before.

I began to grow impatient with all the talk of how wonderful my country was because it seemed that what he was talking about, the shrines, the clothes, Noh and Kabuki, was not my country at all, or at least only a part of it, a very small part that we Japanese call to mind at certain, special times, when it suits us to adopt again this special sense of Japan, of being Japanese. For Stephen, the special part was all there was, and in his unwillingness to see the rest he was missing so much; he was missing the truth.

When he said his ambition was to return in the spring to

view the cherry blossoms I asked him why and he seemed unable to understand my question. Yet how could I have explained to him with my broken English the utter wretchedness of Ueno Park in April, when you can smell the stench of beer three hundred metres away from the entrance, and see the clouds of cigarette smoke which rise through the blossoming trees? How could I explain the sordid spectacle of the drunks sprawled on old newspapers and shreds of cardboard boxes, vomiting their rice into the trampled dirt, or the salarymen swinging from the broken branches like so many inept apes? I had other things to talk about. I wanted to tell Akiko of my plans to escape, and I could not. I could not, because everything her husband loved was a part of what I longed to escape from.

When, at last, we were able to go, Stephen said that we would, all of us, be welcome to stay with them should we ever come to London. Akiko, defeated by the conventions that obviously meant so much to her husband, was forced to at least bid her three friends farewell in her own language. I had a little contentment from that, and more from the fact that I might well take up her husband's offer of hospitality much sooner than either of them thought.

I returned to Tokyo, and there was a letter for me from Professor Kobayashi. He said he had made some enquiries for me, both in Tokyo and abroad. A scholarship was out of the question for the immediate future, but if I was willing to undergo language training, and was able to pay the fees, I could attend a course beginning in the last week of January at the Greenlake School in Reading. Then, in the autumn, he had been assured by Mr Camley, I would be welcome at his college in Cambridge. With that place secured, a scholarship could be more easily arranged.

The letter closed by saying that he would telephone. There was nothing else, no plea for me to stay, not even a sense of regret that I was leaving. It was a business letter, nothing more, and the business that had been between us through all those years was at an end. He did not even seem glad that it was so. That at least would have been something. When I had finished reading his letter I wept again.

Yet there was something else. He did telephone and then, after the talk of what I should do, where I should go, he proposed a visit to Nikko together. We went on a Friday afternoon, intending to stay only that night and return to Tokyo the following afternoon. After that first time in the Hotel Fuji View I would not stay over a Saturday night when the hotels were likely to be filled with men like him, and their companions, girls like me.

We travelled separately, as we always did on the few occasions when we went away together, and although we took adjacent rooms at the hotel, they were quite separate. We stayed at the Kanaya, of course, and he wanted to be careful. Well, he always wanted to be careful. But sometimes, just being careful is not enough.

There were few guests, for it was a cold Friday in early January. The New Year holiday had just finished, and there was no snow to tempt photographers. The bright colours of the shrines seemed dull beneath the leaden skies, and a bitter wind blew. We ate in the hotel dining room, alone for most of our meal.

He spoke gently to me at the table, and I knew he would want me to sleep with him that night. He called me Miss Miura. When we returned to our rooms I bathed quickly, and went out into the corridor in my robe, with the other things I would need then and in the morning in a small bag. I knocked and entered his room, and found him waiting in the bed for me. I do not know, even now, what I felt for him then, if I really felt anything at all. I do not know for certain that I have ever, really, felt anything for any man, even Michael, yet I believe I was pleased that he still had a passion for me, that I could still inspire this in him, for him.

Afterwards, he would not sleep. He wanted to talk to me, but the room had only twin beds in it, and they were too small for us to lie together comfortably. So I moved to the other bed and lay alone, listening to the sound of the river falling from the mountain in the darkness on the other side of the window, and the words falling from the lips I had kissed in the darkness of the room. With the sound of water and words it seemed I was a child again, and for a moment I thought I might become afraid but it seemed I had forgotten how. That forgetting made me think I had grown up.

I do not remember everything he said that night because I kept dozing. It was a speech really, it sounded like a speech and I was constantly coming in and out of it from sleep, as if I turned the dial of a radio but always found the same station.

He said how happy it had made him that we should have these last few hours together before I went away. He said how he had tried to teach me some of the things that he had learned of life. He said he felt he had prepared me for my own life in the best way that he knew. He said so much and with so few pauses, unless he was stopping to think in the moments when I lapsed from consciousness, that he might have been reading from a script. It almost sounded rehearsed. Well, I suppose that even then I should have known it was hardly likely he was expressing these sentiments for the first time. I did know it then, it was simply that I would not accept the knowledge.

How long he went on I cannot say. I woke some time in the early morning, perhaps four or five o'clock, and I left his room in the darkness. We checked out at ten o'clock and did not bother to walk the short distance to the shrines for a last look, but took a taxi straight to the station where, although we boarded the same train, we travelled to our separate homes in separate compartments. In Ueno station, when we got off the bullet train, I caught sight of his grey head once in the crowd, and then he was gone. I was to hear his voice, in anger, once more, and receive a final letter, but I would never see him again.

There was suddenly so much to do. I went back to Kyushu the same day I returned from Nikko. My mother acted as intermediary with my father, for he would not speak to me directly himself. I did not really care, all I wanted from him was his agreement to my plans and his money, but when I asked my mother the reason for his silence she said that he was very busy at his work. I stayed with them for three days, and then made the long journey to Tokyo once again. I did not say goodbye to my father. My mother was to come to

Tokyo when my travel dates were fixed. She would see me off from Narita. I did not expect my father would accompany her.

It was all done in a little over a week. I had been to the British embassy and received a letter of consent; I had arranged for all my clothes to be packed and shipped. I resigned from my job and gave notice on my apartment, for which my father would have to continue the rent over the next two months. There was much business and few good-byes. It was only during those last few days before my leaving that I understood, I think, my loneliness. There was no one to regret my going, even at my office. I had been a part-timer, and so set apart from the others. Only Mr Yamada, the boy who cut my hair, said he was sorry I would not see him for some time, and wished me luck. I had not told him I was leaving, I had not meant to, but he had cut Miss Sekiya's hair the day before he cut mine and she had mentioned it.

He said that he might come to England some day, and would visit. I told him that he would be welcome. We knew neither of us meant what we said, yet the words were urged by kindliness on both our parts, and this we also knew.

It was on the afternoon of my last day in Tokyo that I heard from Professor Kobayashi again. I was with my mother and my Aunt Mie. My telephone was in the kitchen in that apartment and so I was able to excuse myself to take the call.

He was angry. I had never heard his voice filled with anger before. He was not the man I had known, or perhaps I should say, I had not known the man he was.

He told me that I was diseased, and that I had passed the disease on to him. He was, for once, quite specific and it was not left to my imagination just what kind of a disease it was I had given him. All I could do was wonder if what he was saying was true, for I, myself, appeared to be completely healthy. I tried to tell him so, but I was inhibited by the proximity of my mother and my aunt, and anyway, his anger would not admit an interruption. He said he had always trusted me and that I had betrayed him. I had betrayed not only him, but his family, for his physician had insisted that his wife receive treatment as well, and now he must find some way of justifying this to her.

It was not a long conversation. I was not given the opportunity of making either a denial or a defence. In the end he called me a tart and rang off. I can still hear him saying the word.

It took a little while for me to prepare my face for my mother and my aunt again, but I did so. I sat with them through the afternoon and early evening, and walked with them to the station. I would see them both again the next day, my mother was staying with my aunt, and both of them would come with me to the airport in the morning.

When I was alone I thought about the disease I carried within me. I supposed it had come from Miss Yumi, carried to me by Satoshi Mizuno. If it was so then he had had his full revenge of me, but there had been other men and it might have been that he had carried the germ from me to her and not the other way around. It did not matter. I would have to seek treatment, or at least be tested to see whether or not I needed treatment. As I had wanted to tell Professor Kobayashi, I did not, myself, appear to be ill. I would have to seek treatment, and I would have to seek it here. How could I have done otherwise? I could not, I would not, have gone to a doctor in a foreign country with something like — with something like that.

I waited until I thought my mother had arrived at my aunt's house and then I telephoned her to say that I would not, after all, be travelling to London in the morning, that I would not be travelling to London on the day after either. When she asked me why I simply said that I had changed my mind and then I put the telephone down. I waited for it to ring again, but it did not, my mother, evidently, having decided she did not wish to pursue our conversation.

ELEVEN

I made my father truly happy when I cancelled my journey to London, for he was able both to have me stay in Japan, which was what he wanted and, at the same time, to berate me for being a wilful, selfish girl. I am sure he cannot have enjoyed himself so much for years.

He came to my apartment with my mother the day after I was supposed to have left wearing his indignation as if it were a suit of clothes from Saville Row. My mother sat passively as he ranted on at me, calling me ungrateful, worthless, the great disappointment of his life, the shame of the family. I wanted so much to tell him my reason for not going so that his insults might have a little more focus to them.

When, finally, he was done my mother said that my father had decided I was to return to Kyushu with them that night. I was to live at home until such time as a suitable husband could be found for me. I remember I looked at her with the full force of my contempt in my eyes. I said I would not go back to live with them, I would not marry against my will. I expected another outburst from my father, but it did not come. Instead my mother continued, as calmly as ever, saying that if I did not return with them then I must fend for myself. My father, she said, had worked hard for me all of his life and his reward was that I had turned out quite the opposite of all a dutiful, and how she stressed that word, daughter should be. I was not fit, she said, to use my father's name. She told me I might stay in Tokyo if I so wished, but I must make my own way. My father would not continue to pay my rent. My father would not continue to pay my allowance. There was a flight back to Kyushu that evening and my seat was reserved. I had the rest of the afternoon to come to a decision. With that they left me, sitting in the wreckage of my apartment, my suitcases waiting by the door uncollected, my passport and my ticket to London on the table.

I cannot pretend that I was unaffected by what my mother had said, but as I sat there it came to me that the situation was not quite as dark as it perhaps might appear. My rent was paid for the next two months and so I had the right to continue living in my apartment for a time at least. What was more, I was confident that my father would not yet have closed my account; if I acted quickly I could withdraw most of what was in it from a cash dispenser that afternoon, and anyway, I had a large amount of money in traveller's cheques, more than enough to see me through the rest of the month if I lived carefully.

I made myself a meal with the few pieces of food I had left in my kitchen and then, just before the bank closed, just before the time when I should have been boarding the flight back to the south with my parents, I emptied the account my father maintained for me. It is true that having so much cash in my apartment made me a little nervous, but it was not that which made sleep so difficult to find when I went, at last, to my bed. No, it was excitement denied me my rest, excitement at the sudden smell of freedom I had in my nostrils. I had sought freedom in escaping from Japan, when all I had ever really wanted to escape from was my family, my mother, my father. Most of all, my father.

My sensation of euphoria lasted almost all the next morning. I was brought back to reality by an interview I had with the factor in charge of letting my apartment, an elderly man with long white hair and yellow teeth, who spoke to me from behind a thick curtain of tobacco smoke. He might have passed for a professor, a man of learning; certainly the things he had to say about my apartment startled me more than anything I ever heard in a lecture hall.

It seemed that, while I was within my rights to remain in possession of my accommodation during the period for which the rental fee had been paid, I must, should I wish to continue my possession, enter into a new contract with the agency. To do so would require the payment of a sum equivalent to six months' rent in advance. I left the office with the imagined hoard of my father's gold as diminished as my sudden sense of liberty.

Of course, I knew I must find work, and find it as quickly as possible. I suppose I could simply have returned to my job with the translation agency I had quit so recently, but my pride would not let me. My pride did, however, relent so far as to allow me a telephone call to my former editor at the agency, one of the few people I had ever begun to like or admire there. I explained the sudden cancellation of my travel plans, although not, of course, the reason for the cancellation. I asked if she knew of any translation work from which I might actually earn a living. She was quiet, and then told me what I already knew, that such things were difficult.

When I put the telephone down I have to admit to feelings that were close to despair, but then it rang suddenly and I heard my former editor's voice asking me how I felt about romance. For a moment I was confused, I did not quite know what she was suggesting and started to say that I had had quite enough of that with men, but then I realized she was talking not of romance itself, but romance fiction. Perhaps the two are not really so very different. No, I do not mean that, I quite definitely do not mean that. They are very different, I only wish that they were not.

There was, my former editor said, the possibility of regular work as a freelance with Heartbeat/Columbine Books. They had just established their own office in Tokyo prior to beginning independent publication in Japan. They were looking for translators now. She knew an editor there, someone she had been at university with years before. They were not close friends, but she could still, she thought, give me an introduction. Perhaps I would like her to speak to her friend, to write a letter of introduction for me.

Two days afterwards I returned to my apartment from the Heartbeat office with a photocopy of the first and last chapters of something called *The Restless Heart*, my test piece for the company. In addition, I had ten or twelve other romances, titles already translated, that I had bought from a bookstore I passed on my way back. I remember it was a Friday evening and as soon as I got in I began to read. I had two weeks to complete the test piece, and I intended to have the work done long before the final date for submission, but first I wanted to read, I wanted to know as much as I could about romance, or, at least, about this sort of romance.

I read, reluctantly at first, two books, *Island of Dreams* and *Love's Harvest*. I read reluctantly because I knew, without ever having opened such a book before, that I should despise what was in it. I was reading, I told myself, only to acquaint myself with the style of the thing, for my own translations. The text itself was nothing, the text itself was only something to be translated, as the technical gibberish I had used to work with was only something to be translated.

I did despise what I read that first evening, and then on the morning which followed. Yet, for all that, I continued to read in the afternoon, when I returned from my few small errands. I continued to read in the afternoon, in the evening and on into the night. I read, and could not come to terms with the conflict in my feelings towards what I was reading. I did despise it, the compounded stupidities of character and plot, yet I found myself, some part of myself, responding to what I read. I could not understand why, I only knew that it was happening.

I was wakened early on the Sunday morning by a telephone call from my mother. Her voice was hushed, as if she was afraid of being overheard by someone, my father presumably. She asked me whether or not I had reconsidered returning to live with them. I said I had not and put the receiver down. A few moments later it rang again. My mother said she would speak to my father for me, that she would ask him if he might continue my allowances. I told her that if she spoke to my father she should do so on her own behalf, not on mine, for I had nothing I wished to say to him. My mother said she would telephone me again when she could. I said nothing, only the single word 'yes', indicating my understanding of what she had said and my disinclination to continue the present conversation further. It was as cold and cruel a goodbye as I could manage.

I had meant to go out for a short walk that Sunday morning, but I did not. After talking with my mother I went straight back to bed, straight back to the books I had piled upon the floor. I went back to them because, talking to my mother, I had understood why I continued to read in spite of everything I felt. I understood why my objections to style, the hackneyed story lines, the contempt I had for those who would read such trash, slowly slipped away. I understood that it had to do with love. It had to do with the expression of love.

All my life I had wanted someone, anyone I suppose, to tell me that I was loved, that they loved me. In the books, for all the things that happened to the heroines, the mistakes and the misunderstandings, the brutalities even, to which those girls were sometimes subjected, in spite of all this, in the end, they were loved. In the end there was someone to say 'I love you' to them. That is why I read what I had previously affected to despise. I read because I found in those books what I had not found in my life, a message of hope. One day, some day, each story said to me, there will be one who will tell you he loves you, also.

I did not give even one second's thought to my mother's telephone call and what it might imply. I was in a spell, and the spell could not be broken even by the fact that my father might, possibly, be relenting towards me, that my money worries might be as insubstantial as the dreams of romance themselves. I let my reading take me into another world, a world where every man was a hero, handsome and strong and, in the end, kind, and I was every heroine, every girl whose sadness was banished with a kiss.

It was after midnight when I finished my reading, and I began the translation of the test chapters without waiting for the light of the morning to come. I knew I could do the work. I knew I could do it well. I knew I could do it better than anything that I had read. I did. The chapters were ready in three days and, on the fourth, I presented them to the editor at Heartbeat. A week later, two weeks later, I cannot really remember, I was called back to the office where I signed a contract to translate my first romance, *Concerto*. When I put my name to the contract I was asked to specify a completion date. I said that I would deliver the finished translation in a month. The editor seemed a little taken aback and asked me if I would not, perhaps, like to take a little longer, but I was firm in my resolve. I would, I repeated, have the translation ready within one month.

It was like writing my thesis all over again, doing that first book. I did not really sleep, I did not really eat, I worked, always I worked. There were times when I thought perhaps, after all, I could not do it. Times when I would wake from an hour, a half-hour perhaps, of unconsciousness on the couch that was now my bed; times when I would gag at the steam rising from another ordered bowl of noodles. But, after all, I went on. I completed the work.

It was good, the work, that first work. My editor, whose surprise when I appeared at her desk transformed to an all but imperceptible concern as she took the pads from me and skimmed through the first pages, was impressed. I left with another book, another contract, another set of translation pads all packed so neatly into the bag with the Heartbeat/ Columbine logo on the side. When I arrived back at my apartment I went to sleep in my bed for the first time in four weeks. When I woke the next morning I cleaned and shopped, and then, in the afternoon, began the new translation, working on the rough draft as I read. Within a week the draft was complete and I was ready to begin putting it into shape.

Of course, I did not work as I had worked on *Concerto*. I could not have done so and lived, I knew that. Besides, there were other things to which I had to attend. I opened a bank account for myself, the first time in my life I had an account of my own. Well, what I mean is that for the first time in my life I had an account that was not maintained by my father. I opened it with his money, of course I did. It was what I had left from the traveller's cheques and the other money I had taken from my old account. In return, along with my bank book, I was given a small gift signifying the bank's appreciation of my custom: it was a fluffy figure of Paddington Bear. I told the clerk that this was not suitable as I had no children, but she replied that the gift was for me, that it was what was usually given to young women. When I insisted that I did not want a toy I was provided with a packet of dusting cloths.

I completed that second translation in six weeks. What was it? *Stormy Weather*? *The Bachelor Boy*? I really cannot remember. What I remember is that when the second payment was made I had earned more than one million yen. I was not rich in any real sense of the word, in, say, my father's sense of the word, but in my own way I was. I was rich because, for the first time in my life, I not only had money, I also had the freedom to spend it in any way that I wanted. I decided that I would find a new apartment.

It did not take long. I found a place, a tiny place, in a mansion block in Denenchofu. I had not been in that area since the time I stayed with Akiko's uncle the night before we were to take the entrance examination at the Blessed Martyr, Akiko, Reiko and I. It gave me a strange feeling moving there to live, as if the past had never really let go of me.

It was tiny, that place — one room, a little kitchen area and a bath. I moved in, taking nothing with me from my old place except a suitcase full of clothes. The rest I sent back to my parents' house without a letter or a telephone call to explain my actions. I slept the first night on the floor without a mattress, covering myself with my coat. Then I set about furnishing my new home, my first home.

I so enjoyed buying things that I liked. For all the time that I could remember it was my mother who had chosen everything for me, mostly sending to Tokyo pieces of furniture she did not want or no longer needed herself. The only part I had in any of it was to show my gratitude at the end. Even my clothes were selected by her, and if I did happen to buy anything myself, it was only ever with her permission, in shops she had sanctioned in advance. I think that one of the few times my mother ever expressed approval of something I did was when I first said I wished to buy clothes from Hanae Mori and Jun Ashida. I remember her telling my father, who paid, of course, that it was a sign I was growing up and becoming more responsible.

Well, now I was responsible. I bought carpets and furniture. I bought curtains and crockery. I bought pictures and plants. And I paid for them, all of them, with money that I had earned.

I remember that little apartment so well. I remember the sunshine upon my bed in the morning, and the sunshine upon my desk in the afternoon. And I remember, once, it was the first evening I was in the apartment when everything was settled, when everything was in place, I was tired and I stopped what I was doing for a moment, only a moment, and I looked about me at my room, at my things, in the light of the lamps I had bought: a white teacup, a plate, the chrysanthemum petals already fallen from the heavy heads in the vase, the dark wood of the table I had bought from the salvage shop for a few thousand yen and polished until it shone and the room smelt of wax and lavender. I remember thinking then that it all belonged to me, everything I let my eyes fall upon, my plants, my books, my things.

Perhaps I was, perhaps I am, selfish, but it mattered that all of this, the things I could touch, the things I could not touch, the light, the sunshine and the smell of wax and lavender, all of this was mine. And it mattered that it was mine because I had made it mine. It was not given to me. It was not chosen for me. It was mine.

The things in my old apartment I had taken to my parents' house by the removals company my mother had retained just before I was to go to London. The same company took my things, my own things, just yesterday, the table and the pictures, the white cups. Mr Ueno told me there was no room in his mother's house for my possessions. He might have added for my memories as well. I comfort myself with the knowledge that if his mother could know my thoughts today there would be no room for me, either, no matter how much she desires to have me as her victim.

I had been living in Denenchofu for a little under a month when, on one day, I received two items in the mail, and a visitor. One of the things I found in my post box that afternoon was a very handsomely printed post card announcing that my hairdresser, Mr Yamada, was to open his own shop in Daikanyama in a month's time. The card expressed the hope that I would honour the new establishment with my custom. I did not, somehow, think that I would. Although he was a good hairdresser, although he had cut my hair just before I was due to go to London, cut it to my satisfaction, to more than my satisfaction, Mr Yamada was from my old life. The life I was to have in Denenchofu was to be my new life. I was determined it would not be soiled by anything, or anyone, from what had gone before. I was determined, but I was wrong.

The other thing I found in my post box was also from the old life, but I did not know that at once. It was a package, and I did not have time to open it because I had a visitor waiting for me at my door. It was my mother.

She had come at my father's bidding, of course, to do my father's bidding, of course. She told me that I had hurt and shamed my father by my actions. She said that I had not behaved as a daughter should behave. She said that my father was a good man, a man who had worked all his life for me and that I had repaid him poorly for all he had done. As she spoke I sat and listened or, at least, pretended to. I did not really need to listen to my mother's speech for I knew it all already, and, as if I were the prompter in some play, heard each line in my head before it was actually spoken. It was only when she strayed from the text that I actually listened to what she was saying as she said it.

She told me that, in spite of everything, my father had decided to forgive me. They knew all about my new life, she said, my job, my apartment. I supposed they had set a detective on me. It would not have been difficult, or, indeed, unusual. My father maintained an account with a large investigation agency as a matter of course. He used the agency to check into the background of his workers to make sure he did not employ anyone with even a suggestion of the taint of Korean blood. For the first time during the interview I was angry with my mother and I asked her, pointedly, how she had come by so much information. I asked her if they had used a detective.

It had no effect of course, my directness. It never did, never does. My mother deflects it with a technique akin to deafness. She continues with what she intends to say as if I have been silent all along. She did it then, she would do it now were I to leap suddenly to my feet and scream my thoughts at my wedding guests instead, simply, of thinking them. Well, that day, her voice continued as the flow of a stream continues, on and on, until she reached the matter she had come to me for. My father wanted me to return to Kyushu with my mother. He wanted, my mother said, to be reconciled with his daughter.

It would have been useless to argue with my mother. Instead, I complied with the request she had been sent to convey to me, although I did not do so immediately. I said I would not, could not, go back with her as my father wished, but I was willing to return, alone, and only for a short time, a weekend, a long weekend at most. I had my work, I said.

My mother told me that she understood, and left. I walked with her to the station and told her I would telephone her and tell her my plans. Afterwards, when I got back, I cleaned my apartment.

I believe I opened the package I had taken from the post box with Mr Yamada's card after my mother left, but I did not look closely at the contents until the following morning. It was a book, and I received so many sample text books from publishers who had me on their files as a teacher that it was my habit to simply toss each one into the waste-bin. This book was different. I suppose what made me examine it more closely was the envelope, which bore signs of only having been forwarded to me from my last address. Usually this sort of mail carried on it the address of every place I had lived since graduating from the Blessed Martyr. Clearly the person who had posted this particular package to me knew where I had been living until only two months beforehand. As far as I was aware none of the publishers who most regularly squandered their money on such importunings had this knowledge.

In fact, this book was not from a publishing house, at least, not directly. This book was from Satoshi Mizuno. It was also by Satoshi Mizuno. The book was a critical study of Jean Rhys, hastily put together on poor paper, with the usual murky photographs of people and places identifiable only from the captions underneath.

I read it standing by the sink in my kitchen. The printing may have been done in a hurry, but the writing itself had taken no time at all or at least had taken Satoshi Mizuno no time. The book was nothing more than a translation, line by line, of the thesis I had written for my master's degree. Even the title was mine, *Casualties of Love*. At first I had thought that, at least, was original. It was not. The title seemed foreign to me simply because it had been rendered into Japanese. Picking the book up again that morning I had thought it must be a piece of romance fiction and not the school text I had imagined the night before.

It was Satoshi Mizuno's revenge, of course, and it was really rather a good one. It was one, as well, which continued for, slight as it was, hastily done as it was, the book gathered some applause. It was reviewed in the newspapers and journals, and at least one reviewer took the opportunity to welcome the author back into the tight little circle of foreign literary criticism in Japan after too long an absence. Yes, it was well done, so well done I almost found I was able to admire it myself.

Two and a half weeks after my mother visited me, after Satoshi Mizuno's book came, I returned to my parents' house. It was quite late when I arrived. My mother met me at the station, as she always did, and prepared food for me, as she always did. My father, of course, was not at home. I was tired from the journey, and not at all hungry. I made a gesture towards consuming the meal my mother had made, but then quickly excused myself, bathed and went to my room to sleep.

It was the next morning when I saw my father for the first time. He was eating breakfast. I prostrated myself before him as I always did, as I did this morning. I said that I was Sachiko, that I had returned to his house. He did not pause. He did not look at me. He uttered several grunts through the soup and fish with which he continued to fill his mouth. I took these to be sounds of recognition and assent. For a moment I thought he might even be choking, but he was not. I got up and left him to his food, which clearly interested him more than his daughter did.

It was my mother who told me of my father's insistence that I should marry before the end of the year. My mother said that he was angry because I had thrown away the opportunity to travel and he could see no point in my remaining single, wasting my time in Tokyo, squandering the money he gave to me. It was time I accepted the responsibilities of life. As I had failed him as a daughter it was time I was a wife. It was time I was a mother.

My mother said that a marriage broker had been engaged and that my father had selected one of several eligible young men for me to meet. She said that I was a very lucky girl to have a father who was willing, after all the disappointments I had supplied him with, to take into account my own preferences in finding a husband for me.

Part of me wanted to take hold of her then, to seize her hair with my fingers and pull her head this way and that, screaming the truth into her stupid face, her expressionless eyes. I wanted to say that I had no intention of marrying anyone my father thought suitable, that the very fact of his approval must at once disqualify the man. I wanted to tell her that I had no intention of marrying anyone at all then, because I had found, at last I had found, something I wanted to do. I wanted her to know that my new work was important to me, that it was important to me because I was good at it, but more than that even, because, for the first time in my life, I was free of her, and I was free of my father. I wanted her to hear from my own lips that my intention was to return to Tokyo, to take up my work and hope, pray perhaps, that a little of the magic I found in the books I translated might come into my own life, bringing me a man I would marry because I loved him, and because he loved me.

I said none of this, of course. I formed instead the trite phrases of thanks and acceptance so easily plundered from our language's treasure house of insincerity, and only then sought to tell my mother of my new work.

I was less than a week in my parents' house, and in that time I think I saw my father twice. The only communication I had with him was through my mother, except for the night when he came home at ten o'clock, drunk of course, and cursed me for an hour before he fell asleep at the kitchen table. I helped my mother get him to bed, and afterwards I washed myself as if I had touched some indescribably filthy thing.

It had been decided by my parents that I should stay with them until I was married, but, in the end, I was allowed to return to Tokyo on the condition that I came back for the meeting with the young man they had selected for me. At least my father approved of my new address, although my mother said she had not told him about the size of the building. It was her way of letting me know she would have preferred me to live in close proximity to my landlords so that, through them, she might better monitor my comings and my goings. The relative anonymity of where I now lived disturbed her, but this, of course, was precisely why I had determined to live there. My mother saw me off at the station, as she always did. I sat alone in the train, the space next to me bought and paid for by my father as it always was.

Two weeks passed and I journeyed south again for the encounter my parents had arranged. Of course, I refused the man, I had not intended ever to do otherwise. Afterwards, my father raged at me, threatened me. My mother sat through it all. When we were finished and he had gone to bed, she told me that I would be married, and by the end of the year. I said nothing and returned to Tokyo again the following day. On the train I began the first draft of my new translation, a story set in Africa called *The Mountain of Shadows*. I remember it because the translation was very popular and I was featured in the Heartbeat newsletter the month after the Japanese edition of the book was published.

I enjoyed my life then, I believe: the apartment, the work. Even the trips back to Kyushu for the meetings with men my parents had arranged were only minor irritations. I think I was happy, almost. Yes, I think I was happy, almost. It was like that for a year or so, before Mr Camley came again to Japan.

I believe it was the day I received his letter saying that he would be coming to Tokyo that I decided I should seduce him. It had been forwarded to me with all my other mail, and it came, as Satoshi Mizuno's book had come, as a surprise. I do not think I had given Alistair Camley one thought since the time I had seen him last. I did not even remember having given him my business card, although I suppose I must have done or else I do not know how he could have had my former address. Unless he had obtained it from my former lover. That thought came to me then, I must admit. It came to me at much the same time that I decided I would seduce Alistair Camley. It came to me at much the same time the idea came that Alistair Camley would be the instrument of my revenge against my former lover, Professor Kobayashi, and against my former lover, Satoshi Mizuno.

He was quite perfect for it really, quite perfect. He was known to both men, and was a friend to one. I knew that word of what I was to him after I had made him mine would be carried to them both, somehow, would be whispered in the ears of both, somehow. The English have an expression about how the world is a very small place. Well, Tokyo is a smaller place than the world, a much smaller place, in spite of the millions of us that live here. No, it is a smaller place because of the millions of us that live here.

And Alistair Camley, Mr Camley, was perfect because he wanted to be seduced. He wanted to be seduced by me. He had wanted me to seduce him the first time we were alone together. He told me so. He told me he had only ever come to Japan to sleep with Japanese girls: the lectures he gave, the books he worked on, even the money he earned, all of these were mere pretexts, excuses for his presence here. He told me he had dreamed dreams of me and I had disappointed him for I had not made any of the dreams come true. When I had failed to take his hand and lead him to his room, when I had not taken his clothes from him and knelt before him, when I had not dressed in a kimono and fed him pieces of raw fish, had not turned to display the nape of my neck, had not let him raise my robes and let him take me from behind in the position of the peacock, he had been forced to go to a bathhouse to have his needs attended to. There he had been required to pay.

Of course, all of this was in the future then. Then there was only his letter telling me that he would come to Tokyo again, that he would stay for seven months to work with Professor Kobayashi on their book, that he would be happy to see me and that it was his hope, his dream, that we might be friends. And then, too, there was only my plan of revenge.

I do not know why I have begun referring to Alistair Camley by his name, for I do not believe I ever once did in all the time we knew one another. Michael is the only man I have ever called by his name, and it took weeks before the unease of doing so was gone entirely from me. Professor Kobayashi, Satoshi Mizuno, I always referred to as 'teacher'. The other men I was with so briefly, there was no need for names. Alistair Camley I always used to think of simply as the man from Cambridge. Of course, at the time of his letter, I do not believe I thought of him even in those terms. He was simply to be my revenge, and for that he did not need a name. When I wrote to him it was simply a post card, telling him I would be very happy to help him again during his stay in Tokyo, not a word about friendship of course, and giving him my new address and telephone number. I remember congratulating myself on my reply, on the polite precision of my English.

I met him, for the first time, at the Borsalino restaurant in Roppongi. I chose it for our rendez-vous. In part, this was because it is situated close to the International House of Japan where Mr Camley was staying at the beginning of his time here. Mostly, however, I chose the place for the quality and price of its cooking. It was a place I felt Mr Camley would endure only with a certain amount of unease, as to the decor and food, the attentiveness of the waiters, and the coming of the bill. I intended that throughout our time together he should be placed at my disadvantage. Well, I was a little stupid then.

He was as uncomfortable as I had hoped he would be. The menu baffled him, for he read neither Italian nor Japanese, and he was entirely dependent on me to make any sense of it at all. That was how I had intended things should be that first evening. It was how I intended things should be all the times we would be together. He would never know what would be on the menu. He would take what he was given. I would choose, for myself.

That he had a passion for me was obvious that evening. That he lusted for me was even more so. I had no intention, however, of letting him have his moment with me then. I wanted his appetite whetting. I wanted to watch him hunger for me. Besides, I was still receiving treatment for the infection I had unknowingly cultivated in my body and given to the man whose friend I was even then beginning to seduce. It was to be another week, the doctor who was treating me said, until I could safely resume sexual activity, although I had doubts I would receive his sanction even then to judge from the manner in which he treated me. He was an Englishman, and dispensed disapproval as freely as he did the antibiotics which were meant to cure me. I can still recall the element of relish in his voice when he described the nausea his capsules would almost certainly induce in me, as if that were to be my punishment for the sins in which nature had found me out. Still, he was, this doctor, beyond the reach of my parents, which was why I had gone to him.

Mr Camley, of course, knew nothing of this. Mr Camley wanted me to return with him to his room, so that we might discuss in more details the ways in which I could be of help to him, he said. I would not. He was disappointed. I know he was disappointed. When we parted he tried to kiss me, as he had kissed me on parting once before. He aimed his mouth at my cheek, but I turned aside and because he had his eyes closed he stumbled when he found only air in the space where he had anticipated my flesh. He looked at me afterwards and misery and desire were written upon the pasty slab of his face. I returned to my apartment in Denenchofu with the memory of that, and it cheered my heart.

I let him have me three weeks later. I had been helping him to find more permanent accommodation but in the end someone from the university to which he was attached secured a place for him. We had arranged to meet with the intention of viewing two apartments, and when he telephoned to tell me that this was no longer necessary, I took pity on him and said that we should meet anyway. The gratitude in his voice told me that he was mine to do with as I liked. I decided that I would go to bed with him that day. It was a decision I made quite on the spur of the moment.

Now, I cannot believe that I could have been so stupid. I imagined I was in control. I imagined I dictated events. All the time that Alistair Camley was in Japan I never once dreamed the car dream. Now, it seems to me, I was in control of nothing. Now, I think, I should have dreamed the car dream every time I went to sleep.

I was excited meeting him. It was like the feeling I had had that time with Satoshi Mizuno, when I took him home with me and I knew what he could only hope. But it was different as well. It was different because I had not been with a foreigner before, and I wondered what it would be like, what he would be like.

There was some uncertainty when we got to International House because Mr Camley seemed suddenly afraid. He would not let me go up to his room with him, but told me to wait for ten minutes and then follow him. So I waited and watched the wedding guests milling about, for it was a Saturday and here, and everywhere else, there were people going about the business of marriage, just as now, today, here, I go about the business of my own marriage.

I had not been in one of the guest rooms before and I was interested to see what his was like but I had no time to look about me. Almost as soon as I closed the door behind me Mr Camley started trying to pull my clothes off.

This really was not what I had intended at all, not at all. I had determined that I would tell him that he might have me. I had prepared myself to initiate what should happen between us, and to order its progress. Now I was neither in command of the situation, nor even quite certain just what the situation was, for Mr Camley had buried his face inside my coat, looking for my breasts, I imagine, and while one hand held me to him, the other was beneath my skirt and pulling at my legs so that I was in very real danger of falling.

At odd moments of our struggle, for that is what it was, Mr Camley's head would emerge from out of the folds of my clothing and hover in front of my face while he attempted, I thought, for I could not understand much of what he was saying, to engage me in conversation. He was quite breathless, as well, which made it even more difficult to understand his words. Most of the little I could grasp was in the form of questions. He repeatedly asked me if I was hot, so much so that, finally, I said yes, I was hot, I was extremely hot. This appeared to be the answer he sought, for he closed his eyes then and took a very deep breath before returning his little face, grown quite red with effort, to the quest for my bosom. I remember thinking even then that he was going to be very disappointed when so much effort would result in so little reward.

I do not know how long all of this went on, not more than a few moments, I suppose, but it seemed like a very long time indeed. I was holding on to Mr Camley very tightly because I was afraid, very afraid, of falling. That, however, was the full extent of my involvement in what was happening for the excitement my anticipation had elicited had been quite vanquished by the sudden turn events in reality had taken. I passed the long minutes of our embrace trying to keep my feet upon the ground and looking out through the window which allowed a generous light to fall into the room.

When next Mr Camley pushed his face in front of mine I was startled, for I had been thinking of something else entirely. There was a passage in the book I was then translating that was presenting me with many problems. It was a rather graphic love scene, I mean graphic in the physical sense. I had not come across one like it before and, because the translator's guide supplied by Heartbeat required the deletion of all mention of the body below the waist, and that even those parts above should be referred to in the most modest and shadowy of terms, I was unsure how exactly I was to proceed.

Mr Camley's face, when it appeared, was very red indeed now, and his silvered hair had so been disturbed by whatever he was attempting to do inside my clothing that I could see plainly the baldness he had tried with such art to disguise.

He asked me again if I was hot, and again I said yes, I was hot. He asked me then if I was so hot I was melting. I did not know the word 'melting', but I said that I was melting. I remember looking for the word in my dictionaries when I returned to my apartment that night. When I found it I thought of the day I had run to the Takarazuka theatre, and my excitement on that day, my anticipation of what was to come. What I had felt earlier with Mr Camley was not at all like that.

Next, Mr Camley asked me if my knickers were on fire. I did not know the word 'knickers' either, but guessed that it was a plural noun and said yes, they were on fire. This reply filled Mr Camley with such ardour he tried to pick me up, but could not because, so fearful was I of falling, I would not let go the little purchase I had upon the ground. In the end we gestured towards the masculine passion he had so obviously wished to demonstrate and went awkwardly towards his bed, for all the world like contestants in a two men, three legs race.

He let go of me just before we reached the bed, and I sat upon the edge expecting him to go to wash while I arranged myself, but no sooner was I seated than Mr Camley threw himself upon me again, causing me to fall backwards. He threw my skirt up and for a moment I could not see, which made me suddenly very frightened, but then I felt him pulling at my tights and underthings, and not wishing to have him tear them, I raised my hips and helped him slide them off. When he had my things past my knees he mounted me and there was the most terrible pain in my groin, as if I had been pierced with a nail. I think I may actually have screamed, I cannot, honestly, remember, what I can remember is the pain. I think I may have screamed because I remember too that Mr Camley put his hand across my mouth to quieten me.

He did not, himself, enter me that first time. It was the prong of his belt buckle that probed my flesh. What Mr Camley thought he was doing I have no idea, from the stains I found there afterwards he obviously enjoyed his brief but ecstatic congress with his sex between my buttocks and the top cover of his bed.

I do know that he mistook my pain for passion, and worked himself vigorously against me, causing the metal spike to push itself repeatedly into me. It did not last long, less than two minutes I suppose, but when he had done I was weeping, still too much in pain to be properly thankful that it was over.

Mr Camley moved away, and I closed my legs to him, turning on my side to try and soothe my hurt. He touched my tears, and his fingers were gentle upon me, almost timid. Then he went to wash himself.

There was blood, of course there was. I suppose he found some on his belt, or on himself perhaps, because when he came back to me he said he had not known, had not imagined even, that I was a virgin. I did not disabuse his ignorance for mixed in with his concern there was pride as well and I remembered Mayumi, my student, my little acrobat, and how she said she had sold her virginity again and again, and for a high price each time. I did not think she could ever have known the pain I had just known, and I was determined Mr Camley would pay, again and again, for what he imagined he had taken from me, and that, each time, the price would be a high one.

TWELVE

And so I began my affair with Mr Camley, a professor of Cambridge University, a famous man. Another famous man. I was a very expensive lover for him. After that first time, I always insisted that we go to hotels, proper hotels, not the love hotels he wished to go to with me. Yet, for all that, money was the whole extent of the price he had to pay for me. If I used him it was in a kindly enough manner, for he was kindly enough to me. He only wanted me for his pleasure, it is true, but his pleasure was not in harming me. The harm he did he knew nothing of. The wound in my groin healed with time, and the disapproving care of my English doctor.

Anyway, I believe he thought that I was worth the money, the money he spent. I practised all the tricks that had been forced upon me by Satoshi Mizuno, as well as deceit. There were not that many, I suppose. Even the imagination of the pornographer is limited, finally, by the finite possibilities of our body's form. Only in the anticipation of the event is there room for exaggeration. Mr Camley was like most of the men I have been with in that he was given more to speculation upon his desire than its actuality.

But he was not a cruel man. The wound in my groin was made unconsciously, and healed in time. The one true cruelty I witnessed at his hands was done not to me, but to his wife, for one day after we had been together for the weekend in a room at the Keio Plaza Hotel, he took me home with him and introduced me to her.

Of course, I did not know that I was going to meet his wife. Until I met her I did not know that he was married.

We were together for a weekend, for the first time. After he paid the bill and we were out in the street he asked me if I would go back to his apartment with him for tea. I was a little unsure. I did not really wish to see where Mr Camley lived, just as I did not wish him to see where I lived. Hotel rooms were where we transacted what was between us. When he sensed my indecision swerving towards rejection he said that I was expected, that he had already made the arrangements. I could not help wondering what arrangements were necessary for the boiling of a kettle, but then he said that he had arranged for an English tea, a meal, to be served to me. I could not then, graciously, have declined him.

Mr Camley had spoken the truth when he said he had made arrangements. He had made his arrangements with his wife. I knew, as soon as he opened the door to his apartment, that there was a woman inside. I do not know how I had that knowledge, it was a sense that came to me, as perfume carries on the breeze of someone's passing. But even though I sensed that there was a woman there I did not know that the woman was his wife. And I did not know that she was Japanese.

He told me afterwards he had met her fifteen years before, when he had spent a year, as now he was spending a year, teaching in one of the women's colleges in Tokyo. She had been a student of his. He had a wife in England at the time, he said, but the marriage was not a happy one, and they divorced soon after his return. Then his wife, his Japanese wife, had gone to Cambridge and they married shortly after her arrival. Her name was Masako, and she came to greet us just as Mr Camley was closing the door. We were expected. He had told the truth in that at least.

I spent two hours in that apartment, two hours with that woman, and afterwards, after I left, I never saw her again. I heard of her, of course; indeed, I saw her name just this morning in the Asahi newspaper. They have been running a series of articles all this week on Japanese living in England. Masako Camley was being interviewed on the subject of education. I can only suppose she was chosen because of her husband, for she herself is not involved in education and she has no children. When I saw her name this morning it shocked me, even after all this time. The shock was almost the same as when I saw her there in the apartment.

I had slept with married men before, of course I had — Professor Kobayashi, Satoshi Mizuno, the others. I had thought, often with dislike, sometimes contempt, of the wives of those men. I had not, however, until now, met one of them, and I had never been taken home to have tea with one of them, with the odour of her husband's seed still upon my skin. I was angry. I was, as well, ashamed, and I felt her humiliation as I felt my own.

We sat together on the sofa, speaking in Japanese, with Mr Camley opposite us in a chair, his face suffused with a look like doubtful sunshine, for he spoke not one word of our language and he must have been wary as to what, exactly, we might say to one another. He need not have worried. Nothing was said, although I am quite sure his wife knew what I had been doing with her husband in spite of his story that we had been in Osaka at the conference of the Japan Literary Society. He had, he said, taken me with him as his secretary.

I suppose she was used to his lies, as used to them as she was to his girls, for I was not the first. Later he used to boast to me of the girls he had in Cambridge, of how he posed them in his rooms in college there, and then, when he had no hand upon his flesh other than his own, he would turn to their photographs in the album he kept in his desk drawer, and he would comfort himself in his loneliness. One day, he added my photograph to his collection. It was his little ceremony, he said. Perhaps taking his girls back to tea to meet his wife was a ceremony also.

But nothing was said. The things we spoke of, his wife and I, were quite inconsequential: the weather in England, the life in Japan. For two hours we spoke and we said nothing.

Yet, I believed then, and I believe now, we understood one another very well, Mrs Camley and I. Yes, we understood each other very well indeed.

At last I could stand it no more and made some excuse to leave. Mr Camley said he would accompany me to the subway station. I was silent as he walked with me and he marked my silence, asking me what was the matter. I told him that taking me to meet his wife had been a very wicked thing to do after he had just spent the weekend with me. He was embarrassed by my words, although, of course, they passed into the air like startled birds, unnoticed by those around us in the street. Had I spoken to him in Japanese as I did in English then I, too, would have been embarrassed but to speak in English it was as if I were transported to some foreign land where, at last, I was at liberty to say what I wanted, to do as I liked, all checks and inhibitions fallen, the striped poles of so many border posts littered along my path to freedom. The words I used to speak of my displeasure meant nothing to those walking near us, as the words he would teach me to say, later on, the words that so excited him when he was inside me, meant nothing to me.

That night I told Mr Camley I did not think I would see him again. It was a threat, and I understood that it frightened him but the gesture was an empty one. I knew it as I made it. I saw him again three days later. I needed him for my revenge as much as he needed me for — for whatever it was he needed me for. I did my best to forget the meeting with his wife. What was between them was between them. I had not begun it, and I knew my going away would not end it. He was a man who had to have women, and who had to have oriental women if he could.

He had to have his women, and I had to have my revenge. I had it, in a small measure. After two or three months there was a letter for me from Professor Kobayashi. Well, it was not exactly a letter, more a note really. He said that it had come to his attention that I was — what was the word he used — consorting, yes, consorting with Mr Camley. He said that he, Mr Camley that is, was quite notorious in Japan for his activities as a womanizer and he cautioned me to be careful. He also begged, yes, he actually begged me, to say nothing to Mr Camley of our former friendship. He wrote, 'If what was once between us had any meaning to you at all, you will respect my privacy.' I still keep that note, somewhere. Of course, I told Mr Camley everything. I even showed him the note one Saturday afternoon when we were in bed together. He laughed about it, called it a great joke, but sought to dismiss it. Yet his ardour, after I had shown it to him, was quite remarkable, not at all as it usually was. Yes, he performed quite well that day.

It did not last of course, the ardour or the satisfaction of my revenge. It did not last because I did not really like Mr Camley, or the things we did together. He imagined he was very fine with me, very fine for me, but he imagined this only because I let him. I had watched Miss Yumi at work and I knew how little is the deception needed to please a man, to convince him of his prowess between a woman's legs. They believe because it is necessary for them to believe. And it did not last because, at the end of the year, which was not really a year but only eight or nine months, Mr Camley returned to England and I was alone again. It was then or, at least, it was shortly after his leaving, that I decided I should, in fact, marry. I decided I should marry my hairdresser, Mr Yamada.

I had not seen Mr Yamada for such a long time, and my hair was really awful, long and uncared for. I wanted to begin again, I suppose, another of my many new beginnings. I decided to start with my hair. I telephoned his shop and went over. It was in Daikanyama and very small. Yet it had been beautifully done, with veneers of red brick applied to the walls, and dark stained wood for the chairs and benches. There were plants everywhere, palms and ferns that seemed to luxuriate in the unlikely air of heat and chemicals. As well as Mr Yamada there was a girl receptionist and an apprentice, a boy, who washed hair and then stood to watch Mr Yamada at work, learning his skills by imitation rather than instruction.

I had made a late appointment, and I was late even for that so it was almost seven-thirty when I arrived and Mr

Yamada was busy with another customer. Yet, when he saw me, he asked me to wait and then, although he sent his assistants home, kept the shop open himself to attend to my hair. Afterwards, as I was paying my bill, he asked me to go to a nearby café with him so that I could tell him more of the time that had passed since I had seen him last, the time he imagined I had spent in England, and the new work I was doing.

I was surprised. Had we ever spoken before, other than the usual exchanges of the hairdresser and his customer? I do not think so. Perhaps that was why, in the end, I decided to marry Mr Yamada. He was the only person who ever seemed to want nothing from me, who ever seemed pleased to see me simply for myself, or care that I had come back when, in fact, I had never been away.

What happened then? Well, I suppose we began going out, although it was a somewhat desultory courtship, for Mr Yamada was always so busy. He kept the shop open every day of the week because he dared not do otherwise, and he kept it open until eight o'clock each evening. He gave his assistants the day off on Mondays, but he was always there in their absence, attending to the few customers who came to him then.

When I asked him why he worked so hard he said that he had no alternative. It was not so much his fortune as his reputation that he was seeking to establish, and he felt obliged never to turn customers away, especially when singers or models, as so many of them were, people who had followed him from the salon where he had worked before setting up on his own, called asking for special appointments. He was already famous in his way, and his name was often to be seen in the credits beneath the photograph of this or that famous or familiar face in the fashion magazines. He paid for it, of course, going to the shop at five o'clock in the morning sometimes if a girl had an early session with the photographer, and then travelling with her to the location in order that he might see that what he had done was not undone by the weather, or by some other stylist. He paid for it with me as well in the end.

When I saw him it was usually quite late in the evening. I would meet him and we would eat somewhere, or else he would come to my apartment and I would cook for him. But I did not see him often, perhaps that is why we got on as well as we did for as long as we did. He almost never stayed the night with me, although we became lovers quite quickly; he was uncomfortable with me in the mornings, as if sleeping through the night in my bed was not somehow quite proper. There was something almost endearingly old-fashioned about Mr Yamada.

I believe he told his parents he wished to marry me before he told me. Certainly the first time I visited them I was greeted as a prospective daughter-in-law. Mr Yamada's family, his two sisters and younger brother, were all there, and seemed not the least embarrassed when his father, an old man who even then seemed to be approaching the senility that at last consumed him, asked me pointedly how many children I would have. I believe he expressed himself of the opinion that four was the proper number. I said nothing, for my disbelief at what he had said took any reply I might have made from me. It was afterwards, on our way back to Tokyo, that Mr Yamada formally asked me to live with him. I told him that I would consider his proposal, but in fact I had already decided to accept.

Why did I agree to marry Mr Yamada? I suppose I liked him well enough, although I am not sure I liked him well enough to marry him. Yet he was a decent man, and I do not believe he ever lied to me or purposely harmed me in the time we were together. He was not married, of course. Perhaps it was the novelty that I could actually do so which made me agree to be his wife. Yet he was very dull, somehow the glamour of the people whose hair he cut and styled into such fantastic elegance was not contagious to him. In bed he was unimaginative, and he did not like the things I had come to believe men liked. I think the only real sensory satisfaction I ever afforded him was when I cleaned his ears, stealthily probing the deep, tight curled orifices on either side of his head with my thin wooden spatula and wadded piece of cotton wool. Then he would whimper with joy in a way he never did as he loosed his seed in me.

The truth is, I suppose, that I agreed to marry Mr Yamada because I was so hard pressed by my parents. I knew I could not long hold out against the almost monthly meetings they arranged for me, and the subsequent storms of bile and recrimination that followed my rejection of the latest candidate. I knew that the only way I could circumvent my father marrying me off was to do so myself. I knew, as well, that in choosing Mr Yamada I would so infuriate my father he might die from the rage that would ensue from my telling him. I would have enjoyed that.

I am lying to myself again, once I had decided that I would marry Mr Yamada, I did not tell my father. I told my mother, and she broke the news to him. I suppose she exaggerated the little I said to her, for my father, while he was not happy that I should have chosen my husband myself, was not angry enough to forbid the match outright. He agreed to meet the man I could not, even then, conceive of as my future husband although I had agreed the match. I suppose my father also set his detectives to work examining the substance behind what my mother had told him.

My father must have received the detective's report before he met Mr Yamada because he was, even by his own standards of boorish behaviour, extremely rude to him. Mr Yamada had closed his shop for two days in order that he might visit my family, but in fact spent less than twenty minutes in my parents' house. He stayed the night at an inn, not far from the house, and came early the next morning, before eight o'clock, for his interview with my father, who said he was too busy to see the poor man at any other time. They talked in the room where my grandparents' shrine is, the little house of death, and when he came out again Mr Yamada looked as if he might spend his next night's sleep there with them, for his face was so white. When I asked him what had happened he could say only that he must return to Tokyo at once. He left the house and I did not see him again until the next evening when I called in at the shop.

I went to the room where my father was after Mr Yamada

had gone, and for the first time in my life I was not afraid to enter there, nor did I bow on coming into my father's presence.

I asked my father whether he was satisfied with the man I intended to marry, and he said he was not before he had properly understood the exact phrasing of my words. When he did understand there was a moment of silence so deep I felt my courage failing before he restored it by screaming the foulest abuse at me. Even my mother, who came in from the kitchen, stood back by the door, repulsed by the language he was pouring upon my head.

It was a terrible day. When my father was calmer and therefore a little more in control of his feelings, he merely shouted at me. At one point he even attempted to reason with me; he began to list the lowly professions I might as well marry someone from as Mr Yamada, who he would not refer to by name but only as the barber. I could, he said, take a fishmonger for a husband, a pork butcher perhaps or a noodle vendor. He paused then, desperately searching for some other trade's practitioner to add to those he had already mentioned. I supplied one for him. A chicken fryer, I said, and walked away.

It went on and on, late into the night. When he screamed at me that I might marry this peasant but I should not bring him again into his house, I asked him why. He stared at me in disbelief so deep his eyes were like holes, burnt in the scarlet fabric of his face, as if I had quite lost my reason. Then I said I was simply following an example he had set himself, for my grandmother had repeatedly told me my mother was a peasant and yet he had married her and brought her to the house. I told him he was a model for me in this as in so many other things.

I left for Tokyo the next morning, my mother accompanying me to the station. My father was still in his bed. He had complained of feeling ill during the night, and my mother had sent for the doctor. When my mother told me this I said that no doctor could cure what was wrong with my father, only death could do that, and with such medicine I wished his illness a speedy end. My mother did not answer me. She telephoned that night, of course. My father had been taken into the small clinic his doctor maintained and so, alone in the house, she could speak freely to me.

She asked me if I was determined to marry Mr Yamada and when I said that I was, told me to be quite sure of my purposes in doing so. I believe she suspected my motives, that she knew me better than I cared to admit. Yet, when I told her I thought I could make a life with him, she asked me only to wait, and in the time I should give her she would seek to reconcile my father to my wedding and to my choice of husband. She did so. It took a long time, almost a year, but she did so. Of course, by then it was too late.

My mother was perfectly correct to be suspicious of my motives in wishing to marry Mr Yamada, and yet I might still have done so had Alistair Camley not returned to Japan.

He came after much the same length of time he had lived here last: ten months. It was not a surprise that he came. I had exchanged correspondence with him several times since his leaving. His first letter arrived perhaps a week after he had gone. It was not much of a letter, really. All he said was that he missed me, he missed me and the things we used to do together. He wrote that I was the most beautiful girl he had ever known. He asked that I write to him, that I at least write to him, and then he added that I should on no account send any letters to his home address but always to the college. I think it was that last admission which prompted me to write, for, with me at least, Mr Camley was never anything other than what I knew he was.

Unable to have me in reality, Mr Camley turned to his memories. He would write of the times we were together, and the things we had done with each other then. His letters were not in any sense poetic, they were pornographic. Several of them ended with his saying that he must masturbate because the act of remembering, and of writing down what he remembered, had so aroused him. One of the letters contained the stains of what he said was his seed that he had splashed upon the pages as a momento.

As our correspondence grew the letters came to contain other things as well as memories, for it soon became apparent that the act of remembering our past times together was not enough for Mr Camley. He had also to delineate his present adventures as well.

Once he sent me an envelope marked 'photographs' on the outside. It held several polaroids of Mr Camley in various sexual positions with a woman. Two of the photographs were close-ups of his sex in the act of entering, first, between the woman's legs, and then her mouth. I was horrified initially that he should send me such things. My only thoughts were what might have happened had the letter been intercepted and opened by the Post Office, and that I should destroy the pictures at once.

I did not destroy them. I did not obey the instruction of my first thoughts. I was drawn back to those photographs again and again to look. I thought of showing them to Mr Yamada, but I did not. Instead, I kept them in the drawer where the materials for my translations were stored and, often when I was at work, I would stop and gaze at the photographs Mr Camley had sent.

The woman was European, the wife of one of the other faculty members at the college, at least that is what Mr Camley wrote. She may have been a prostitute, but I think she was not. She did not look like a prostitute. She did not look as if she was being paid for what she was doing. She seemed to be enjoying it. What does a woman who takes money for sex look like? I had only to confront my own appearance in the mirror to know that. Besides, he had told me before of his affairs with women in Cambridge, and I had no reason not to believe him. But it was Asian women he sought out most.

He told of journeys he made during the year, to Copenhagen and Hamburg, and to Amsterdam. Always he went for sex, oh, the excuse might be this or that conference, a public reading, a book fair perhaps, but the reason was sex. He said that in Amsterdam he found a girl from Thailand and took her because she so reminded him of me. I was not entirely flattered by this comparison.

He said how he had become excited undressing her as he pulled up her skirt to reveal little white panties which clung tightly to her buttocks. He always wrote that, no matter who or what the girl, each one was possessed of the same anatomy, the same single piece of underwear.

Before the photographs came I thought that most of what he wrote was fantasy, that, after all, with the exception of myself he had had no other girls, and yet, if fantasy it was, then it was fantasy organized with an energy he did not expend elsewhere. I went to look for his work in the bookshops here once. There were two slim volumes, that is the description the English reviewers use so often, of his own verse and then a number of translations from Japanese, but always undertaken with a native speaker. Well, he could not have done it unaided for he spoke very little of our language himself.

Yet his sexual career was massively documented, complete with maps and illustrations. He had photographed me once when we were together, posing me in his academic cap and gown, but otherwise naked, with my legs apart. And there were maps. He told me he had a map of the world upon the wall of his study in Cambridge with flags pinned on it. A blue flag designated the country from which his latest conquest originated, a green one marked the place in which the conquest occurred. When I indicated that I did not believe him he sent me a photograph. Of course, all of this, the maps, the photographs and diaries, he said he kept a diary, the published works of pornography, were stored in his rooms, a place to which his wife had no admittance.

I did not, do not, understand how he kept his two selves, his two lives, so separately, but he did. I am sure his wife suspected that he was unfaithful to her, certainly she knew that I had come to her house from his embrace, but whether she had any proof further to her sense of what he was doing I am unaware. His professional reputation had not one single smear upon it, not even the shadow of a smear.

And did I encourage his letters? I suppose I did. I replied to them, not in kind, but I did reply. Why I did so I am less sure. I suppose I enjoyed hearing from him in a way. It seemed harmless, the thoughts of a naughty little boy. Anyway, he was so far off, so distant from my life. I did not think that he would enter it again, although I should have thought so. I knew he was a visitor to Japan, to Tokyo, not a frequent one but a visitor nonetheless. The letters made him seem even farther away, like memories of something that was once but now had ceased to exist. Perhaps it was part of something I wanted, not to hold on to exactly, but not entirely relinquish either.

Besides, my life was generally so dull, so ordinary. Mr Yamada's company seemed like an investment I had made which was providing me with increasingly diminishing returns. I hardly saw him, and when we were together he was so tired he would fall asleep in minutes. He slept when he was with me in my apartment and so I suggested that we meet in public more often. Occasionally I managed to persuade him to leave the shop a little earlier, he had three assistants now, one of them a senior stylist who was more than capable of dealing with things in Mr Yamada's absence. Then we would go to the cinema, but he always fell asleep. When he dozed off during the first few moments of a symphony concert I had begged him to attend with me, I walked out and left him sleeping in the auditorium. I would not speak to him, would not return his calls for a week after that.

My life was dull. I had my work, of course I had my work, and I found a magic in that, still. I say I had my work, but the translations were not work to me, really. I lived in those books the life which life itself denied me: the strong and handsome men, the passion and the love, and, at last, the happy ending. I surrendered myself entirely to each work I translated. What I produced was very popular. The chief editor said people were beginning to ask for my translations by name, or at least, by the pseudonym I worked under. I understood why, for what I wrote I wrote in a rapture, a delirium of the senses; the language flowed from me onto the page. I was translating a novel a month, but it was not a task, not a drudgery as some of the other translators, when I spoke with them at editorial meetings, said it was. To me it was delight. It was — I suppose it was love.

Yet the rapture of my work ended. It could not be

sustained. Each book had a final page, and the pain of parting with the world I had shared and, in my own tongue, shaped, was bitter. I was always returned to reality.

When I spoke with Mr Yamada of my feelings he would tell me things were sure to be better once we were married, yet he would not marry me. He said it was not proper to marry without my father's consent, without the payment of the money to my family. I said I did not care about any of this and that, if he delayed, he might lose me. Mr Yamada would smile at me then, saying he was too careful to lose me. Afterwards, after our talks, he would sleep or go back to his shop.

Mr Camley arrived in Japan just before the Christmas period, as he had done that first time, that first time I met him. I knew he was coming because he had told me so, putting the information in the form of a postscript at the end of a letter in which he described his pursuit of the wife of a well-known writer as she drove to her home after he had encountered her in a supermarket. She had pushed herself against him provocatively in the queue before the cash-desk, he said, and indicated that her use of the vegetables in her shopping basket was not exclusively culinary. Mr Camley was driving his wife's car, and it was no match for the woman's Jaguar so that the word pursuit does not quite describe the progress they actually made once his quarry was certain she was being followed.

As soon as they were out of the town, she pulled her car over into a lay-by and he had her, he said, on the back seat. The radio was blaring Tchaikovsky's second piano concerto as she pulled off her underthings and straddled Mr Camley, the Jaguar's windows already misted with the body heat their passion had engendered.

Mr Camley said that he was serving on the committee of one of the literary prizes for which the latest work of this woman's husband was entered. Mr Camley said he felt the least he could do was vote for the book after the brilliant performance the wife of the author had given.

I knew he was coming, and yet I was surprised when he telephoned me from his hotel. He was in Japan to work with

Professor Kobayashi, this I also knew. I was certain then that discretion or, at the very least, good manners, good taste perhaps, would prevent him from contacting me. Why should it, when it had not done so before?

I did not mind receiving letters from Mr Camley, in truth, I rather enjoyed them. They were so outrageous, fantastic even, they made me laugh. I did not want to see him again, though, not after all that had happened. I told him when he telephoned that I was to be married, but although he congratulated me, although he joked with me that my fiancé was a man to be envied, still he insisted that we meet, and, finally, I agreed. I would not let him come to my apartment, however, I met him in front of the station in Shibuya, and I took him then to Daikanyama to meet Mr Yamada. I felt I had to convince him that I was telling the truth, that I did have a fiancé, and I could think of no other way to do this than by showing Mr Yamada to him.

Mr Yamada was busy with a customer when we got to the shop, but he set one of the apprentices to work with the hairdryer so that he might talk with us. I introduced Mr Camley to him as a teacher from England, and explained why he was in Japan. Of course, Mr Yamada had no English, although his salon was advertised as 'international'. He knew a few phrases that I had taught him, words to do with his trade. Mr Camley had not come to have his hair styled, however, he had come for me. And he got what he came for, or, at least, he got permission for it.

Mr Yamada spoke through me, saying that he was very busy, too busy to be with me very often. He said how sad it made him that I spent so much time alone, and that he was glad my friend had come from England because he could see how happy it had made me. The poor, good-hearted fool. He asked Mr Camley to take me out, to spend his time with me, entrusting me to him, a man I would not give the care of a mongrel dog to if it were a bitch.

We went out of the shop into the hurrying night and I knew I would not marry Mr Yamada, not now. Taking Mr Camley to him had been, I now saw, a test, a test of how much I was valued by the man who wished to be my husband. Of course he did not know into whose hands he was giving me, he could not know, but the test was in whether he would give me into anyone's hands and he had failed the test. When I had decided to marry him I did so, in part, because I thought that at least I had found someone who, if he did not love me — I did not expect anyone to love me — valued me. I knew now that he did not value me enough.

I stopped a taxi and got in with Mr Camley. I asked him where he wanted to go and he suggested a love hotel. Half an hour before and I might have slapped his face, but not now. Now I gave the driver instructions for the hotel I had been to with Satoshi Mizuno, not caring what the man might make of it, a Japanese girl going to a known love hotel with a foreign man. Well, whore is what he would have made of it. I could think only that I had been passed along to another man again, as if I were a parcel.

I suppose Mr Camley must have thought his Japanese girl, his dream girl as he had sometimes called me, had come back to him. He was right in a way to think so. We secured our room and I at once undressed him. I bathed him in the great seashell bath as the girls in the soaplands bathe their customers. I brought him to the edge of his passion and then took him, still wet, to the towel-covered bed. I lay down for him and I opened my legs and he went to mount me, and then — it was as if I was back in the garden where my grandmother had left me in the darkness to wait for the demon — I began to scream.

I began to scream and, as I screamed, my head rolled from side to side. My head rolled and my body shook, my whole being went into spasm. At first Mr Camley was concerned, I know because I remember his face close to mine, his restraining hands upon my head. I imagine, for I do not know, that very quickly his concern transformed itself into fear. I know only that at some point I stopped screaming, the fit gone from me as it had come, with neither prelude nor warning. I could hear someone knocking on the door of the room, demanding to know what was happening. I answered that everything was all right, but the knocking and the questioning continued until I opened the door and stood naked in front of one of the women who had care of the hotel. When she was satisfied that a murder was not being committed she left, and I turned back to the room to find I was alone. I spent the night in that room, I slept in that ridiculous bed, and in the morning I paid the bill. I neither saw nor heard from Alistair Camley again.

Things seem in retrospect to have happened so quickly after that, although, in reality, they did not. I went to my parents' house, as I always did, for the New Year celebrations, and there I told my mother that I would not, after all, be marrying Mr Yamada. My mother carried the news to my father, but said that she would never again act as intermediary for me or attempt to shield me from the consequences of my actions. She was as good as her word.

I continued to see Mr Yamada when I returned to Tokyo because, although I had determined that we should not marry, I was not yet ready to let him go. I wanted to hurt him a little before that. I made things between us very bad very quickly, and it is one of the actions in my past that I now regret the most for he was, Mr Yamada, a good man in his way. He was hurt and, more than that, he was confused, unsure of the reason for the spite I had let loose upon him. In the end I could not, in the face of his hurt and wondering innocence, long continue my attacks, and so I went to the shop one evening when I knew he would be alone to tell him I would not see him again. He did not question me, and I left him in the same manner in which I had found him, alone among the palm trees and the ferns, as I walked away into the night.

When was that, February? Yes, it must have been for the next month, in March, Professor Kobayashi died.

I heard of his death when it was announced on the television news, and then the next day I read the article about it in the newspaper. It was cancer and it had taken him with a terrible speed. There were obituaries, of course, and then the announcement of the funeral. I decided I would attend, for I could not do otherwise.

I remember the weather and how it was completely wrong

for what had happened. It was a day of sunshine and soft warmth, the wind a promise of the coming season, not, as it should have been, the afterbirth of a bitter winter. It should have been. It should have been a dark, cold day, a day as dark and cold as in the poem he had read to me once on the death of the Irish poet Yeats. Yet the weather, no matter how sunny, could not disguise the winter I carried in my heart. I dressed myself in black that day not only for my ex-lover but for myself, for my life, for the frozen space in my womb where no child had ever lodged. I was, I knew, attending more than one funeral.

As it happened I did not attend the funeral, not properly. My courage ebbed and I stood on a corner opposite to the temple and I waited. I waited until it was over and I let the mourners pass me by, a dark stream in the sunbright hours of the morning. I watched his widow and his children leave. I watched so intently I did not see who it was that took me by the arm and pulled me so roughly into the middle of the narrow street. Even then, when I saw the face of the person who held my arm, I did not recognize Miss Sekiya until she spoke, her face so close to mine she spattered my cheek when she demanded to know what I was doing in that place on that day.

She took me to a coffee shop. It did not matter that I could not speak, it was not her intention to engage me in conversation. My role in what would ensue was simply to listen. She had ordered cognac with her coffee and they poured her a glass at the table from a cheap, domestic blend. She did not touch it, she had no need to, for there was in her enough bitter spirit already, strong with the years' distilling. She said she had something to tell me and what she told me was so astonishing in its obviousness I was made quite rigid with shock.

She knew what I had imagined no one knew, the fact that I had been his mistress — she called me his mistress, she would not use the term lover. She said she had known it from the beginning. She said she had known it even before the actions which brought that fact into being were played out.

He had seen me, she said, the great professor, he had

selected me from among all the other girls and he had asked about me, asked her about me. When it turned out that I was her pupil, everything else was so much easier. They had conspired together for him to have me. Each event that I had taken as chance had been planned, my tutoring of Mayumi, the meeting in the corridor, the dinner appointment she had made and not kept, his own timely arrival. In everything she had conspired to present me to him.

She told me this and she made to leave. As she did I could form only the question, why? She spat at me again, her words more like the snarl of some animal than human speech. She answered my question by saying that before me, he had taken her, her and all the others. It was, she said, the way things were.

I sat for a long time after she was gone, ignoring the girl who, at length, removed the untouched cups and glasses, the salarymen who came in at the lunch hour and filled the room with noise and smoke. There was something I had to do. I ran the past through my head as if it were a tape that I could stop and start, slow down or speed up. I watched again all the things that I had experienced with that woman and at last understood them: the comments she had scrawled upon my essays now I saw were symptoms of the jealousy that consumed her; the terms of endearment she had sometimes used in fact were phrases of contempt.

She must have known, even before it happened, that he would choose me, she must have thought it likely, because it had happened so many times before. It had happened to her, and then again and again, through her. She had raised me, cultivated me, knowing he would take me from her, and that then, inevitably, I would take him, again, from her. I had once possessed all that she had once possessed, and I had possessed the man who had taken all she once possessed from her.

I still do not know why she spoke to me as she did that day. I was not the only one. I suppose that, even at the time of his death, there was someone else, someone else she had provided for him. All I had then that she did not was the inescapable fact of my presence there, a reminder, perhaps, of what I had done to her, of what she had helped me do to her, guiding my hands along a fretted panel, as if she were a teacher of the blind.

THIRTEEN

This wedding will be over soon. One of Mr Ueno's friends, someone from his student days, is speaking, treating our ears to a rhetoric of imprecise sexual innuendo and vulgarity. It was to be expected, as the carrier bags filled with expensive, unwanted gifts that will be pushed into cupboards, their wrappings undisturbed, are expected. Even now, before the last plates have been removed and the coffee and liqueurs served, the waiters are busy, moving with their accustomed stealth about the room, slipping the presents beneath each guest's chair, unlikely Christmas fairies bestowing gifts out of season.

The guests are laughing at what they hear, watching the pale face of Mr Ueno's friend, which must be half-obscured by the microphone in front of it. No one is displaying the slightest curiosity as to what those bags they are sitting on top of contain.

They will leave, soon enough, the wedding guests. They will go out into the warm night, with their faces flushed and the shine heavy upon their black clothes. They will carry their shopping bags filled with gifts. They will mingle with all the other shoppers in the streets and in the stations. Perhaps, on the trains they will take to carry them homewards, some will sit with other returning guests, those who have mourned the dead, and only the colour of the men's ties will separate the ones who have celebrated from the ones who have mourned. For the mourners too will have their little packages with them: the handkerchiefs, the tea and the salt. On such occasions we seldom leave empty-handed.

They are laughing now, even Mr Ueno is laughing although it is not expected, it is not quite right for him to do so. I suppose he is beginning to believe that this marriage is actually happening, that he has taken me for his wife, because his friend is telling him that it is so, is flattering his ego and his virility. Perhaps the wine he has drunk has helped. He managed to spill most of his champagne at the beginning, but his hand has steadied with each glass since then. He may even manage a show of masterfulness when we stand with our parents to say farewell to the guests and receive their good wishes, but I doubt he will have drunk enough to carry his masquerade as far as our hotel room.

Everyone is laughing, except my mother and the waiters. I suppose the waiters have heard it all so many times before they no longer see the humour in what is being said. As for my mother, well, I cannot recall hearing her laugh, not once, in my entire life. Why should she laugh at my wedding? Of course, I am not laughing either, but I cannot decide whether it is that I am like the waiters and know the jokes already, or because I am, after all, my mother's daughter and understand that what is being alluded to here is really no laughing matter at all. Perhaps it is that, for it is true that, even when I have been amused by sex, I have seldom found it funny, at least, not in the long run.

I see now how like Mayumi, my former pupil, my little acrobat, I am. I, too, have twisted and turned through life, somersaulted, tumbled to avoid my fate. All that movement, shifting from house to house, so many lies, so much deceit, and to what end? We were both caught, finally. For me there seems now to be only one window left to leap through, and I wonder if, when the time comes, I shall make as supple and graceful an exit as she did, the night she so astonished me, turning her body through space to land then, at least, upon nimble feet. Were I to jump I doubt I should ever feel the ground beneath me again.

When I told my parents I was no longer to marry Mr

Yamada I gave myself entirely into my father's hands. I think it was only because his vanity was thus so overwhelmingly flattered that I was not married at once to someone else. I asked my father's forgiveness for having flouted his will. He, in turn, was happy to let me suffer the consequences of what he deemed my waywardness, the false and foolish pride I had shown in myself. There would be no marriage for me yet to anyone. To my father I was a broken reed that needs must mend itself, or, were I to use a less poetic and, for my father, more likely image, damaged goods requiring repair before being put back on the market. He saw my sorrow and imagined it to flow from the grounding of my hopes of matrimony; it was of course no such thing.

If I suffered it was because I knew something of myself that I had not known before, but should have. It was not simply that Miss Sekiya's revelation had shocked me, it had as well insulted my intelligence. The way in which I had been seduced ought from the very beginning to have been as obvious to me as it was to the others. There was, as well, the knowledge of how I had always been used, always handed from man to man, even when I had imagined I acted of my own will, that I gave myself. I knew this now to be untrue. I knew instead that I had been the passive article and not the active, the possessed and never the possessor.

I coped in the manner I always did with such difficulties, I moved. I found an apartment, two rooms, a small kitchen, toilet and bath, built above a family house near Inokashira Park. I took it at once, although, from the sitting room, I could see the great trees of the park swaying in the wind, wrapping the horizon in their leafy arms. Since childhood I have been fearful of the sound of the wind moving through trees. Perhaps I thought it was time I faced my demons.

My mother approved as well, although her liking for the place was based upon the fact that I was once more living close to someone she imagined she could rely on to monitor my comings and goings.

My mother deceived herself on this occasion. The owner of the property, who did, it is true, live just beneath me, was an old woman whose age seemed somehow to have excused her from caring for either my, or anyone else's, moral health. The afternoon my things were delivered to the house she stopped me in the garden, touching the greening buds of the hydrangea bushes as she spoke and said she did not mind if I brought men home with me, as long as I maintained some degree of quiet.

The unexpected frankness of her speech took me aback a little, but I was resolved not to test her liberality. It was not my intention to bring anyone home with me, anyone at all.

I disposed my furniture about the rooms; I hung the pictures I had bought on the walls; I sorted my books and placed my plants upon the bright window ledges. When it was done I settled myself at my table and at once began a new translation. I settled myself at my table and, as I did so, I settled into my new life, one that I accepted I should live alone.

Of course, I was not entirely without company. I went in to the Heartbeat office each month to deliver my completed translation and collect a new assignment. My mother continued to fill my life with telephone calls and parcels: instructing, directing and compelling me in the complex social relationships which for her made up reality. For myself, I preferred, increasingly, my own company.

Customarily, I would go to return my work and pick up the next book I was to translate on a Friday. My editor liked me and always took me to a tea-room after we had completed the formalities of whatever business there was to do. Sometimes we would go with the other women from the office, and I cannot say I did not enjoy these occasions, the laughter, the good-natured conversations, but I was always happy to return to my quiet rooms, to bathe, to spend the evening listening to the wind in the distant trees, to turn the pages of my book.

After some time in my new apartment, my new life, after a month, six weeks perhaps, I began to go out in the more accepted sense as well, to films, sometimes to a concert, but always alone. And in my solitary state I noticed other women on their own, sitting apart in cinemas and concert halls, as if their lack of a man to escort them carried with it a sentence of isolation from the rest of society. Well, if sentence it was, then it was one I was more than willing to serve. I found that, by myself, I could at last define myself, that I did not need the personality of a man to throw my own into relief. I would shape my own life now. I would live alone in the best sense of those words.

During the months that followed my break with Mr Yamada, and the death of Professor Kobayashi, I began to find a happiness it seemed I had not known hitherto. If there was anything from what had gone before then it was — how shall I describe it — a very small thing, a dull and almost unremembered ache, a little emptiness perhaps, a hollow somewhere in the soul. The small thing grew smaller with each passing day. I had no thoughts of looking for romance, if I wanted that I had only to pick up my work. I was resigned, no, it was not resignation, I was resolved, never to be with a man again. Until I met Michael.

It was December. I went to the end-of-the-year party at the office and I surprised myself at how much I enjoyed it, so much so I followed some of the women to a second party at a bar in Shinjuku. It was a small place, and already crowded when we got there with others celebrating the coming turn of the year. There was music in the bar and people singing, badly, for the most part, but with too much happiness for anyone to care.

They were all from the same company, these others, and there were foreigners with them, two men and a woman. Everyone sang, even the girls that I was with were each asked for a song, the warm atmosphere embracing us, drawing us in. When it was my turn I sang an old song I remembered from my childhood. It had been old even then, something one of the maids would sing as she worked in the kitchen of my father's house. When I sang the others laughed that I should know such a song.

One of the foreigners sang then as it was expected, at last, that they too should join in. He was not an accomplished singer, but his effort too was rewarded with applause. The woman, however, would not be persuaded to take the microphone, and so the other man got up. He would not take the microphone either, but that was because he said he did not need it. Nor would he choose one of the songs for which there was a backing tape which he might sing against. He simply stood at the table he had occupied with his friends, clasped his hands in front of him and began.

I thought my heart would stop with the beauty of his voice. A pure tenor, it rose through the clouds of smoke and laughter, the cheap perfume of beer and whisky, as a swallow's wings in the last light of the summer day. He sang of lost love and secret sorrow, a wedding day that did not come. There was such quiet in that bar when his song had ended: for a few moments no one spoke, no one laughed. Afterwards, after those quiet moments, the talk, the amplified sound of music, the foolishness, returned, drifting back like children now chastised to the scene of their little crime. But my ears were deaf even to the chatter of my companions. In my head I held the sound of his singing.

Oh, Michael, your sweet tongue confused me. You showered words upon me like a stream of golden coins, so many, I took them for the legal tender of the heart and they were not. I should have listened to your singing with more attention and less rapture. I should have heard the song and not the singer.

I stayed on when the others from my office went out again into the night and, when I could, I spoke to the foreigner. He had come to the bar to order more drinks for himself and his friends, and he seemed surprised when I spoke to him in English. I found his accent strange, a little difficult to understand, and when I asked him where he was from in England he laughed and said he was an Irishman, a real Irishman from a place called Sligo. He seemed surprised when I said I knew about Sligo and when he questioned my knowledge I repeated the lines of the Irish poet William Butler Yeats about bare Ben Bulben's head. He did not know what I was talking about.

He invited me to join his friends, but when I said that I could not, that I was shy, he took them their drinks and came back to where I was sitting at the bar. I was embarrassed, and protested that he should not desert his friends so readily to talk with a stranger, but he said they were in love and could get along without him very well. He asked me my name and I told him, and then he told me his. Michael — he began, and before he could finish I completed it for him, adding the word Furey, Michael Furey.

Again, I confused him. He had not read his country's writers, and so knew nothing of the dying boy who walked once through a night of rain to bid his true love farewell. His name, he said, holding up his hand to silence any further interruptions that I might have made, was Michael Joseph Devitt.

So we talked, Michael Joseph Devitt and I, until I said I must leave to catch my train. He came with me to the station, for he was tired and wanted to get home as well. He had to work, he said, the next morning. We walked to the station, and before we parted we exchanged cards. It was only when I was trapped in the crowd on the train to Meidai-mae that I looked at his address and saw he lived but a walk across the park from me in Kichijoji.

I thought of him a lot in the days that followed. I was translating a book set in Miami then, called *Holiday Romance*. Although the hero was an American his face, when I visualized it, was Michael Devitt's face, and I heard his voice as Michael Devitt's voice. He interested me, this Irishman; it seemed unusual for a foreigner to be here and not teaching English. Michael Devitt was a computer software designer, or at least, that is what it said on his card. Quite what this meant I did not know, but there was so much I did not know about him then and so much I wanted to know: why he was working for a Japanese company, why he had come to Japan to ply his peculiar trade. He was as tall and handsome as any of my fictional heroes, and to me, quite as mysterious.

I was in Kyushu, of course, for the holidays, enduring what I always endured when I was there. The only moments of happiness were those spent in the company of Reiko and Setsuko, but they were few this year, husbands and children, family interests, had come between us; life had come between us. If Akiko was there I was not told.

For the rest, I worked with my mother as if I were one of

the servants, cleaning the house for my father's guests, preparing the food and drink, serving them and then cleaning up the mess when they had gone. All the time I found myself thinking of Michael Devitt.

I hoped I might find a message from him when I got back, but the tape in my answering machine was as blank when I returned to Tokyo on the first Saturday after the holiday as it was the day I left. I wondered if it would be proper for me to telephone him, but I did not, I could not. I waited, and I waited, but the call I waited for never came. I went back to my work and, gradually, the image of Michael Devitt began to fade; the face of the hero dissolved, and the voice I had heard so clearly died away, until both were once again simply words that I read, black letters on the white page, as they had been before.

When I had accepted that I would not see Michael Devitt again, when I was sure that he had no interest in me at all, I met him by accident when I was walking in Inokashira Park. I should have expected it really, for it was something taken out of the books that made up so much of my life. He was standing alone, looking at the dark, chill waters of the lake on a louring Sunday afternoon in February. I saw him there, and did not know whether I should speak to him or simply pass him by, worried that if I touched his arm or said hello he would not recognize me when, for no reason I was aware of, he turned and he saw me and his smile dispelled the greyness of the cloudy, wintered sky.

He took me to drink coffee in one of the little places that line the narrow street leading down into the park from Kichijoji. He remembered my name and used it, the word falling from his tongue as if it were a blessing. I felt, for once, my name bore witness to its meaning.

We talked and talked until the day had gone and the street lamps burned in the darkness and the cold. He asked if I was hungry, and, when I told him I was, took me to eat in a small French restaurant he said he had discovered, announcing the fact with such a flourish he might have been a true explorer, a voyager on mighty seas, setting his foot where none of his kind had been before. I did not tell him that I already knew the place he was taking me to, that I frequently ate there at lunchtimes during the week, and it embarrassed me as much as it did him when the waiter who met us at the door greeted me by name. Yet, for all that, the food was good and the wine was good and our talk was better. It was after eleven when we wished one another a goodnight, and I went back to my apartment believing him when he said he would call me.

He did call — oh, it was a week later and I had despaired again and again at the thought that I had lost him — but he did call. We went to a film at the little Baus Town cinema in Kichijoji. It was one of the comedies of Eric Rohmer, so popular with the young in Tokyo that year, and I enjoyed it. Only afterwards, in the restaurant where we went to eat, did Michael tell me he spoke no French and could not read the Japanese subtitles. So he had sat through the film, his understanding of what was taking place confined to what he could deduce from the movements on the screen. I asked why, why had he agreed to take me to a film he knew he would not understand, and his answer warmed me more than the richness of the wine in my glass: he said it was for me.

He worked very hard at his company and at his apartment, yet he found time to share with me. We would meet at the weekends and once, twice even, during the week. We did not go far; usually I would call him and ask if he had time to see me and then I would run to catch the train to take me the short distance down the line to Kichijoji, or, if it was the weekend, Sunday afternoon perhaps, I would walk through the park. We found a café, a restaurant, a bar we liked, and we would meet in one of them, depending upon the day and time, to eat, to drink, to share coffee with our conversation.

He was not a cultured man in the sense that I understood it. He never read literature, he once dismissed novels as elaborate lies. He said it was hard enough to get the truth about the world set out before us without making up stories around it. Michael read history books, and told me he laughed at most of them.

He laughed when I explained to him how I earned my living. He said at least no one could take that sort of thing seriously, and I laughed as well, and said of course not, no one could take that sort of thing seriously.

Yet there was always something for us to talk about. All we did was talk. Well, at least, I talked. Now, it seems to me, Michael mostly listened. I think that is why I fell in love with him. I told him things, things I had not even told myself, and he listened. Before, with the other men, I had been the one who listened. Michael gave me space and time, and he allowed me to tell him of my life, or as much of it as I could.

He was a generous man. He gave me so much, and got so little in return. Sometimes I was able to help him with things he could not manage by himself because he did not speak Japanese very well; setting up a standing order to pay his monthly bills, or going with him to the Immigration Bureau in Ikebukuro and then the local ward office to register the extension of his visa. But this was nothing. I gave him nothing. And giving him nothing, I worried that I would lose his friendship, lose it before it turned to love. I knew that I loved him, I think the moment I heard him sing I knew that I loved him. I wanted time to make him love me.

Perhaps I should not have worried for, in those early weeks, his generosity did not falter. He sent me flowers once, roses in a box from Rose Gallery, because I had said, mentioned really, that once, just once, I would like someone to send me flowers in a box. It was not serious, I think I was telling him about it because of the book I was translating at the time. It was called *Flowers for the Lady*, and the hero, at last, won the heroine's heart with a box of roses from Harrods. I remember then asking him if there was something he wanted and he said there was nothing.

I invited him to my apartment for dinner, but he would not come. He said he could not see why I should cook for him when he had not cooked for me and then he turned the invitation around, asking me to be his guest.

It was a Saturday when I went to the mansion block where he lived. I worried in case, that night, he asked me to sleep with him. I worried because my time was very near that month and I could not be sure when I might start to bleed. If he asked and I refused him, he might not understand and, not understanding, might not ask again. I wanted to sleep with him more than anything. I wanted to be his lover. I wanted that more than I wanted a box of roses.

I was nervous in his apartment. The rooms themselves made me nervous. It was — it was not what I had expected, the bareness of it. It was a clean white space, and there was nothing in that space that he had not consciously and carefully placed there. The tables were grey, as if the colour had been washed out of the wood with time and much, much effort. There was a chrome and leather chair, and a long couch, hard and uninviting. A set of shelves constructed from steel and glass held a small television, a small video recording unit, a compact stereo unit, four small black speakers. On the walls he had three large photographic prints in stainless steel frames. The prints were all black and white reproductions: a woman's face, a vase of dying tulips, a black man's torso. I recognized the tulips from the poster advertising an exhibition of the photographer's work at the Parco gallery in Shibuya the year before last. Even the kitchen where he had cooked our meal was immaculate, as if no one had ever worked in it. When we ate we did so at one of the grey tables, taking our food from white plates with stainless steel forks. I felt that I was eating underwater.

There was nothing in those rooms that did not have some purpose, and I thought with shame of my own cluttered, fussy surroundings, the apartment through which in a few months I had strewn the litter of years. I had bought flowers for him at the station, but when I offered them I was ashamed of the mixture of colours, the faint, haphazard quality of their arrangement, the fussy bow the florist had tied. After taking the bouquet from me, Michael left it in the sink because he did not own a vase.

My nervousness made it impossible that I should enjoy the food he had prepared, even when I had drunk the wine which accompanied the meal. I did not know what to say, what sort of conversation could possibly complement the shaped austerity all about me; I was afraid of spilling my drink or letting the food fall from my glistening fork on to the black tiles of the floor. I laughed when nothing funny had been said, and sat dumb before him when he made a joke. In the silence he got up and put on some music, but it did not warm the air that hung, heavy with frost it seemed to me, between us.

To make some sort of table talk I asked him what kind of food the people ate in Ireland. He laughed and said the Irish formed their diet from fantasy and potatoes. Then he laughed again and added that they found such food doubly palatable because it nourished their starvation. I did not understand him. I understood only that his laughter had no warmth, like the music, like the room. He said he came from a nation of dreamers, harmless souls, but for the fact they had the power to blow the head from off the shoulders of anyone who stood between them and their vision of unreality. Again, I did not understand. It was only later that I realized he had shown me a little of the great reserve of bitterness he held within him.

Perhaps we were both nervous. It was a little better after we had eaten, after we had finished the wine. I asked about his work and he showed me the computers he used when he was at home in the apartment. But he said that what he did was boring, a means to earn money and nothing more. His real interest was photography. He showed me some of the things he had done. I expected pictures of his family, his brothers and sisters, his parents; I feared the ones of his wife. But there were none. What he showed me was not unlike the work that hung upon his wall. Pictures of a dark and threatening sea, a mountain half hidden in the mist, stones and winter trees.

When I expressed my admiration he said anyone could take photographs, the skill lay in processing them into pictures. He talked about the varied effects that could be obtained with different papers, and techniques to make what was light dark, what was dark light; he showed me prints from which half of the original had disappeared, others where parts of two or more photographs were fused together to make an image that had never, actually, occurred.

I said it was like magic. He shook his head and told me it was not magic, it was only another kind of history.

I did not sleep with him that night. I went back to my own bed, and the next day I called him. I asked him if he thought it was a good idea for us to continue to meet. He did not answer me at once, and I felt the distance, the space that was between us, not only Michael and me, but all of us, all the men and all the women. When he spoke he startled me. He said my question was not something that he had thought of and so he could not make a response. He said that if I had asked such a thing then I must have thought about it a good deal, and, having thought about it, would already know the answer.

He was to come to my apartment for lunch the following Sunday. I told him I still wanted him to come, and that I was sorry for the foolishness of what I had said. I put the telephone down and knew that I would ask him to sleep with me, not then perhaps, but soon, sometime soon.

Well, we did not sleep together when he came to lunch but soon after that, after that Sunday, we did. It was in Michael's apartment. We had been to see a film at a cinema in Ginza and, although it was quite late when we got off the train in Kichijoji, he asked me to come back with him for something to drink. I still do not know why, but it seemed like the right time to let him know what my feelings were for him. He had made tea for us, but when I told him that I wanted to be his lover he took a bottle of whisky from a cupboard and opened it.

We began to drink, and I think Michael did not drink whisky all that often because he became intoxicated very quickly. He told me that he liked me, but liking, he said, was not enough. He said there should be more, liking was in the mind but there had to be something in the heart as well. He said there was nothing in his heart, not for me, not for anyone.

I do not know when my tears began, then I suppose. He came to where I was sitting and put his arm about my shoulders. We stayed like that for a long time and then I told him I would leave, but he would not let me. Perhaps he felt sorry for me; perhaps he feared I might try to hurt myself — I do not know. I know only that he spoke very gently to me.

He said he was sorry for having hurt me. He was not a good person, he said. He asked me if I loved him and when I said yes, I loved him, he held me closer to him. When he let me go, he stood, taking my hand as if to pull me to my feet as well. I thought he wanted me to go and when he said that perhaps, after all, we should try I did not understand. I asked him what we should try and he said perhaps we should try to love one another.

I went with him to his bedroom and we undressed, like children almost, almost hiding our bodies each from the other's eyes. When I could not help but let him look at me he told me I was beautiful. He came to me and we kissed, our first kiss, a clumsy kiss, before he pulled back the covers of his narrow bed.

When we lay together he told me it had been a long time since he had slept with anyone. I thought he meant a month, two months perhaps, but he did not mean that, he meant it had been years, three years. It was the first thing Michael ever told me of his past.

I believe he spoke to me then in the way he did because he was afraid that when we made love it would not be good for me, that he would finish very quickly. I said it did not matter, and to me it did not matter, because most of the men I had been with finished very quickly. It was something I was used to, something I expected. But when we made love that first time, and all the other times as well, it was never the way I was used to. I knew more passion with Michael than with any of the others. He filled me. He satisfied me. I was complete with him. Afterwards, in the little time before I fell asleep beside him, I knew I had never made love before, never been loved before. Before I had only ever been used. Those others had used me as carelessly and casually as they might have used a urinal. I understood that then.

Some of the men I had been with made love wanting to hurt me, and some of them fought me, as if I had something, some possession, they must take from me by force. It was not love with them, it was struggle, a fight from which they were determined to emerge the victor. Michael never took from me, he only gave.

Perhaps he was too careful of me. He approached my body as if it were some fragile, precious thing. He kissed me and he caressed me with tenderness, and when he entered me it was as if he entered some holy place. Inside me it always seemed he had complete control and curbed his own pleasure until I begged him to release it, knowing that I could not find more myself, that already I had found too much. Yet, always there was more for me, one more piece of pleasure as he came to his, as I felt him abandon the hold he had upon his senses; then I would go with him on the journey, carried along by his momentum.

He was the perfect lover, he was; and yet it hurt me that he gave so much but could not gladly take the little I offered in return. I remember the first time I had my bleeding when we were lovers. He said it was all right, that he did not mind my blood upon him, but I could not allow myself to be pleasured by him then. We went to bed that night and he held me. When we kissed I felt him stiffen against me and I moved to take him in my mouth, but Michael stopped me. It was not necessary, he said. He would wait, he said.

I told him it hurt me that I could not show my love for him in this way and the next night, when we lay together, he was silent as my lips found him, and the hands he lay upon my head, while they did not restrain me, did not urge me to my task either. I felt he had no joy from the passion I gave him with my mouth. It was a response from the body, but not his heart, and when I put my face to his again, he would not meet my eyes, as if he had done some shameful thing. I did not understand him then, and I do not now. I did not seek to touch him in that way again, I thought I should wait until he asked me. He did not ask.

It was not a conscious decision that we should live together, it simply happened that I stayed with him one night during the week and then, somehow, did not leave. It was an accident really. It was not usual for me even to see Michael during the week then because he so often worked late at his company, or else took work home with him to do for the following day. Anyway, I hardly ever slept the whole night with him even at the weekends because of my mother telephoning me.

I had to some extent dealt with this problem of my mother. I had bought a telephone answering machine that could be programmed to relay calls to a specified number. Now, if I was with Michael when my mother telephoned, she would be answered by the machine which then called me at Michael's apartment a few moments later. All I had to do was telephone my mother, saying I had been in the bathroom washing my hair or some such excuse, and she could never know that I was not at home. Of course, it was not quite as easy as that, I still found it difficult to lie with equanimity to my mother, and I was sure that she could tell from my voice when I was doing so; but the rules of our particular little game held and I knew she would not question me as long as I preserved at least the appearance of propriety.

So, in a way, it was a combination of Japanese technology and manners that allowed us to live together, and perhaps the assurance I had that I could always answer my mother's calls let me slip from my apartment and into Michael's. I stayed that first night because he had called me and asked me to come over. He was busy with something and he needed me to help him. Well, it was not that he needed my help, as such, he needed help and I was glad to give it.

It was not much that I did, but by the time the task was completed it was too late for me to take a train, and although I tried I could not find a taxi. Michael offered to walk me home across the park, but that seemed foolish when he was already so tired. In the end I went to sleep in his arms, something that, romantic as it sounds, we had little choice about. There was not room for us both in Michael's bed unless he had his arms about me.

The next day I stayed on in the apartment when Michael went to his office, and I was there to welcome him home at night. Somehow after that I never went back to my own rooms for more than an hour or two at a time, and then I would bring some of my things across, my clothes, my work. Soon, almost all that I owned was in Michael's apartment, and, without either of us having made a decision about it, we were living together.

It was not easy, especially for Michael. He found himself surrendering to me more and more of that perfect space he had created. I tried hard not to violate it, but somehow there would always be something out of place, a book left upon the floor, the stereo on, when he came in. We bought a larger bed, and although we knew it was right to do so, even I could see that the bedroom had been changed, would not, could not, be the same as it once had been. Michael said nothing. When he returned from his work and found my translation pads scattered about the floor, Michael said nothing. Once, I tried to clean the apartment for him, but I could not replace the things I moved when I dusted the shelves, or site the chair and couch exactly as he had sited them. He came in and I could see his eyes moving about the room, noting each irregularity while he talked to me, exchanging the greetings of the one who has been away to the one who has remained. When I came from my bath later in the evening I found he had put everything I had moved back in its proper place. I said I was sorry for what I had done, but, still, Michael said nothing.

The first time he ever shouted at me was when I had cooked for him. There was grease on the kitchen floor in front of the gas table, and vegetable peelings floating in the sink. He frightened me. Afterwards I knew it was not anger as much as distress that made him raise his voice, but I had never seen him like that before, never heard such emotion in his voice. I thought he might hit me, and although I heard each word he said I could not understand what he was saying. I knew only that I had done something so wrong he would tell me to leave. I would rather he had hit me than that.

Of course, he did not hit me, and he did not tell me to go. His anger flared for a moment and then it was gone. We cleaned the kitchen together and, if we ate the meal I had made in a silence, it was a silence from which ill-feeling had been banished. He held me afterwards and we talked about what had happened; in talking we healed our wounds, but I understood for the first time that I did not know Michael, and I understood for the first time that I could not get to know him, that there would be always some part of himself not open to me.

Michael almost never spoke of his past, or, if he did, it seemed to me it was simply a version of his past he presented. There was something missing; something left out. Sometimes, when the mood was on me and he was not at home, I would search through cupboards, empty drawers, looking for the things he had left out. I thought there must be letters, there must be photographs, but though I searched everywhere I found nothing or, at least, there was nothing in what I found. There were letters, of course, but they told me nothing and the photographs were all the same, mountains, breached stone walls and ruined houses, fields, the dark and empty sea. I came to feel that Michael's past was like his photographs, all the figures had been cropped out of the picture until only he remained.

But there were other things I did not know of Michael, as well, better things, like the gaiety that could fall upon him. He would sing songs to me then, foolish songs that I could make no sense of but laughed at all the same. He would dance for me as well when the mood took him, like a crippled ballerina, lurching from room to room and, if I ran from his foolishness, he would pursue me, transformed into a monster, the creature from the black lagoon, he called himself.

We would laugh and laugh, but somehow the laughter never quite filled the space around him, the space behind him. One night I dreamed I was asleep upon a mattress in which the body of a woman had been concealed, her blood defying logic to seep upwards into my nightclothes. I did not speak of my dream, but the memory of it stayed with me through the rest of that day. Perhaps it stayed with me through the rest of all the days we were together.

Yet we were happy, if I remember it all there was so much more happiness than unhappiness. I was the one who allowed the ghost into our house, not Michael. I called her to me, and I kept her with me. She, of course it was a she, was my familiar.

Michael tried only to make me happy. He called me princess, he treated me like a princess. He took me shopping for clothes because he said I dressed like an old woman. He took me to have my hair cut because he said I should show more of my face, that it was too beautiful to hide it away behind a fringe. We went to shops I had never been to, shops I had never heard of. With my new clothes, with my hair cut as short as any boy's, I looked in the mirror and I did not know myself. I was a new person. I was a new Sachiko.

Michael ran in the morning before he went to his company, getting up when the light outside the window was still grey. He never disturbed me, moving about the house like — like a ghost, another ghost, I suppose. After a little while I asked him to take me with him. I wanted to run, I wanted to shape the body beneath my new clothes, beneath my new face.

We began slowly, at night. He did love me. I know he did love me. He would come home tired from the day's work and he would run with me, ten minutes at first, and then twenty, and then thirty. When I could run for thirty minutes at a time I started going out with him in the mornings to circle the lake in Inokashira Park, once, twice, three times we ran, round and round. We ran through the dawn and we ran through the seasons, the time of fullness, when the rain drops sat fat and patient upon the petals and the leaves, so many little crystal frogs, and through the time of the falling of the petals and the leaves. We ran in winter. We ran in spring. Through the time of bareness and through the time of budding.

My body sleeked itself, the baby fat I had carried all my life fell from me. I looked in the mirror and I did not know who I was. Only that I was a new person, only that I was a new Sachiko.

I was a new person. I was a new Sachiko. And it was not enough for me. I haunted myself with the ghost of Michael's past that I had conjured up. It was not even as if he never spoke about the past. He did. He talked of his boyhood, his home in the west of Ireland. He even said that, one day, he would take me to Sligo and we would stand by the wild sea that beat upon the shoreline beneath a slate-grey sky.

He told me that his parents were dead, that his brother was somewhere in America. He never said that he was married, that he had a wife and children somewhere, but then he never said that he did not. In the absence of his denial I took his silence for confirmation that he did. But if he had a wife, then why did he propose that we should marry? But if he had not, why did he run away, why did he leave me?

He hated Japan. Is that why he left me? Once, when that angry flame burnt within him again, burnt bright again, he said my country was a nation of carrion eaters, that we had grown fat, bloated, on the corpses of Korea and Vietnam, of Rhodesia, of South Africa. Wherever the other peoples of the world drew back in horror, the Japanese rushed in, ankle deep in blood, to shovel money into their pockets.

He called us hypocrites. I answered that I knew nothing of any of this, nothing. I knew only that if he hated my country, if he hated my people, then he must hate me, and yet I loved him, I had never offered him anything but my love.

I do not think he even heard what I was saying of love, he spoke only of money and the way the Japanese disguised the fact of their avarice with the lies of history and culture, the unquestioned assertion of their uniqueness among nations. He said our history, our religion, our culture, were artefacts, lies given the force of truth through constant repetition. He ridiculed Japan as a country that could not admit its past, that lied and bent the truth, shaping a past that never was: our ancient state religion established only with the Emperor Meiji, the awkward truth that before then the emperors had been Buddhists not Shintoists hidden, conveniently forgotten. He spoke of the archeological sites closed as soon as any evidence of a Korean civilization older than our own was unearthed. Of the tombs of our first twenty emperors, the children of our mother the sun, all built during the 1930s and filled only with echoes of the workmens' spades. He said that our national anthem, the song our prime minister said would mould and unify our young, would shape a Japanese identity, was written by a German. Our history books, he said, dismissed the years of war we made upon Asia in a few paragraphs, as our Emperor dismissed it, a misunderstanding, denying the massacres, the horrors, to show the bombs of Hiroshima and Nagasaki falling from unreasoned skies upon a people wholly innocent.

I pleaded with him that I did not know. I begged him to stop, please stop. It was as if a fever came upon him and only my tears, at last, could break it. Then he was gentle with me, then he was comforting to me. Then he answered my question. He did not hate me. It was the lies he hated, it was not me. We lived in a country of lies. He had been born in a country of lies himself, and he knew the cost of lying to a people. It was the lies he hated, not me. I was happy to believe him.

I was happy to believe him because he said he would marry me — no, he said we should, we ought to, marry. Early on, soon after we had made love that first time, he said to me that if I became pregnant he would take care of me. I remember I asked him what he meant and he said he would marry me. That was the first time. The second time, the time he said we should marry, was not because I was pregnant, it was because of a telephone call from my mother.

It was quite late, I remember, when the telephone rang. He answered it. It was agreed that he would always answer the telephone in case my parents had set the investigators to follow me again, sensing perhaps that something was wrong. It was a message for me and so I took the receiver and pressed the buttons on the keyboard that I might hear it. It was my mother, and I dialled the number of my parents' house.

My father was at home, I could hear him in the background, and he was drunk. I could hear that he was drunk. He was shouting at my mother. I asked her if something was wrong. She said, yes, something was wrong but she did not wish to discuss it with me now. She would come to Tokyo early in the next week and we would talk about it then. She had nothing else to say to me after that, and she put the receiver down.

Michael had gone to bed, and I went in to him. I said I

must go back to my apartment at once, I must stay there that night and for the next few days. He asked me why and I told him I was certain my parents knew I was living with him. I did not hear what else he said because the fit that had come upon me when I was with Mr Camley in the love hotel came again. I began to scream. I began to roll my head from side to side. Did I lose consciousness? I do not know. I only know that at some point my eyes saw again, and I was lying on the bed with Michael's face above mine.

We both slept at my apartment that night, and it seemed that we were Adam and Eve, driven from Paradise. My rooms smelt of dust, and the light inside was tired, compromised. I hated being there, but I was so afraid my mother might call again.

Michael did not go to work the next day. He stayed with me, he cared for me, and we talked. He said he never wanted to see me afraid again as he had seen me afraid that night. He said that we should marry. He said that when my mother came to Tokyo he would meet her, and he would tell her we were to be married. It sounded so easy as the words came from his mouth that I believed him.

As it happened, Michael did not meet my mother when she came. He wanted to, he said he wanted to, but I had begged him to let me see her alone this time. I would talk to her. I would tell her. I did. I met my mother at Tokyo station and we walked to Nihonbashi. In the tea room at the Takashimaya department store I asked her why she had telephoned and what it was she had to talk to me about. It was my marriage, of course, or rather, it was not my marriage but the fact that I was not yet married. I shamed my father, my mother said. Among his business circle he was alone in having an unmarried daughter, he was alone in having no grandchild.

I understood at once. My father had come home drunk and maudlin at the way his daughter treated him — the Christmas cake was growing steadily more stale upon the shelf — and his mood had changed to anger. Now my mother had been despatched to bring me his ultimatum. I was to marry within the next year or my father would stop my allowance once more. Not only that, he would delete my name from the family register. Even my mother seemed embarrassed at such frankness, and in so public a place.

For a moment I had it in my mind to ask if, when he deleted my name from our family list, he would add, in its place, that of his bastard son, but I did not. Instead, I told her that, if my father wished it, I could be married in a month, a week even. She asked me what I meant and I told her.

My mother was to have stayed for two or three days in Tokyo, as it was, she returned to Kyushu the next morning. Before she left she said she would not speak to my father for me on this matter, but she would tell him that I was coming to see him, and that I would have something important to say.

I planned to go and see my father at the weekend. What was left of the week went quickly. I went to the ward office and asked the requirements in the matter of marriage between a Japanese and a foreigner. It was not so much. I had to provide some documents from my family's place of residence, and Michael must present a paper from his embassy in which he swore that there was no impediment to his marriage with me, and a translation into Japanese of that paper. I told Michael this, and he telephoned the Irish embassy to make an appointment there. We would go together the day after I got back from speaking to my father.

I took the train to Kyushu. I always took the train to Kyushu, I never took the train home, as others did. The seat next to me was unoccupied as it always was because my father still could not tolerate the thought of a man sitting next to his daughter. I wished that Michael was there with me. He had said he would come, but I denied him. I told him it would be better this time if I went alone, that his presence would only complicate matters. But when I left him at the station I wished that I had not spoken, that he had come with me.

I was to stay four days in my parents' house, and I did not speak to my father of my marriage until the morning of the fourth day. I went with him to his office. I spent the day with him and in the evening, when we were driving back to the house, I told him I should like to marry. He said only that it seemed like a good idea, and it was after we had eaten, my father, my mother and I, that I told him I had met someone, a foreigner, that it was my intention to marry this man. I said I hoped for my father's blessing, but if he could not give it, if he would not give it, then I should marry anyway. When I had finished speaking my father lent across the table towards me and struck my face with the palm of his hand, once, twice, three times. He began to shout at me, worse, worse than he had shouted at any time before. As his words fell about me, as the marks of his fingers bloomed upon my cheeks, I tasted blood inside my mouth.

I went alone to the station the next day because my father had forbidden my mother to accompany me, and for the first time in my life I left the house without bidding him farewell. I went first to the ward office to collect the documents I would need for my marriage, and then I looked around me at the town where I was born. I did not think I should see it again, and I felt no sadness. At the station, before I caught my train, I telephoned Reiko and Setsuko to tell them what had happened. They wished me well — dear friends — they said they would come to my wedding, they would witness the papers for me.

Michael was not there to meet me when I got to Tokyo, but he had said as much. It was often difficult for him to get away from his company at night. I would see him at home. He might be there even now, waiting for me, cooking for me. I telephoned, thinking I would let him know that I had arrived, but there was no reply, only his voice on the answering machine.

But he was not there when I got to the apartment, although it was almost midnight, and when he had not come by one o'clock I called his office. There was no one there, only the night janitor. Everyone had left at six, he said. I waited. Perhaps Michael had been forced to go drinking with the people from the office. It happened sometimes. I waited. At two o'clock in the morning I decided that I would call the police, and it was only as I lifted the telephone receiver again that I noticed the photographs were gone from the wall, the empty frames stacked against the chair. I went to the cupboard where we kept our clothes. Most of Michael's were missing. I went to his study. He stored his prints and slides in a special cabinet in there. It was empty.

Even then it took a long time, a long time for me to understand that he had left me. I went and I lay down on our bed, and I think I slept. When it was light outside I got up and I started to collect my own things together. It was just eight o'clock as I carried the first bag of clothes across the park to my own apartment, moving among the crowds of schoolchildren, the businessmen. There was a foreigner jogging beside the lake and I thought for a moment it might be Michael, but it was not. He had run faster than that man and he had run further

It took me a long time to move my things. When I had them all back in my apartment I sat down to weep. I had told myself that I would not weep until I had closed the door of his apartment for the last time and I had thrown his key into the lake in the park. I had done that, and now I was ready to weep but I found that I could not. Instead I telephoned the Irish embassy to cancel the appointment Michael had made for the afternoon.

I did not weep, and I did not tell my parents what had happened. I shopped for food; I cleaned my rooms and put my things away. The next morning I ran in the park, and afterwards, when I had showered and fed myself, I took up my work again. I told myself that all was well, that I was well. It was not. I was not. I became tired with a tiredness the deepest sleep would not subdue, and felt so weak I had to stop running. I went to see the English doctor who asked me if there was any possibility of my being pregnant. I told him there was not, but then, when he gestured his ignorance of what might be wrong with me if I was not pregnant, asked to be tested. When I left his surgery I knew that I was almost six weeks gone with child.

For another week I thought that I should keep the baby. I thought that I would at least have this to remember my love by. Then I dreamed of the kittens Grandmother Miura made me drown when I was a child. Until that dream I had forgotten all about them.

How old was I when it happened? I do not remember. I remember only that an old cat came into our garden, half-starved. I fed it with some kitchen scraps I begged off one of the maids. The next night, of course, the cat returned. It came again the following night, and again and again. I came to think of the cat as my cat. I gave a name to it and would call it in the evenings by the name I had given to it. It came, of course it came, for it was hungry. It came for the food, but to my childish mind it came for me. It came out of love for me. It was forbidden for me to have any animals, and I knew that I should be punished if I was discovered in what I was doing. I trusted the maids with my secret, but no one else. I did not believe they would betray me.

I made a little house for my cat in the garden, behind the place where the gardeners, when they came, threw their rubbish. It was not much of a house, a cardboard box, but I furnished it with a woollen sweater of mine that I thought would not be missed and I stole two old plates from the kitchen to hold the food and water on which I nurtured my cat.

I did not know the cat was female, and when it started to grow fat I imagined it was with my love and with my kindness. One day I found my cat curled up in its box with six quivering babies, I suppose not more than an hour or two old, sucking at its teats. I was both fascinated and, at the same time, horrified by my discovery, so much so that, as I stared into the box, I did not hear my grandmother approach behind me.

She had found my secret before I had, and as I stood dreaming of the games I would play with the kittens when they grew, she was preparing to drown them. Seeing me there by the rubbish tip confirmed her suspicions that it was I that had attracted the cat to our garden in the first place, and then contrived to keep her there. For this reason, she later told me, it was necessary to teach me a lesson.

My grandmother had with her a bucket of water, I remember clearly it was an old galvanized bucket, and a small cotton sack. She told me what her intentions were, and although I pleaded with her to spare the lives of the kittens she would not. More than this, it was her intention that I should right the wrong I had done by acting as their executioner.

She made me take the kittens from the mother one by one, and drop them in the sack. Then, when she had tied the neck closed, she made me, she made me, put the sack into the bucket.

I had imagined the sack would sink at once. It did not. I had imagined the kittens would die at once. They would not.

My grandmother took my hand in her hand and forced it onto the sack, forced it to push the cotton under the water, forced it to hold the sack down as the water soaked through the thin fabric. It took so long. It took so long. And then the cries of the kittens began and though I screamed, and though I wept, neither my cries nor my tears could keep the mewing of the kittens from me. And neither my cries nor my tears could break the hold of that strong hand upon me, a hand which was like death, a hand which was death.

I do not remember how long it took until the mewing from beneath the water stopped, but it was a long time, a long time. Afterwards Grandmother Miura threw the sack onto the rubbish pile and took the box, in which the little lives she had ended had begun, back into the house. The cat itself was gone and I never saw it again.

That night I was sent outside to put some rubbish into the dustbin and coming from the darkness of the garden I heard one of the kittens calling. I know I heard it. I could do nothing, of course. I could do nothing, only run inside the house and shut the door upon the sound, which is what I did.

I dreamed that dream, and I had the tears and the cries of the drowning kittens again, and when I woke my pillow was wet and my head ached. And when I woke I telephoned an abortion clinic because I knew I could not keep anything that I might love. Oh Michael, I wanted once to run away to a foreign country to escape the life that I had here. I found you and you were my foreign country, but you would not let me stay. I found you and I thought I had re-written the story of my life, but you went away with less than half a chapter done. You gave me love and somewhere, somehow, I lost it. You gave me a child and I lost that as well.

The woman I spoke to on the telephone told me when I should come and whom I should see. She said there would be some forms to sign, and that I must obtain the written consent of the man involved in the case — she used those words exactly — I must have his signature on the form before the abortion could be performed. It was the law, she said. I explained that the man involved in the case had left Japan, but she only repeated what she had said before. I thought about what I should do, what I could do, for a long time, and then I telephoned Mr Yamada.

A woman answered. Mr Yamada was not at home she said. She sounded annoyed, and I was not sure she would pass on the message I gave her, asking him to call me back. I did not hear from him, and so I called him at the shop the next day. He was surprised and, I felt, a little uncomfortable. I did not mention that I had called his apartment. I asked if I might see him and his voice betrayed him. I said I had a favour to ask, that it would not take long.

I saw him in the evening. We met in the coffee shop we had gone to that first evening. It was the only thing that remained the same from the time when we were together. He was to be married, he said, to the girl who had worked for him as his receptionist. She was pregnant. They expected the baby in January. He asked what the favour was I wanted and I knew that now I could not ask him. I could not ask him because he was such a decent man he would have felt compelled to agree to my request. I said it was just that I was thinking of getting my hair cut with him again, but I wanted to ask if it would embarrass him first, I did not want to just walk into the shop. He said he would always be happy to cut my hair.

When I got back from seeing Mr Yamada I sat for a long time wondering what I was going to do, and in the end I knew only that I did not have any idea what I was going to do. I still did not know three weeks later when I saw the first spots of bright red blood on my panties, and I began to lose the baby.

I telephoned my mother when I got out of the hospital. I told her what had happened. She said she would come to see me. When she came to see me she said she had spoken to my father. She had told him a little, not all of it, but a little. He had agreed that I should come back to live with them. She asked me if I would go back with her, and I said yes, I would go back with her. We travelled together at the end of the week.

On the train she told me I should not worry anymore, that my father was a good man, a hard-working man. She said that I had suffered enough and now he would see that I was taken care of. When we got to the house my father was waiting for us. I knelt before him, and I told him I was Sachiko, I told him I had come home.

FOURTEEN

I must stand up now. I must stand up and walk around this table to where the man from the hotel is waiting with the bouquets of flowers. I will take one of the bouquets and Mr Ueno will take the other. Together we will go to where our parents are standing at the back of the room, I will go to his mother and father, he will go to mine. We will bow, we will offer our thanks to our parents, and then Mr Ueno will give his flowers to my mother, as I will mine to his. There are roses in my bouquet. I wish I might stab my finger on a thorn and fall asleep for a thousand years, a hundred thousand years, sleep and sleep until I am awoken by a prince's kiss. Or perhaps I am already asleep. Perhaps I have been asleep since the day the prince left me. He left and he did not return.

I do not know why Michael went away. Did he have a wife in Ireland? Or was it fear that made him run? I do not know. I know only that he went and he has not come back, will not come back. I know only that I am to be married — that I am married to someone else.

I give my flowers to that woman, and I stand with my husband as my father takes the microphone in his hand. This will be the final speech. It is usually given to the groom's father to make this speech, but my father's money has ensured that he will have the last word again.

I know what my father intends to say. I saw the speech as

my mother was writing it for him, or rather, putting the thoughts that he had set out for her into some sort of order. He will tell of his sorrow today because his only child, his only daughter, is leaving him. He will say how precious I am to him and how his heart is breaking because now I am forever lost to him. He will tell stories of my childhood, the times we spent together, the games we played. He will tell of the laughter and the tears we shared. There will be little anecdotes to illustrate each of these points, and as he relates them my father will cry, because by now he is convinced that every word he is about to speak is true.

He will cry as well because it is expected that on such occasions the bride's father should cry. And it is expected that I should cry as well. The men from the hotel will shine their spotlights in my face so that all those who hear my father's words can share my tears. Michael was right about one thing, we are a people who live in a world of lies. Well, my guests are going to be very disappointed in me for I will not cry. I will not cry because what my father intends to say does not move me even as a fiction. And I will not because I do not, now. The tears did not come · for my baby, for Michael's baby. They will not come for my wedding.

Anyway, I will be too busy to listen to what my father has to say, I have to think, I have to think what I am going to do now, what I am going to do about Mr Ueno, what I am going to do about my wedding. I had thought I would kill myself. I would give him his wedding night, and in the morning, before he woke, I would leave the room and walk to the subway. There I would wait for a train with all the others, the salarymen and the students, the office ladies, and at the right moment I would step off the platform and out of my life. It is still the best plan that I have, but I wonder, I wonder if I lack the courage for it, after all.

For a long time after I lost the baby I thought lovingly of death, but I did nothing. I could not take my life, but I wished it might be taken from me. On the flight to Europe with my mother I hoped, I prayed, that our aircraft would fall from the skies, that I might tumble and tumble until I was broken on the cold and unforgiving snow, or plunged into the ocean to merge with the fish that swim, indifferent, to and fro. Now, perhaps, I do not want to die.

The truth is I do not know what I want, except that I do not want to be married to Mr Ueno. I have thought that I might leave him while we are in Europe. I have my money still, I have my work, and soon I shall have my passport. I could run to Alistair Camley. He would hide me, I know he would hide me. By the time my parents had been told I could be anywhere. I could be in Ireland, waiting by the cold sea for Michael.

I know I must find Michael. I must find him because I have to know why he left me. Only that, to know why he left me. One day, perhaps tomorrow, perhaps not tomorrow, but one day I will die. I do not want to die without knowing what it was that made him go. I only want to know that, to know why.

My father is crying and so is Mr Ueno. I look at them because I cannot see beyond the spotlights shining in my face. I look at my mother. My mother's face is quite untouched by tears. My mother's face is as I always remember it, formed, set, without emotion, accepting. I look at Mr Ueno's mother and I see that she has won. She probably agreed with my father that he should make this speech instead of her own husband. She would see it as a declaration of surrender, a passing of the spoils. She would see it as the final reading of the bill of sale. I am hers now. I belong to her and she will do with me as she pleases. I can almost smell her satisfaction. It oozes from her like sweat.

It is finished. Even my father's fiction could not be sustained indefinitely. The men must dry their tears while the master of ceremonies makes the guests ready to depart, although, now the lights are back on, I can see that many of them already have their carrier bags upon their knees. The wedding is over. My wedding is over. I must leave now to take up my position by the door, before the eager guests. I must stand by my husband and I must bow to those who came to see my marriage. I must accept their good wishes, I must return thanks for thanks. It is my first duty as a wife. I shall do it.

And afterwards I shall go with Mr Ueno to the second party that his friends have arranged in another room in the hotel, where there will be more speeches, and more to drink. It will be some time yet before I am alone with my husband. In our room, when we are alone, I shall dispose myself for him as he wishes, I shall give my body to him, if that is his desire, and if it is not then we shall sleep, at some point we shall sleep.

Are these my choices then, death or marriage, death and marriage? Is this all there is? Are the books right in this as they were wrong in so much else? I wanted a hero, but there are no heroes. I waited for a prince to come, but he came only to leave again without me. I wanted to be loved, but I am not loved. I wanted a happy ending. Well, perhaps some books are right, and some are wrong. Perhaps some tell us what we want, while others say merely what we can have.

What shall I do now? I shall sleep, yes, I shall sleep, but after sleep the morning will come and then what will I do? And then what will I do? I know only that there will be no more fictions. I was a daughter and now I am a wife. My imagination will not help me now. What will I do? I do not know what I will do. I do not know what I will do, yet.